SO
HAPPY
FOR YOU

Also by Celia Laskey

Under the Rainbow

SO HAPPY FOR YOU

CELIA LASKEY

HQ

ONE PLACE. MANY STORIES

HQ
An imprint of HarperCollins*Publishers* Ltd
1 London Bridge Street
London SE1 9GF

www.harpercollins.co.uk

HarperCollins*Publishers*
1st Floor, Watermarque Building, Ringsend Road
Dublin 4, Ireland

This edition 2022

1

First published in Great Britain by
HQ, an imprint of HarperCollins*Publishers* Ltd 2022

ISBN: HB: 9780008481056
TPB: 9780008481063

MIX
Paper from
responsible sources
FSC
www.fsc.org
FSC™ C007454

To anyone who's ever been a bridesmaid

SO HAPPY FOR YOU

PART I

1

If you want to know the story of how my best friend and I ended up trying to kill each other, I should probably start with the night she asked me to be her maid of honor. Before that I guess I should clarify that at that point in our lives, we were more like best-ish friends. We had been actual best friends in high school, but as we got older and I became more and more of a "rabid feminist" and Ellie became more and more focused on meeting a man to marry and have kids with, we kind of started to resent each other. But neither of us could seem to let the friendship go.

Anyway, it was a number of years ago now, when we were both thirty-three. Ellie had asked me to meet her at this new bar in Brooklyn Heights called The Uncurious Cat or The Skinny Pig or some other super-clever name that consisted of an animal preceded by an oxymoronic adjective. Picture any bar in any affluent Brooklyn neighborhood and you've got it: gleaming white subway tiles on the wall behind the bar, a chandelier made of dozens of Edison bulbs, an accent wall covered in a vintage flamingo print, tea lights flickering on the tables, oversize ice cubes in drinks, and men in checkered oxford shirts sitting across from red-lipsticked women, their hair in donut-shaped buns.

I watched from outside, shivering in the spring jacket I had prematurely donned that morning—it was early May and it had just unexpectedly snowed *again*—as all the couples flirtatiously smiled and eagerly nodded and placed their hands on each other's knees. One couple was already vigorously making out in the corner. I probably rolled my eyes and thought something like: *God, straight people, we get it: the world is yours.* Because I was gay and frequented dive bars instead of swanky ones, I thought I was better than them. At that time in my life, I thought I was better than most people.

When a woman sitting next to the window went to the bathroom, the man sitting across from her took out his phone and started scrolling through Spouse Spotter, the most popular dating app those days. It was known for giving each member a "marriageability rating," abbreviated to MR, on a scale of zero to one hundred. A man's MR was determined by his age, height, looks, wealth, IQ, emotional intelligence, sexual capacity (don't ask me how they determined this), and willingness to make a long-term commitment. Women were rated by their age, looks, height, bra cup size, weight, academic degrees, personality, and family background. Women who hadn't married by twenty-seven were labeled "leftovers," and women who were still single at thirty-five were "rotten." These labels appeared right next to their profile picture. Men who hadn't married by a certain age weren't called anything at all.

An app like this sounds a little fucked up to us now, but you remember how things were then, right? After the divorce rate soared to 76 percent and the marriage rate dwindled to 21 percent, fewer people were buying houses and having kids, which meant suburbs became ghost towns and cities became wildly overcrowded, which meant rent prices and STI rates skyrocketed, which meant the economy and the health of the nation were at risk, which meant the government finally decided they had to take action, even though Americans were happier than ever according to the World Happiness Report. Happiness was not good for capitalism or the patriarchy or white supremacy, i.e., business as usual.

So the government gave a ridiculous amount of money to The National Organization for Marriage, making it the most powerful lobbying group in Washington. They also tripled tax breaks for married couples, gave out loans for weddings and homes at bargain-basement rates, and severely restricted access to abortion and egg freezing. Every month, in every capital city in the US, there was a government-sponsored blind date event. Rom-coms dominated the box office, and family sitcoms were all you could find on TV. Women nearing the age of twenty-seven were targeted with daily countdown ads that displayed the number of days until they became "leftovers," and women nearing thirty-five got countdown

ads until they were "rotten." Thanks to the government's efforts, it was clear that people (not only the straights but your
basic gays, too) were suddenly desperate to get married in a
way they hadn't been since the '50s—maybe even more so.
Thus why the Uncurious Cat was crowded with young people hoping to spot their spouse.

Ellie had asked me to meet her at the bar because she had
"big news," and I could only assume it meant that she had
finally gotten her boyfriend Kaivan to propose (even though
they had been together for less than a year) or that they had
broken up. I was hoping for the latter. To everyone but Ellie, I
called Kaivan "the enema," an even worse form of douchebag.
His parents were hippies, the kind who tended to appropriate
from other cultures to show how "open" they were, and they
named him Kaivan, a Persian name, even though they were
white and pronounced it just like Kevin. Because of his name,
his dark hair, and his tan skin, people sometimes assumed he
was Middle Eastern, and when he thought it worked to his
advantage, he didn't correct them. He worked in the start-up
space and created an app for cheaters called DownLow that
would hide secret text messages and calls—he claimed he
would never use the app himself; he was just "filling a gap in
the market." He rarely came out because Ellie claimed he always had some networking event, and the rare times he did
show up, he'd blab on about his countless "projects," dropping names of tech people no one knew. Once, when Ellie
was falling-over drunk, she told me he never went down on
her because he "hated getting his face wet." The next time I
saw him, I asked him if he took showers or liked to go swim-
ming, and he just looked at me blankly. Despite all of these

aforementioned flaws, Kaivan seemingly wanted to get married and start a family just as badly as Ellie did, and in this way, they were a good match.

Deciding I couldn't delay it any longer, I took a deep breath and pulled open the heavy door to the bar, scanning the faces until I saw Ellie's Polish features: round cheeks and round blue eyes, hair so blond it was almost white, and nearly translucent skin to match. She was wearing a billowy white silk blouse and a delicate gold necklace. She looked up and waved, and as she lowered her hand, I saw it: a huge square of diamond hanging off her ring finger, reflecting the tea light on the table. My chest constricted like someone was tightening a screw, and I realized just how much I had been hoping for a breakup. Not because I wanted Ellie to be unhappy, but the opposite. I wanted Ellie to find a guy who wasn't an enema; a guy who wouldn't force me to lie to her about being happy for her engagement. After ordering an old fashioned and a water, I forced a smile and walked toward Ellie, steeling myself for the coming conversation.

"I guess congratulations are in order," I yelled over the din of the bar as I gestured to her hand, then gave her a hug. "Are you so happy?" I said into her coconut-scented hair.

"Mostly relieved," Ellie said, pulling out of the hug and sitting down. "I know you think it's ridiculous, but the last few years I've had this frantic feeling, like a buzzing that keeps getting louder and louder until you can't hear anything above it, and it's finally quieted down. The day I get married, it'll be gone for good." She leaned back in her chair, lolling her head and letting her arms hang at her sides, then released a long sigh. She *did* look more relaxed than I had seen her in ages.

I laughed, then shook my head. "That *is* ridiculous, Ellie."
At that point I had been with my partner Aimee for nine
years, and we both agreed we wanted nothing to do with
marriage, a patriarchal institution that started as a way to reinforce the idea of women as property and had excluded queer
people until only recently. When everyone was campaigning
for gay marriage, I would have rather campaigned to abolish
marriage entirely—now *that's* equality. Once, earlier in our
relationship, Aimee had suggested we could just go to city
hall with a few friends, so we'd be married but without the
big, silly wedding. *Wasn't that kind of subversive in its own way?*
she had said. When I pressed her about *why* she wanted to
be married, she couldn't articulate it. She said it was just the
way she felt; that it would be a nice way to celebrate our love
for each other. I asked if she was dying to save some money
on our health insurance and taxes, or if she liked the idea of
the government having a vested interest in our relationship.
It was strange to me that people correlated marriage with
romance, when a state-sanctioned partnership seemed like
the *least* romantic kind. People who didn't get married but
stayed together simply because they wanted to always seemed
so much happier. After we talked about it a few times, Aimee
came around and admitted the reason she had wanted to get
married must have had to do with societal pressure, and now
that she saw marriage for what it was, she was happy to simply be my partner for love's sake, not the government's.

"You know it's different for women who want kids," said
Ellie. "We're on a timeline, whether we like it or not. I was
only two years away from being rotten." She saw me open
my mouth and added on, "And don't start a fight with me

about adoption." She pointed her finger in my face. "We're here to celebrate my engagement."

I held up my hands in surrender, then forced myself to ask for the proposal story.

"He did it while we were in Montauk last weekend." Ellie smiled like she was trying to crack nuts with her cheek muscles as she fingered the ring's band with her thumb. "He had the chef at the restaurant hide the ring inside this scallop, and at first I was like, 'what the fuck is in this scallop? I'm going to rip this restaurant a new asshole on Yelp.' Then I realized it was a ring and I just started screaming."

The diamond was so big it leaned against her pinky, like it was tired from hauling its weight around. Kaivan's app must have been doing well. "That ring fit inside a scallop?"

"It was a pretty gigantic scallop."

"Wow. What a proposal." It always seemed like the more flimsy the relationship, the more elaborate the proposal—I was surprised Kaivan didn't get a flash mob to do a choreographed dance to "Marry You" by Bruno Mars.

"And you know how Kaivan and I have been talking about moving to LA?"

"You mean the place New Yorkers go when they've given up? Yeah, you've mentioned it. Remind me why?"

Ellie rolled her eyes. "Well, you know my mom lives there now since it's where her whole side of the family is from. When Kaivan and I have kids, it'll be great to have her around to help out. Plus, I'm tired of winter, and the rat race, and the literal rats, and running to catch a train that never shows up, and living in apartment buildings with other people above and

below and on either side of me. It makes me claustrophobic. I
want a house with a yard and a pool and a Prius and a dog."

"I want two kids," said the woman sitting next to us to
the man across the table. "And a gross household income of
at least two hundred thousand." It's wild to remember that
this was the way people talked to each other on early dates
then, like it was a numbers-based negotiation instead of two
unique people getting to know each other.

The man nodded, typing a note into his phone. "I always
liked the idea of three kids, but I can meet you at two," he
said. "As long as we raise them Jewish."

"You were never really cut out for New York anyway," I
said to Ellie. We had both lived in Brooklyn for ten years at
that point. Ellie had moved right after me, when I wouldn't
stop talking about how amazing it was—how you could get
a slice of pizza at 3 a.m., and the subway could take you literally anywhere, and there were bodegas on every corner for
anytime you had a craving, and there was always something
to do, like a robot-themed roof party in Bushwick or a new
exhibit at the MoMA featuring miniature models of imagined cities or photos of some faraway place like Kazakhstan.
Granted, as I edged into my thirties the days of roof parties
were long gone and getting to the MoMA over the weekend
when none of the trains were running was a complete ordeal,
but I had never thought of leaving. Ellie had been thinking
of leaving ever since she arrived—she was always complain-
ing about the inconvenience and the noise and the crowds.

Ellie widened her eyes and made an incredulous face. "I
wasn't *cut out* for it? God! You're so mean."

I *was* pretty mean, back then. It was a way to feel briefly powerful in a world where I felt powerless, but of course, I wasn't fully aware of this. I just knew it felt good. The thrill some people got from shopping or exercise or driving fast, I got from being mean. "It's not an insult," I said. "Different strokes for different folks."

Ellie blew air between her lips. "Sure. Says the person who can't stand when anyone does anything differently from her."

A waitress came by and took our order for two more drinks. "So when would you move?" I asked.

"Soon, I think. Now that we're engaged it doesn't feel so crazy to move across the country together. Our lease is almost up and I don't want to spend another winter here. I don't want to get married here, either. Your options are either a tiny restaurant in the city for a million dollars or a dilapidated barn upstate. Now we can do it somewhere beautiful near the ocean, like Malibu. My mom will probably force me to have it at this country club place our family owns. It's kind of a dump but it has a gorgeous view of the Pacific."

A man in a checkered oxford appeared beside our table. He had a face like he had drunk a glass of milk every day of his life. "Hi. I was just wondering—" he started.

Here we go, I thought. I had been cursed with a cherubic, open face that tricked strangers into thinking I was an affable person, and men especially got the wrong idea because I didn't immediately read as gay: I had shoulder-length red hair that I would have cut short in the Universal Lesbian Cut if it wasn't for my round face and undefined jawline—in pictures, I always zeroed in on the excess skin right below my chin, like a tiny pouch, even though I was a thin person. Otherwise, I had evenly proportioned features that I thought were boring but that most people would categorize as generically attractive. Usually I wore a little bit of makeup, to even my blotchy skin tone and define my almost nonexistent eyebrows, and even though my style wasn't overly feminine, it wasn't *un*-feminine. If certain lesbians could be classified as high femme or butch, I was somewhere in the middle—mid-femme? I loved prints, mainly floral and animal and fruit. That night I was wearing a black sweater with little pink T-rexes on it. No one in the bar knew to look for my short, unpainted nails or knew that underneath my sweater were hairy armpits that hadn't been shaved in years, especially not the man hovering beside our table.

"No," I said, looking up at him and shaking my head.

He scrunched his eyes. "What do you mean, *no*?"

"No to whatever you're going to say."

He huffed out some air, something between a laugh and a perturbed sigh. "But you don't know what I was going to say."

"Yes, I do," I said. "Please spare us and just leave us alone."

He crossed his arms. "What was I going to say?"

I sighed, leaning my head against my hand. "You were going to try to start a conversation with one or both of us that would lead to getting our phone numbers or going home with you. Neither of us is interested."

Ellie smiled at him apologetically. "She has a partner, and I'm engaged." She held up her hand, waving her fingers so the diamond twinkled.

The man smiled like everything made sense now.

"God, Ellie," I hissed. "Men don't need a *reason* for us to be left alone."

"You could have just let me finish my sentence," he said before walking away.

Ellie gave me an admonishing look. "That's two quarters for the mean jar tonight."

I scoffed. "He'll be fine. Men like him will *always* be fine." I lifted the hair from my neck with one hand and fanned at it with the other. "I need to get out of this bar."

"Wait, wait," Ellie said. "Before you leave, I have a question for you." She folded her hands on the table and straightened her back, then took a deep breath. "Will you be my maid of honor? I know it's early to ask, but I feel like I can't picture the actual day until I can picture it with you by my side." She smiled at me expectantly.

My stomach dropped. I had been so hopeful Ellie and Kaivan were breaking up that it hadn't occurred to me to prepare for the question. I took a gulp of my old fashioned. "Aww, Ellie, that's so sweet."

"So that's a yes?"

I twisted around in my chair like a toddler being forced to finish their meal. "You know I don't really believe in marriage, much less weddings." After being my cousin's bridesmaid a handful of years before, I had vowed to never be in a wedding party again. I had spent thousands of dollars on the flight, the accommodations, a ruffly pastel dress that I threw directly in the trash the day after, gaudy hair and makeup and nails, all my cousin's expenses over the course of the weekend, and a cocktail shaker, the cheapest item from their registry. The rest of the bridal party consisted of straight women who loved romantic comedies named after holidays, gender-reveal parties, living in small towns near their parents for the free babysitting, floppy hats, bible verse tattoos, long dresses to cover the cankles they didn't actually have but constantly talked about, using the word *blessed* unironically, and fighting in public with their husband about who did more chores but calling him their "best friend" in date night photos posted on social media. In these photos the pose was always the same: their left hand pasted to their husband's chest, proudly displaying the ring that meant more to them than the man they'd received it from. Most of Ellie's female friends other than me leaned toward this category of woman.

"Trust me, I know how you feel about weddings," Ellie said. "But I won't do any of those crazy wedding charms or whatever. I promise." She held her pinky out toward me, but I didn't want to do our usual pinky swear, since it felt like agreeing to being her maid of honor. Wedding charms were what couples euphemistically called the increasingly unsettling rituals that accompanied weddings in the past few years, like replacing floral bouquets with bouquets of garlic and sage (to ward off evil marriage-ruining spirits), lengthening the train of the gown until it stretched fifty-plus feet (to signify the eternal length of marriage), kidnapping the bride the day before the wedding and keeping her tied up and blindfolded in a basement or a shack (in case she changed her mind), or the guests tearing off pieces of the bride's dress (hoping to get some of the bride's luck for themselves) as she and her new husband walked down the aisle, which of course escalated to tearing her whole dress off and she'd be left in her strapless bra and thong, crying through her waterproof mascara.

If you were paying attention, there were hints that the rituals had recently gotten even more sinister. On the local news the anchors laughed about a "bonkers" soon-to-be bride who was arrested for digging up a coffin to steal the bones inside, and when the police asked her why she had done it she said the bones were from a woman who had been married for eighty years. She planned to grind them up and eat them on her wedding day in hopes that her marriage could have such longevity. A maid of honor posted in the "That's it, I'm Wedding Shaming" Facebook group that the bride asked her to get a pair of lovebirds from a pet store, saying they'd be used in the wedding ceremony, but they never were. When the maid of honor was helping clean up after the wedding, she saw the lovebirds in the dumpster behind the venue with their tiny feathered throats slit. An ER doctor wrote a long thread on Twitter about a woman admitted with multiple stab wounds in her lower abdomen who claimed to have been attacked by a group of bridesmaids attempting to cut out her ovaries, but they couldn't finish the job. The woman died and her killers were never found, but the ER doctor was haunted by it. When isolated, each incident seemed like a freakish outlier, but taken together, the dots started to connect. The problem was, no one at that time was connecting the dots; not even me.

"Still," I said. "I don't know if I'm the right kind of person to be a maid of honor."

"You're my best friend. That makes you the right person." Ellie reached across the table and took my hand in hers, squeezing tighter and tighter until her pointy manicured nails dug into the soft flesh of my palm. "Please."

I tried to pull my hand away, but she had it locked in her talons. There was a weird, intense look in her eyes.

My skin stung underneath Ellie's nails. "Ellie, you're hurting me."

"Oh, I'm sorry." She gave my hand a final squeeze before letting go, and I felt one of her nails pierce my skin in a soft *pop*. She blinked and her eyes returned to normal.

I snatched my hand back across the table and examined the damage: four deep purple half-moons, the one on the bottom smeared with blood. I took the napkin out from under my drink, slightly wet from the condensation on the glass, and wiped at the spot. Years later I would remember this moment and ask myself if Ellie already knew the reason she wanted me as her maid of honor, or if she didn't decide until later.

"What is it?" Ellie said. "You don't think Kaivan and I are a good match?" She said it lightly, jokingly, but there was a challenging tone underneath, and right underneath that, a pleading one. Like she already knew they weren't a good match and was waiting for me to tell her the truth she needed to hear.

I looked down at my old fashioned and took a drink, even though all that was left was the oversize circular ice cube. It slid down the glass and bumped against my nose, cold and wet.

"Oh my God. You *don't* think we're a good match, do you?"

I raised my shoulders a millimeter; the world's tiniest shrug.

"Well, go on," Ellie said, crossing her arms. "I know you're dying to tell me."

The waitress dropped off our second round of drinks. Everyone knew it was a Rule of Life that you didn't tell your best friend you hated their significant other, especially their fiancé. But Ellie had given me the opening by asking. She had to know the answer, and still wanted to hear it. She had always looked to me for my strong opinions, sometimes to a fault. Frequently, I wasn't sure what Ellie's opinions about most things were. Politics, a movie we had just seen, a meal at a restaurant—she always seemed to fall at the complete ambivalent midpoint, like the fulcrum of a seesaw. Like she was waiting for someone to hop on one end and tilt it up or down.

Maybe she didn't want to marry Kaivan and just needed confirmation it was the right choice. And maybe, if I was being honest with myself, confessing how I felt about Kaivan might be my way out of being Ellie's maid of honor. I took two big gulps of my fresh old fashioned, which was stronger than the last one and burned my throat. "It's just..." I started. "He let his biggest investor think he was Iranian because they wanted to give their money to a minority-led start-up. His app is for cheaters, people who habitually lie to the person they claim to love. His favorite writer is Norman Mailer, who stabbed his wife and wrote an essay called 'The White Negro.' And remember the first night he met me, when he asked if it would still be cheating if Aimee slept with another woman?"

Ellie's pale face had gotten redder and redder as I talked, and it was now the vibrant magenta of bougainvillea. "He apologized for that."

"The problem is that he thought to say it in the first place."

Ellie leaned her head against a balled-up fist. "Listen, he's a man. An imperfect man, as all men are. We can't all be lesbians, Robin."

"Well, I think you could find a man who's a little less imperfect. Who brings out the best in you."

She sat up and pulled her face back. "Meaning you think Kaivan brings out the *worst* in me?"

"I didn't say that," I said, even though I supposed it was what I meant. Everything I had just mentioned to Ellie about Kaivan, Ellie had at one point defended: his app wouldn't have been funded unless he'd let the investors think he was a minority; innovators couldn't always be tied down by morality; and you had to admit Norman Mailer was a good writer—couldn't you sometimes separate the art from the artist?

Ellie shook her head, shaking it faster and faster until her face and hair became a blur, then abruptly stopped and took a few long, deep breaths. "Sometimes I really don't know why we're still friends," she said before standing up and leaving.

2

As we got older and became more different, I had often questioned why Ellie and I had remained friends, too. There were times I wondered if it would be better if we just went our separate ways, but I still felt close to her on some molecular level that must have formed when we were teenagers, like we had branched apart but still shared the same trunk. I met Ellie junior year of high school when my older sister, Beth, who had been my lifelong best friend, had just gone to college. Right before she left, we had a fight so bad that I physically shook whenever I thought about it. I was a raw wound, desperate to replace that deep connection only a sister can fill.

Ellie showed up as a new kid—a rare occurrence in our

small town in Northern Vermont. Her dad was in the military and they had lived in faraway places like Germany and Japan, but then he was diagnosed with ALS so they came back to Vermont, where he grew up and where most of his family still lived. I wouldn't learn this until much later, but Ellie had a twin who died shortly after birth, and because of this Ellie always had the sense that something was missing. That someone was meant to be right beside her, but they weren't. She was plagued by a deep, gnawing emptiness that later led to clinical depression. So she was looking to replace a sisterly bond, too.

My first memory of Ellie is when she showed up to debate club the day we were discussing whether profanity in movies was bad for society. Thankfully, I was assigned to the pro-profanity group, and Mr. Whitman told us we could swear if it helped our argument. I definitely thought it helped. My team's argument, shaped mainly by me, was that profanity in movies was only bad for society if the profanity was directed at someone in a derogatory manner, i.e., "you fucking bitch," as opposed to casual profanity like, "this cheeseburger is so fucking good." Ellie was on the opposite team. Throughout the debate she didn't speak once, and her pale face got incrementally redder like someone was turning up a dial.

Afterward, I saw her outside waiting for a ride and sidled up to her. "What the fuck's up?"

She giggled, her face going red again. "Not much."

"What do you think of our shitty high school so far?"

She shrugged. "Debate club wasn't too...shitty."

"I take it your parents don't swear a lot."

She shook her head earnestly. "Never."

"Where'd you come from, some Amish village?"

"Okinawa," she said. As I debated between pretending like I knew where that was or asking, she must have seen the look on my face and added on, "A tiny tropical island that's part of Japan."

"Wow," I said. "What was that like?"

"Boring."

"You were living on a tropical island across the world and it was *boring*?"

"I was barely allowed off base, and the entire island is seventy miles long. That's like, less than half the size of Vermont."

"Still," I said. "It's somewhere else." I thought about how living in Vermont didn't feel so dissimilar to living on a small island, except the ocean wasn't what was trapping my family; it was money. We had never exactly taken a vacation. Montreal was only three hours away and I still had never been. The only states I had visited were the ones that shared a border with Vermont: New Hampshire, Massachusetts, New York. It was strange that Ellie, who had lived so many places around the world, seemed more sheltered than me.

She kept coming to debate club, speaking up a little more each time, and eventually she asked if I wanted to come over after. When Ellie's mom picked us up in their silver minivan, she hollered from the front seat, "So our Ellie finally made a friend, huh?" She never even asked me what my name was or where I lived or anything about me; she just chattered the whole drive about how shy Ellie was and how every time they moved she had to worry if Ellie would make any friends at all; and she didn't know where Ellie got it because she her-

self was such a people person and could talk anyone's ear off
if they let her.

"See, you let me!" she said when we pulled into the driveway.

"And she wonders why I'm so quiet," Ellie whispered to
me. "How am I ever supposed to get a word in?"

Their house was in Oak Glen, a housing complex where
all the upper-middle-class kids lived in large, sterile, cookie-
cutter houses. I was dying to live in one of those houses, as
opposed to my tiny log cabin (literally) with a bird's nest as
decoration in the living room, mismatched wallpaper, and
peeling, graying linoleum in the kitchen. In Ellie's house all
the walls were white and the floors were covered in plush
white carpets, and it smelled like there was a perpetual load of
laundry in the dryer. Each room had a theme. The downstairs
bathroom was USA themed, with stars-and-stripes curtains
and hand towels, and even an Uncle Sam rag doll that sat on
top of the extra toilet paper rolls. The upstairs bathroom was
travel themed, with a world map shower curtain and framed
postcards from everywhere they had lived. The guest bedroom was seaside themed, and Ellie's room was rose themed.
On her wall there was a creepy painting of Jesus holding a
single red rose in His outstretched hands.

"Are you…religious?" I asked.

My parents had been raised Catholic and said they didn't
want to inflict that kind of guilt on me and Beth, so they
raised us completely areligious. Supposedly, they still believed
in God—once, when I asked my dad about it, he said, "Somebody's got to be in charge of all this, right?" Which was such
a classic way to think about God, like He was our boss and
we were His employees. But they never tried to convince me

and Beth of His existence and never really talked about it in general, so we were left to make up our own minds.

"Yeah, aren't you?" Ellie flopped down on her bed that was covered in a rose-printed blanket.

I stayed next to the Jesus painting, examining it. There were red gashes on His hands below His middle knuckle from when He was crucified. The blood of the gash perfectly matched the red of the rose. "No, not at all."

"What do you mean, *not at all*?"

"My parents just didn't raise us that way. I've never even been inside a church."

Her eyes widened. "Really? I go every week."

I sat down on the bed. "So you actually believe in Jesus and God and all that?"

"Yeah," she said in a *duh* voice like I had asked her if she liked ice cream.

"Why?"

She shrugged. "Everyone I know does."

"I don't," I said, even though I was still trying to make up my mind. At that point I was probably somewhere between agnostic and atheist.

Her eyes nervously darted around the room like God was hiding in her closet and had heard me say it. "How can you say that?" she whispered.

"I guess because no one ever told me I *should* believe in Him," I said. "Pretend we're in debate club. What logical evidence proves God exists?"

"Believing in God isn't about evidence. It's about faith." She said it like she was parroting something she had heard a million times.

"But would it even occur to you that God exists if someone didn't tell you He did? What if you were raised by wolves out in the middle of nowhere? Would you think, 'oh, I bet there's this all-powerful being who decides everything that happens on earth'?"

Someone walked by the hallway outside Ellie's room and she put her finger to her lips, waiting until the footsteps receded before talking in a hushed voice. "Look at the history of religion. Every region of the world came up with their own before they knew anyone else was doing it. Buddhism, Hinduism, Islam, Christianity. So yeah, I think people would invent God even without being told."

I frowned. That was a good point.

"Besides, most of what we learn, we're told," she went on. "Would you think the earth was round if someone didn't tell you?"

"But I've seen photos of the earth from space—evidence that proves the earth is round."

"So every single thing you believe in, there's evidence? What about love? How do you know your parents love you?"

I laughed. "I'm not entirely sure they do."

"Of course they do," Ellie said chastisingly. "They're your parents."

I cocked my head. "Wait till you come to my house."

"Well, what about someone who loves you for sure? What's the evidence?"

I winced. Someone who loved me for sure. For most of my life the answer would have been Beth. Now I couldn't even say it was probable. I thought back to the way she used to make me feel, before everything went to shit. "I guess the way that person treats you and talks to you. You can feel it."

"Well, I can feel God's love, too."

I fell back on the bed, grinding the heels of my hands into my eyes. "Come on. He can't treat you any specific way because you don't have interactions with Him because He doesn't exist. When was the last time you supposedly felt God's love?"

"It might sound weird." She looked down at the bed and picked at a thread. "But it was when I met you."

"When you met *me*?" I laughed. "Why?"

"The night before, when I was praying, I had asked God to help me make friends. It's really hard when you're the new kid in a small town. And the next day I met you and just felt like He had sent you to me."

"Did God tell you to go to that debate club meeting?"

"No, I decided to go, but—"

"So why are you giving God credit for a decision you made on your own? And as far as meeting me, you were bound to connect with someone in a room full of people."

"But it felt like more than that. It felt like…like you were the exact person I needed to meet at this exact point in my life. You know when you've had the stomach flu for days and the thought of eating anything makes you want to die, and then someone brings you something that finally sounds good? Like a smoothie or a bowl of soup or some dry Cheerios?"

"So I'm dry Cheerios?"

Ellie laughed. "You know what I mean."

"I don't think us meeting and getting along was God, Ellie. I think it was just…friendship."

She smiled. "Maybe friendship is next to godliness. Maybe it's a form of worship." She saw the look on my face and blushed. "Regardless, I'm just glad I met you."

"Yeah," I said. "Me too, you weirdo."

"Promise we'll always be friends?" Ellie reached her arm across the bed with her pinky extended. The look on her face was extremely vulnerable.

"Promise." I hooked my pinky around Ellie's and we both leaned in to kiss our hands, then pulled away, smiling.

Over our junior year of high school, Ellie and I followed the familiar script of teenage girls becoming partners in crime, even though our version of crime was tamer than most. I had never been a rebel, but I was compared to Ellie, and that was a thrill. She was always ready to follow my lead. We were in the same history class, and our teacher, Mr. Hemming, was a meek man who talked like Mickey Mouse. Ellie and I always sat in the back and passed notes. *What do you think Sally Robbins looks like when she shits?* I'd write. Sally Robbins sat at the front of the class and was probably the most uptight girl in our school. She wore turtlenecks and headbands almost every day and walked like she was balancing a book on her head. *You're so weird*, Ellie would write back. Then I'd mime facial expressions of Sally Robbins shitting until Ellie was silently shaking, tears rolling down the sides of her cheeks. One day I passed her a note that said, *Ready?* I started humming a very quiet, very high-pitched note, then Ellie matched it and we both hummed until Mr. Hemming tilted his head, trying to figure out where the noise was coming from. We'd do this off and on most class periods until one day he stopped mid-sentence, midlecture, and yelled at the top of his lungs, "Can anyone else hear that?" After that we stopped and went back to passing notes.

We'd write soap opera–style love letters and fold them into a football, addressing the outside to a single initial, then leave them in the hallways at school while waiting around the corner to see who picked them up. We had about ten different characters that were very loosely based on people we went to school with—just enough to make people wonder—and the letters gained a cult following. "Did you know that F finally kissed B?" we'd hear people saying at lunch or in the bathroom. "I feel so bad for V that S doesn't love him back." We started hiding the notes in harder-to-find places, taped underneath desks or in the paper towel dispenser in the bathroom, and it turned into a school-wide scavenger hunt. No one ever found out it was us.

The notes were a way for us to bring some excitement into our otherwise dull lives. Outside school, we would spend hours walking around Ellie's neighborhood or the fields and woods by my house, talking about all the things we didn't have: boyfriends (I just went with it, pretending to have crushes on the boys everyone else had crushes on, because I was terrified of Ellie forsaking me), other friends besides each other, sexual experience, invites to parties, breasts, good hair, our license. I didn't have my license because my parents couldn't afford the cost of driver's ed or a car, and I would have gotten a job but my parents couldn't drive me because they were always working: a ridiculous Catch-22. Ellie's parents said they didn't believe teenagers should be allowed to drive until they were eighteen, even though the legal driving age in Vermont was sixteen. They were just looking for any way to keep Ellie more sheltered.

One night as we were walking around Ellie's neighborhood, a white Volkswagen Golf quaking with bass pulled over after passing us. A back window unrolled, letting out a cloud of skunky-smelling smoke and the chorus of A Tribe Called Quest's "Can I Kick It?" Chris Hatch, a senior skater boy who took art class with Ellie and whom Ellie thought was "really talented," stuck his head out the unrolled window and grinned.

"Hey, preacher's daughter," he said to Ellie, which must have been his nickname for her. "What're you up to?"

"Nothing," said Ellie, tucking her hair behind her ears.

"You wanna go for a ride?"

"Sure," she said without even looking at me.

When we approached the car, there was only one empty seat in the back. The rest were filled with Chris's red-eyed skater friends.

"Does she want to come?" Chris jerked his chin toward me like he was working the drive-thru and asking the millionth customer if they wanted fries with that. It seemed like boys could sense my indifference toward them the way dogs can smell cancer.

"Can two of us fit?" Ellie looked at me—a look that said she simultaneously did and didn't want me to come.

"You can sit on my lap," Chris said to Ellie, a glint in his eye. I didn't want to get in the car, but I was afraid of what would happen if I didn't—Chris pressuring Ellie to do something she didn't want to, Ellie having an experience we couldn't share, leaving me behind. Chris moved over to the middle back seat and Ellie climbed in, perching on his lap. I pictured us getting in an accident, Ellie flying forward and crashing through the windshield.

"Ellie, you can sit next to me and we'll share a seat belt," I said.

"I'll be her seat belt," said Chris, wrapping his arms around her waist and squeezing tight as the car started moving.

Ellie looked like she was in heaven, so I clamped my mouth shut and gazed out the window at all the huge houses with every room lit up. I could practically hear my dad yelling about how electricity didn't grow on trees.

"Hey, you're Beth's sister," Chris said. "Beth was cool. How's she liking college?"

I was dying to know how Beth was liking college: which teacher was her favorite, if her roommate was a total weirdo, if she had joined a terrible sorority like she planned to, but we still hadn't spoken since she left. "She's having a lot of fun," I said. "She's gotten like three abortions already."

Chris made a face like he didn't know whether to laugh or say sorry.

Ellie rolled her eyes. "She's joking. She's always joking."

The guy in the front passenger seat turned around and held a lit joint out to Ellie. She hesitated for a second, then closed her pointer and middle finger around it, like it was a cigarette, and brought it to her mouth, taking a long drag. Even I knew you were supposed to hold a joint with your thumb and pointer finger. Neither Ellie nor I had ever smoked weed before—we had never even been drunk—and we had talked about how the effects of marijuana scared us. Would we have a panic attack, would we puke, would we leave our bodies?

I didn't know when she had become unafraid, or if she was just pretending for Chris's sake.

"Damn, preacher's daughter!" said Chris, squeezing Ellie's thigh.

She pursed her lips and blew out the smoke, trying to be sexy about it, but then she sputtered a cough.

"You know her dad's not a preacher," I said.

"I know," he said like I was an idiot. "I just call her that because she's so cute and innocent." He strummed two fingers across the bare skin above her hip bone, like he was playing a guitar.

"I'm not that innocent," Ellie said, smirking. "But you can call me cute if you want."

You are *that innocent!* I wanted to yell at her. *A few months ago you wouldn't even* swear! *If there's anyone to thank for you being a slightly normal teenager, it's me!* I had no idea where Ellie learned to flirt like that, or if it was innate to even the most prudish among us. I shifted in my seat, trying to scooch closer to the window, but there was no room. It felt obscene to be sitting so close to two people flirting so openly.

Ellie passed the joint to Chris, their fingers touching. He took two hits, one right after the other, then held it out to me.

I debated taking it, so Ellie and I would have this experience to share, so when we got out of the car we could talk about what had been going through our heads while we were sitting next to each other, not talking. But I was scared about what would happen to my mind and my body; scared that I wouldn't have my faculties about me if I needed them.

"No, thanks," I said, and no one tried to convince me. I

probably wouldn't have changed my mind, but it would have been nice to feel like they wanted me to.

"So," said Chris, "what were you two doing walking around the neighborhood? Getting into trouble?"

Before Ellie could say something clever, I said, "We walk around the neighborhood all the time. Neither of us has our license."

Ellie shot me a sharp look.

"Really? But you're old enough," said Chris.

"Ellie's parents don't want her to drive until she's eighteen. Driving leads to all kinds of corruption," I said, gesturing around us.

"That's not true," said Ellie, her face already fully red. "I'm starting driver's ed soon."

"Are you feeling okay, Ellie?" I asked, then said to Chris, "She's never smoked weed before."

"Oh, damn," said Chris. "How *are* you feeling?"

She sat up straighter. "Give me another hit, then I'll tell you."

"You sure?" said Chris.

Ellie nodded, and the joint moved through the car back between her fingers. She must have inhaled for five full seconds, then blew the smoke right in my face without coughing.

"This girl is *game*," said Chris. "Can you feel your heartbeat in your pinky yet?"

Ellie held her pinky up, staring at it, then started laughing. "Yeah. That feels so weird."

"That's how you know you're high," said Chris.

We drove around for a little while longer, Ellie and Chris continuing to flirt despite my attempts to dampen the spark, and I mostly looked out the window. When we got out of the car a few blocks from Ellie's house, she slammed the door and quickly walked ahead of me.

When I caught up, she stopped and turned to me. "What the fuck was that about?" She only said *fuck* when she was really, really mad.

"I could ask you the same thing. I didn't even know who you were in that car."

"We talk all the time about how we wish we could do exactly what we were just doing. Why were you trying to ruin it?"

I shrugged. "I guess I like talking about it better."

"Why? Do you actually *not* want the things we talk about wanting?"

"I want some of the things," I said. "Others, not so much."

"Like what?"

I looked up, finding the three diagonal dots of Orion's belt in the cloudless sky above the darkened tree tips, and crossed my arms, trying to contain my heart. It felt like it was going to smash its way through my chest.

"Robin," said Ellie. "Talk to me. Or else I'm just going to stay pissed at you."

I took a gasp of air, then said, "Like a boyfriend."

She threw her hands in the air. "You'd rather be single?"

"No, not single."

"I don't get it. If you don't want a boyfriend but you also don't want to be single—" She stopped, an uneasy expression spreading across her face. "Do you want *me*?"

"Not *you*," I said.

"Oh, thank God," she said, putting a hand to her chest

and laughing. Then she took a deep breath and gripped my shoulders, looking me right in the eye. "Okay, so you're gay."

I nodded.

She shook my shoulders. "Why didn't you tell me before? Why were you pretending through all those conversations?"

"Are you serious? It's not the easiest thing to say. A lot of people aren't cool with it."

"Robin, I'm your best friend. That means I'll support you no matter what, always."

"Promise?" I asked, holding my pinky out to her.

"Promise," she said, locking my pinky in hers, and in that moment I decided sisterhood didn't have to be biological.

3

The day after I got drinks with Ellie, I met with my dissertation adviser, Dr. Gaffney, about the first draft of said dissertation—I was in the fourth year of my PhD in feminist studies at a university that had a very good program but was in Long Island. Most of my cohort also commuted in from the city. I had tentatively titled my dissertation *The Plot to Save Marriage*, about the aforementioned government-sponsored ad campaign to save marriage from obsolescence. People were vaguely aware of the facts behind the marriage craze—the money and the power behind the National Organization for Marriage, the ubiquitous ads for marriage apps and engagement rings and wedding planning services, the decrease in abortion clinics—but

I wanted to connect the dots in such a clear way that it would be impossible to ignore how easily we were manipulated, and how unhealthily obsessed it had made us.

I also wanted to show that this wasn't the first time we fell for an ad campaign: up until the early 1900s, weddings were informal gatherings held in homes with no white dress, no double-ring ceremony, and no expensive gifts. It wasn't until the 1920s through the 1950s, when businesses were struggling financially due to the depression and then the war, that they saw an opportunity to create a new money-making industry. They created a powerful advertising campaign that literally *invented* the traditions we associate with weddings today: the diamond engagement ring, the gift registry, the commercial wedding venue, the white wedding gown, the professionally done hair and makeup, the professional photographs, the live band or DJ, the floral arrangements, the catered food, the artful tiered cake, and finally, the honeymoon. Think how many businesses profit from these invented customs: department stores, wedding planners, jewelers, florists, caterers, bakeries, hair salons, makeup artists, fashion designers, airlines, hotels and resorts, etc. By the 1950s a formal white wedding was considered a necessity, transforming a cultural tradition into a commercial one.

This focus on marriage and weddings led to "the American way of life," or as I called it then, "the ladder," which consisted of marriage, buying a house in the suburbs, and having kids. Climbing the rungs, not questioning if it was actually what you wanted or if it was just what you had been *told* to want. I thought if I could convince people they were essentially being brainwashed, society might look a bit less homogenous, and thus everyone could accept people for who they were and however they wanted to live.

Thankfully, Dr. Gaffney was not a ladder climber. She and her "lover" Arlo were in an open relationship, insisted upon by her, and she loved to tell the class about her rotating cast of other lovers: the vet who liked to be tied up and peed on, the chef with a thing for feet, the therapist who liked to record their "sessions." For her niece's bat mitzvah she gave the gift of a vibrator, and in the thank-you card her niece thanked her for the neck massager, which was apparently what her parents had told her it was. Her office was covered in phallic wood carvings from Bhutan, a country seemingly as obsessed with dick as she was. I studied a purple-painted phallus with eyes on the tip and wings on either side of the shaft as I waited, wet-palmed, for Dr. Gaffney to say something about my dissertation. Feeling a chill from the window, I slipped my jacket on, then took it off when I started to feel warm less than a minute later. I was always either hot or cold, never in the temperate middle. It was maddening.

Dr. Gaffney flipped through the two-inch-thick stack of paper, her black bobbed hair falling in front of narrow eyes that were encased in round black glasses, which extended over her blunt-cut bangs and bulbous nose. Her small, heart-shaped mouth was in its "thinking" position, chastely puckered even though nothing about her was chaste.

"For a book about marriage, it's not very sexy," Dr. Gaffney said finally, twirling the ankle of her crossed leg.

"Sexy?" Sometimes I couldn't believe Dr. Gaffney was an actual tenured professor tasked with educating young people. More than half of her lectures were personal stories—sexy

ones, of course—that had nothing to do with the required reading. You might think this would make her more lax when it came to tests and papers, but her tests were notorious for being impossible, and her feedback for most papers was that it had made her fall asleep.

Dr. Gaffney gave a hard nod. "Yes, that's what I said."

I pulled a hand over my mouth, forcing it into a neutral position. "My feeling is that marriage is kind of the *opposite* of sexy. I don't think the government approving of and having a vested interest in your union is turning anyone on."

"I'm sure it turns some people on. There's a market for everything, you know. But I suppose what I meant when I said *sexy* was just…it could feel more personal, more intimate." At the words *personal* and *intimate*, she made the gesture she frequently made while teaching, like she was cupping testicles in her upturned hand and bouncing them slightly up and down as if to weigh them.

"Are academic dissertations supposed to feel personal and intimate?"

"You know I loathe the style of most academic writing. So cold, so lifeless, so *prudish*." She wrinkled her nose.

I leaned back in the hard plastic chair and crossed my arms. "So your main piece of advice is to make my dissertation sexier?"

Dr. Gaffney smiled at my irritation. "Yes."

"Any thoughts on how?"

She knocked the messy stack of paper against the desk in an attempt to straighten it. "What if you interviewed some brides, or even attended some weddings as a fly on the wall? It would be great to see some of the wedding charms in action, and to get into the psyche of people who are willing to do these things for the supposed luck of a lasting marriage."

I frowned. "I don't really know any people like that." Then I remembered: Ellie was getting married, and no matter how much she claimed otherwise, she *was* a person like that. We hadn't talked since the night before—I had been feeling pangs of guilt all morning, and wished I had just told Ellie I couldn't be her maid of honor because I couldn't afford all the cross-country flights, not because I hated her fiancé. Ellie would still be mad, but not as mad as I knew she was.

After my meeting with Dr. Gaffney, I dragged myself to the building next door to teach feminist studies to my class of antagonistic freshman composition students. They were antagonistic because, admittedly, it was a composition class and not a feminist studies class, but instructors were allowed to choose an overarching topic for the students to compose on, and I thought it was ridiculous that feminist studies wasn't a required class like composition, so teaching it to my students anyway was my way of evening the score. Since working toward my PhD in the topic, I had been called a "rabid feminist" more times than I could count, which I always decided to take as a compliment and replied by saying, "Thank you so much!"

"Who would like to share some of the ways they're privileged or oppressed?" I asked the class. Their homework had been to read "Oppression" by Marilyn Frye and "White Privilege: Unpacking the Invisible Knapsack" by Peggy McIntosh, and the discussion day following those articles was always one I dreaded. None of my mostly white, straight, cis, able-bodied students ever wanted to be called privileged; they recoiled from it like they were being wrongly accused of a crime. They thought it meant they had been raised in a mansion with a silver spoon of caviar in their mouth, instead of just having an easier life than some people. Inversely, they all saw oppression as a well-deserved badge of valor despite the fact that most of them never fought in the metaphorical war.

I also dreaded teaching the topic of white privilege because I was afraid a student would ask me about the difference between race and ethnicity, which I still didn't fully understand despite having read multiple papers about it. There were all kinds of questions my students could ask that I wouldn't be able to answer on the spot, and I lived in constant fear of them discovering this. You'd think someone with so many opinions was smart, but I wasn't. Not then and not now, but now at least I can admit it. I was a good speller, and I read the news every day so I had a decent idea of what was happening in the world, and I could summarize most feminist theorists' ideas, but I constantly had to google foundational things like why World War I started and how bills became laws and where countries like Armenia or Lithuania were—it was like I had been asleep all of high school, or maybe just passing too many notes with Ellie. No matter how many times I found the answers to these questions, I couldn't remember them. My plan, if a student ever *did* ask me something I couldn't answer, was to turn it around and say, "Does anyone know?" while furiously googling on my laptop. Until then, I would just have to forge on with a disguise of aptitude.

"I'll start," I said to the class. "To show you it's not that bad. I'm privileged because I'm white, cis, and able-bodied.

And I'm oppressed because I'm a woman and I'm gay." This was information my students already knew—every semester I tried to come out to my new students within the first week of classes by sliding in something contextually or just saying it outright, and we were already in the third week. Coming out as soon as possible wasn't just a policy I used in the classroom, but in everyday life, as well. It was a defense mechanism I had developed over the years because it was too depressing always having to come out in response to an error—men flirting with me or women thinking I was talking about my nonromantic gal pal when I referenced my girlfriend or people thinking I was talking about my business partner when I referenced my partner. The one small thing I would have liked about being married was that I could call Aimee my *wife*, a word with no ambiguity.

"Who else wants to share?" I asked, knowing no one would answer. After fifteen full seconds of uncomfortable silence, I turned to Dylan, my most resistant student, with his icy blue eyes, cystic cheek acne, and buzz cut. After the first day of class he came up to me and said it was unfair that student athletes weren't exempt from the absence policy. "How do you think you're privileged, Dylan? You can start by giving me just one example."

Dylan stared at me like he'd love to bust through the classroom doors with an AR-15 and fill me with bullets. This was something I frequently worried about, and not just with Dylan but multiple male students. Sometimes I even had bouts of diarrhea in the basement bathroom before class due to these thoughts. But I told myself I wouldn't be able to live with myself if I backed away from hard topics just because I was scared for my own small life. Dylan still hadn't opened his mouth.

"Let's start with your gender. Do you think you might be privileged because you're a man?"

A vein near the angle of his jaw popped. He crossed his arms.

I turned back to the class at large. "I know this can be an uncomfortable topic, but recognizing our own privilege is really important because it helps us take that first step toward dismantling oppression." *Yeah, and we really give a fuck about dismantling oppression*, their scowling faces said. "What do you all think?" I barreled on. "Is being male a privilege?"

"Yes?" said Christy, my in-class rescuer who had gotten As on all her assignments so far.

I leaned against the wooden podium left at the front of the classroom to make me feel like I had some semblance of power. "What does everyone else think?"

A few reluctant yeses were released from between tight lips; a few more heads wearily bobbed up and down.

"Okay, it seems like most of us agree that being male is a privilege," I said. "There are other parts of a man's identity that could render him oppressed, like his race or sexuality, but his maleness itself, taken alone, is a privilege."

Dylan mumbled something and rolled his eyes exaggeratedly.

I took the bait, then kicked myself. "Dylan, you don't agree?"

He pressed his lips together. "No, I don't."

I knew I should just say "Okay" and move on, but instead, I pushed a soapbox toward him and asked, "Why not?"

"I think the very fact that I'm sitting here in this class, being forced to learn about feminism, means I'm oppressed."

My heart spasmed and I took a deep breath, trying to keep my voice steady. "Why do you think learning about feminism qualifies as oppression?"

He huffed. "Because it's all about women. That's not fair."

"Just because we're talking about women's issues doesn't mean women are oppressing you. By definition, women can't oppress men because men are the group in power."

I could see Dylan racking his brain for something to prove me wrong. His icy blue eyes lit up. "What about the draft? Men *have* to be oppressed because of that."

"Yeah, the draft!" said a few other students, then a few more, until the whole room was a chorus.

"The draft hasn't existed for a long time," I said.

They looked at me skeptically. "What? Since when?"

Oh, great. One of those questions I couldn't answer. "Does anyone know?" I asked as I furiously typed "when did the draft end" into my Google search bar.

"Wasn't it like, the 70s?" said Christy.

"1973," I said once the Google results loaded.

"What if a man is really poor?" said another student.

"Yeah, or homeless!" said another.

"Men have to pay for child support!"

"And for dates!"

"Affirmative action!"

"The fact that masculinity itself is called *toxic*!"

"Male babies don't consent to circumcision!"

"False rape claims!"

"Men who are tricked into getting women pregnant!"

The girl who sat next to Dylan and sometimes lent him a pencil piped up. "Yeah! Is there a class where we can learn about all *this* stuff? How men are oppressed? I'd like to take that class."

It took all of my self-control not to pick up the podium and hurl it at them.

"This isn't the first time you've taught this class," said my therapist, Alonzo, who had a thick Tom Selleck–esque mustache and who wore eccentric dangly earrings in just his right ear, mostly sculpted clay food items like cheeseburgers, tacos, or cucumber slices—today he was wearing a fried egg. I adored him. He was the only queer counselor on campus, which I discovered after an initial intake session with a gray-haired white man who told me he was very well versed in "LBTG issues."

"You have to expect that some students are going to react this way," Alonzo said.

"For some reason, knowing it's coming doesn't make it any easier," I said, wiping the back of my hand across my wet cheeks.

"How does it make you feel, when you get into disagreements like this?"

I had been seeing Alonzo for a few months, after my primary care doctor referred me to a cardiologist who determined I didn't have heart palpitations; it was just a reaction to stress. The cardiologist made me keep a journal, recording every time I felt my heart "hiccup" and what had happened just before that, and the results were pretty obvious: my heart would spasm almost every time I got into an argument. So far the therapy hadn't changed the heart palpitations or my propensity for feuds, but I was hopeful. "It makes me upset, obviously." I gestured to my tears.

Alonzo folded his hands in his lap. "Remember how we talked about *upset* being a general word? What's the more specific word?" He pointed at the poster above his head that said "How are you feeling today?" Below, there was one column for positive emotion words and another column for negative emotion words. Alonzo saw a lot of undergrads who had trouble articulating themselves, as I knew all too well—the word *weird* was a catchall for anything they didn't understand, or that made them uncomfortable, and at one point I banned it from the classroom in an effort to make my students more conscious about their word choice, but they just found different vague words.

Even though it felt juvenile, I sifted through the negative emotion words on the poster: sad, angry, frustrated, afraid. No, no, no, no. Then the word *devastated* appeared, hitting me between the ribs. "Devastated," I said.

Alonzo arched his right brow and made a note on his pad. I thought I saw him underline it twice. "Okay, that's a strong word. Why do you think you feel devastated by disagreements?"

I pressed my hands between my knees. "I guess because I take them personally."

"Even if the disagreement isn't about something to do with you, personally?"

"My opinions are personal to me."

Alonzo tilted his head, the fried egg sitting on his shoulder. "Ah, so you see your opinions as an extension of yourself?"

"Doesn't everyone?" I asked. "What are we, other than our opinions?"

He shrugged. "Some might say we're defined by our thoughts, or our actions, or our social role."

"But aren't all of those things based on our opinions?"

He laughed. "I don't think everyone would say that their opinions are the foundation of their self-concept, no."

"Huh," I said. "I don't understand that."

We sat in silence for a few long seconds before he said, "Do you think you would feel less devastated by disagreements if you simply let the other person have their own opinion?"

I blew a puff of air out my nose and smiled. "Of course I would. But a lot of the time, I'm fighting about something political. It feels morally irresponsible to just let someone have a prejudiced point of view. Like, I at least have to present them with the information."

"And how many times has that information changed their mind?"

"Touché."

He flipped to a new page in his notebook. "Have you ever heard of the backfire effect?"

I shook my head.

"It's a neuroscience term that essentially means the more evidence you provide to prove someone wrong, the less likely they are to believe it."

I laughed. "That doesn't make any sense."

"USC did a study a while back where they put people in an MRI machine and read statements that contradicted their core beliefs. So something like 'homosexuality is a sin' or 'everyone should be allowed to have as many guns as they want.'

What they found was that the part of the brain that responds to a physical threat responds to an ideological threat in the same way. So information that challenges a belief is essentially a predator. To keep ourselves safe, we have to shut it out."

"So there's no point in ever trying to change someone's mind?"

"I don't know about *no* point, but the odds aren't stacked in your favor. And don't forget it goes both ways." He pointed his pen at me. "You're shutting predators out, too. So it makes sense that disagreements make you feel so vulnerable. If you see your opinions as the most important part of yourself, then when someone rejects your opinion, they're de facto rejecting *you*."

I blew out a long breath of air, widening my eyes. "That's kind of a lot." I felt like I was going to cry, and I couldn't figure out why. Then my mind raced back to the biggest disagreement of my life, which also happened to be my biggest rejection.

4

If I was to put two apples next to each other on a table, your first instinct would be to compare them. *This one is a little redder; this one has a bruise right here; this one has a more pleasingly round shape.* People do the same thing with sisters, because they're siblings of the same gender who are constantly next to each other. *The pretty one. The smart one. The outgoing one. The shy one.* It was clear that Beth was *the normal one* and I was *the weird one.* It didn't help that even though Beth was two years older than me, our mother always dressed us as twins. "If I'm sewing one, I might as well sew two!" she'd say.

Our mother also cut our hair herself—bowl cuts with clippers, to be exact. Our small Northern Vermont log cabin was heated entirely by a woodstove. The basement shelves were lined with a rainbow of pickled vegetables in dusty jars: beets, cauliflower, turnips, and green beans that were all grown in our garden. Our father hunted deer and hung their upside-down carcasses from the wooden swing post in the front yard. Needless to say, we were what some people called *rural*.

This was the 80s, before it became trendy to "go green." We lived that way mostly because we had to—our dad was a mechanic and our mom was a school bus driver. Part of the reason our parents had these jobs was because neither of them went to college, and part of the reason neither of them went to college was because they both came from six-child families in which their fathers worked three-plus jobs and their mothers spent their days getting pregnant, watching the children, cooking, and cleaning. College was something for people who had the money and privilege to ask what it was they *wanted* to do.

Understandably, they were a little angry about the cards life had dealt them. Okay, really angry. Some might say rage-o-holics. Think Mr. and Mrs. Costanza times fifty. Their rage was equally directed at each other and at me and Beth. A dirty glass left on the countertop, a Q-tip that missed the trash can, or cracking the seal on a new box of crackers when there was one already open all credited a screaming fit so absolute, so pure, that you would have thought the world was ending.

When I was older, it became obvious to me that my parents' anger and their dissatisfaction with their jobs were linked: they were rage-o-holics because they never got the chance to do something they loved; something that made them feel ful-filled. If they had had more of a choice, my dad might have ended up fixing and selling vintage cars. My mom might have designed her own clothes. They might not have had children at all, if that was a thing any couples at that time did. Or maybe they would still be angry even if they had great jobs and no kids. Sometimes I wondered if it was simply genetic, passed down from angry generation to generation. I hated the idea of something being beyond my control like that. It made me worry that the rage was in my blood, and no matter how hard I resisted it, it would consume me just like everyone before.

As children, Beth and I tried to combat all the anger by being extra nice to each other. At night, while our parents battled downstairs, we huddled in our shared single bed and whispered all the things we liked about each other. *I like this mole on your cheek. I like how you always eat my pickled beets when Mom and Dad aren't looking. I like when you tell jokes to the cat.* During the day we set up camp in the woods and played games we had made up. Beth's game was called "other family," in which we pretended to be a normal, happy family where no one ever yelled, and my game was called "other life," in which we pretended to be wolves or aliens or trees.

Even with all our differences, we still saw each other as extensions of ourselves. When our dad whipped out the belt, I felt the sharp, hot sting of it when it hit her skin the same as when it hit mine. As he whapped her my dad would exasperatedly turn to me and say, "What are *you* screaming for?" After I fell off my bike and broke my left arm, Beth swore hers was broken, too. She came with me to the doctor and told him she couldn't move it. "That's not possible," he said, grabbing her arm and violently rocking it back and forth even though she was yowling and crying. "You know girls," he said to my father. "Always so dramatic." That pissed our mother off, so after the doctor's appointment, she stopped at the drugstore and got a sling for Beth. She wore it until my arm was taken out of my cast.

Everything changed when Beth started first grade. At first, she would lie down on the kitchen floor, her body completely limp, and force our father to carry her out to the school bus. (This was before our mother became a bus driver, which would happen when I went to school.) But after a few weeks Beth started walking out to the bus herself, then even running out, a pep in her step. I would follow my mom around all day asking, "What do you think Beth is doing now? What about now?" I drove her so nuts that she started letting me watch TV for hours, never mind the racy soap opera plotlines that went completely over my head. One day when I asked her what an abortion was, she turned off the TV and made me her chore apprentice, showing me how to pull weeds up by their roots and how to tuck in the corners of bedsheets.

At the end of the day, Beth would come home with new friends and close the door to our bedroom, sliding the bookcase in front of it in lieu of a lock. I would sit in the hallway pressing my ear to the door, but all I could ever hear were random spurts of giggles or single words that meant nothing out of context. When they would emerge hours later, Beth would roll her eyes and say, "My little sister is so pathetic." It had never occurred to me that I was the little sister before, that Beth was in a position of power above me.

Our parents got Beth a separate bed and she put it on the opposite side of the room. Late at night she said she was too tired to tell me all the things she liked about me while our parents yelled downstairs. I would stay up, watching her sleep, which after a while turned into messing with her. I would tie her hair in knots, or throw tiny pieces of balled-up paper at her, or draw small dots on her body with ballpoint pen in places she wouldn't tend to look, like the back of her knee or the small of her back. She never said anything, either because she didn't notice or because she knew it would drive me more insane to pretend like she didn't.

This distance between us went on until I started school and my mom could finally get a job. When she became a bus driver for the same school Beth and I attended, it wasn't too long before we became social pariahs. It would have been embarrassing enough if our dad was the bus driver, but kids thought it was an especially funny job for a woman. They'd yank her ponytail and the older kids would throw tampons dipped in strawberry jelly at her while she drove. They'd come up to us in the hall and say, "Hey, my mom wanted to know if your mom can pick me up after school," then run away, giggling. Or they'd mimic our mom, yelling "Sit down!" at the top of their lungs.

Soon enough Beth's only option was to go back to hanging out with me. I told myself I wouldn't forgive her, that she didn't deserve my sisterhood after discarding me so callously and that she was only crawling back now because her friends had discarded *her*. After a few weeks of me always saying no after she asked if I wanted to play Barbies or "other life," she threw herself on my bed and asked me when I was going to get over it.

"When you say you're sorry," I said, realizing I was suddenly in the position of power. "A really good sorry."

"Oh," she said like it hadn't occurred to her. "I'm sorry. Really, really sorry."

I put a hand on my hip. I could get used to this. "For what?"

"For acting like you weren't my friend."

"Why did you act that way?"

She looked out the window. The Bronsons, our neighbors, were raking leaves. The kids and their chocolate Lab were taking turns jumping in the huge pile in the middle of their lawn. "I guess because I wanted to fit in."

"Why?"

"I don't know. Doesn't everybody?"

I ripped a stray thread off the family tree quilt on my bed. My grandmother had made it by hand and given it to my mother when I was born. Written inside the leaves of the tree were the names of everyone who had come before us—my family was obsessed with genealogy and loved to spout that our ancestors had come over on the *Mayflower*—and the four perfectly shaped green leaves on the bottom tree branch said Donna, Gary, Beth, and Robin. "I don't think I do," I said.

Beth tilted her head, considering. "That sounds lonely."

We had many fights in the same vein throughout our life. When Beth had Sara Hawkes over for her first sleepover and I had to sleep on a cot in the living room; when Beth and I went away to the same summer camp and she said we had to pretend not to know each other; when I stopped believing in Santa and the tooth fairy and the Easter bunny before Beth even though she was the older one; when both Beth and I got invited to Lindsey Barnes's birthday party but Beth said I was just a pity invite; when I petitioned the Little League to create a mixed-gender team and Beth told me it would never happen (she ended up being right); when I tried to start a feminism club and Beth told me that was social suicide; when Beth decided to be a cheerleader and I told her that was the most predictable thing she could ever do; when Beth started dating Steve Bass and thought he was all that existed and I told her she'd be sorry for shutting everyone out after he dumped her, which he did, five months later; et cetera, et cetera, et cetera. The cycle of fighting and making up with a sister has an almost circadian rhythm to it, a comforting predictability. I never had a reason to think it would stop.

Around freshman year of high school I started to admit to myself that I could maybe, possibly be just a little bit gay. Everyone was kissing boys, giving hand jobs, and getting boyfriends. The thought of all that made my stomach roil and my bowels clench. But it reached a point where I was becoming that weird girl who had never been kissed, so I let a guy from a different high school with spiky bleached-blond hair stuff his tongue down my throat at the movies. This was the kind of language we all used—*I let him kiss me. I let him touch my boob. I let him finger me. I gave in and gave him a hand job.* Like we were passive vessels, submitting to forces beyond our control. I didn't understand why we kept doing it when we didn't seem to want to. We were always excited by the *fact* of it, the outward trophy of having a boy want us, but we were never really excited by what had happened physically. No one ever had an orgasm, is what I'm saying, despite all the dried cum on the thighs of our jeans. No one even talked about their own pleasure as a possibility.

My orgasms, given to me by myself, were fueled by Nicole Conway, who sat diagonally in front of me in math class. She had long, dark hair and dark facial features, with cheekbones like black diamond ski slopes. She always wore formfitting V-neck T-shirts, and sat with her upper arm extended across her desk and her elbow bent, leaning her head into her palm. When she breathed out, the edge of her rounded breast would ever so slightly rest against the top of the desk. When she breathed in, her breast would rise back up a millimeter, suspended above the desk before she breathed out and it touched the top again. It was mesmerizing and completely distracting. I always got As in every subject, but in math, I got a B-.

Nicole and I were in different cliques, so I barely got the chance to talk to her outside math class. She went to all the parties I was never invited to and played field hockey—at our school, it was what all the cool girls played. My clique was made up of artsy geeks. We didn't play sports, we didn't party, and we didn't date. We mostly hung around in someone's basement listening to Radiohead, watching Monty Python DVDs, and imagining what our lives would look like after we got out of Vermont.

By the end of sophomore year, I had internally upgraded my sexuality status to probably gay. I still had never had a boyfriend and had given one perfunctory hand job at a New Year's Eve party. I had "crushes" on all the stoner skater boys who would never like me back, and my real crush on Nicole Conway was like hitting a tennis ball against a wall—slightly satisfying, but it never went anywhere. Whenever Beth and I talked about boys, my heart would speed up and I would consider telling her the truth, but I always chickened out. I was waiting for her to give me some signal, like saying, "You know you can tell me anything, right?" or "I love you no matter what" or even just giving me a searching look at the right moment. But instead, when there was a pause in conversation that could lead us down that road, she would quickly steer down some winding path and turn up the metaphorical radio. I never knew if she did it on purpose, or if I was just reading into it because I was paranoid.

I gave myself a deadline to come out to Beth before she left for college, but for all the aforementioned reasons, I procrastinated until the last possible day, when she was folding low-rise flared jeans and tube tops into suitcases and rolling up her Counting Crows posters. I sat on her bed watching her, wondering if she could hear my heart beating over "Round Here." My mom was in the kitchen making chocolate chip cookies for Beth to share with her new roommates, and the sweet, buttery smell that was normally so comforting was nauseating me.

I told myself I shouldn't be as nervous as I was. I told myself that after I confessed to liking girls, Beth would laugh and smack my arm and say she had known all along, say of course she still loved me. Besides, it was never people's siblings who didn't accept their sexuality—it was always the parents.

"You want this?" Beth asked, holding up a poster of Adam Duritz, the lead singer of the Counting Crows. He lay in a golden field, sunlight soaking his dreadlocked hair.

"You're not bringing it?"

"Mom said she'd buy me some new ones when we get there."

For some reason the thought of Beth having new posters, and not knowing what they'd be, made me feel so panicky that I started crying.

Beth sat down next to me on the bed and put her arm around me. "Aw, Rob, it's going to be okay. I'll come home all the time and you can come visit me whenever you want."

"I'm gay," I choked out. "I mean, I think I am."

Beth's hand dropped from my arm. We were both facing the same direction, looking at the empty wall where all her posters used to be, the small blue circles of putty still stuck there like a connect-the-dots game. When Beth didn't say anything, I started backtracking. "Maybe I still like guys but I think I like girls, too. Not that I've ever had a girlfriend or even kissed a girl but it's just something I think about sometimes."

"Okay," Beth said flatly, then stood up and kept folding clothes and placing them in a sloping pile in her suitcase. I wondered if she was pretending to act weirded out as a joke; if in a few seconds she would yell "Gotcha!" and come bowl me over with a huge hug. She would do that sometimes, like a few weeks before when she tried to convince me she was going to get a bob haircut and I almost believed her until she fell on the floor laughing. I counted to twenty, each second taking me further away from the possible joke, sinking me deeper into the quicksand of what I had just divulged.

"Beth?"

She looked at me with her brows pulled down, her eyes cold, her mouth flat as a horizon line.

"You're mad?"

"I don't know what I am."

"But you're not happy," I said.

"No, I'm not happy."

"Why not? Why do you care?"

Instead of answering, she pulled four thick yearbooks off her bookshelf and put them in another suitcase. She had won superlatives for "Most School Spirit" and "Most Dependable" and her quote below her picture with her perfectly straightened hair and her frilly blouse was, "The best things in life are the people you love, the places you've seen, and the memories you make along the way."

"You're bringing your *yearbooks*? To college?" I said.

"Not everyone hates high school, Rob."

She picked up her favorite stuffed monkey from childhood, Bibi, considering whether to put it in her suitcase. I pictured the monkey as a baby, Beth as a frazzled stay-at-home mom who looked back at high school as the best time of her life. It scared me, how far away and how close that version of Beth felt.

"Nothing's changed, you know," I said. "We're still sisters. You're still my best friend."

I waited for her to say it back. She might not have been happy, but at the very least she still loved me. As I waited, watching her fold the same T-shirt five times, my sadness flamed then contracted in on itself, shrinking, getting more and more compact, until it was a small, sharp rock in the pit of my stomach. A diamond made of rage.

If Beth hadn't left for college right after I came out to her, we might have been able to salvage our relationship through the sheer proximity of sitting next to each other at dinner, passing each other in the hallway, or watching the same TV show at opposite ends of the couch. We would be bound to talk, to work it out. But she was hours away, and only called to chat with my parents. "You want to talk to your sister?" my mom would ask me after they had finished. "We talked yesterday," I'd lie.

The first time Beth came home was Thanksgiving break. I stayed in my room with the door closed when I heard her and my parents come in, then waited for Beth to knock on the door with her apology. Maybe she hadn't called me because she wanted to talk in person. But hours passed, and when there was a knock on the door it was just my mom telling me dinner was ready.

"What's going on with you two?" she asked, not for the first time.

"You wouldn't understand."

She came in and sat on the bed next to me, reaching over and running her fingers through my hair. The weird thing about my mom was that she could be really tender, in between all the yelling. "You know I have five sisters, right?"

But none of you are gay, I thought. After Beth's reaction, I decided I would wait as long as possible to tell my mom and dad. Maybe I never would. Maybe it would all blow over and I would end up with a guy, anyway. "Do you think your sisters love you unconditionally?" I asked.

"Yes," she said, without hesitation.

"And you love them unconditionally?"

"Yes," she said again. "It's a mix of loving and hating them at different times, but the love always comes back around."

"What's the longest you ever went, hating one of them?"

"Jenny and I didn't talk for almost a year after she told me she was marrying Robert. You know how I feel about Robert."

"How did you start talking again?"

"I apologized," she said. "It wasn't my life. It can be hard to realize that with a sister. That your lives are actually separate. That their choices aren't your choices. I figured if she wanted to marry an asshole, so be it."

"What do you think would have happened if you hadn't apologized?"

She shrugged. "Maybe we still wouldn't be talking. I have no idea."

After dinner I marched into Beth's room and closed the door. "When are you going to apologize?"

She looked up from her laptop. "Seriously?"

"Yeah, seriously. It's been months."

"So you still think you're..."

I crossed my arms. "Yes."

She took a deep breath. As she breathed out, she looked deflated. "Oh."

"Wow," I said, shaking my head at my stupidity. "While I've been waiting for you to apologize, you've been waiting for me to take it back."

"I just don't know how you can be sure. You said you had never even done anything with—" she paused to lower her voice "—a girl. I just think you haven't met the right guy yet."

"You know that's like the complete wrong thing to say, right?"

She threw her hands in the air. "I'm not going to say things I don't mean."

My throat constricted, like someone was tightening a belt around it, and my eyes started to sting. I tried to keep my voice steady. "So you wouldn't mean it if you just said, 'I accept you and I love you'?'"

She looked at me like maybe I had finally gotten through to her, like she was realizing how much of an ass she was being. "I love you, I just…" She looked away.

I shook my head back and forth furiously. "You can't have one without the other. If you don't accept it, you don't love me."

"That's not fair. Everything always has to be so black-and-white with you."

"I would think loving your sister unconditionally is pretty black-and-white," I said. "But I guess I was wrong."

After that I stopped holding out any hope. I had given Beth a second chance—more than I would have given anyone else—and she still didn't come around. Every now and then she'd text me a simple Hi.

Hi, I'd text back, guard up.

What's up?

Studying for an algebra test. You?

Just finished volunteering at the soup kitchen with my sorority sisters.

Sounds fun.

A few seconds pass. What's new?

Nothing really.

Dating anyone?

Was she trying to be supportive or was she hoping I'd say I was dating a guy?

Nope. Still gay, though, if that's what you're asking.

Another few seconds of silence. Okay.

"Okay" like you accept it now? Or "okay" that wasn't what you were hoping to hear?

God, Robin, just okay.

Do you accept me now?

And then we'd have the same fight all over again. After a while it just became radio silence. I stopped going home for holidays in order to avoid her and grew distant from the whole family. "What's going on with you?" my mom would cry over the phone, but I didn't dare to tell her. If Beth couldn't accept it, I didn't see how an older generation would be able to. I waited until I had been with Aimee for two years, long enough for an outsider to see that it wasn't a phase, then sent my parents a two-sentence email: "I'm gay and have been with a woman I really love for two years. If you can't accept this and be happy for me, please don't write back."

My mom called me an hour later and said, "Is this what it was all about? You're just gay? God, I was worried you were a drug addict or had joined a cult!" My dad cleared his throat and said, "If you're happy, we're happy." Sometimes I wondered if it was simply the passage of time—eight years since I came out to Beth, to be exact—that allowed my parents to accept it. The culture had progressed. Don't ask, don't tell was repealed. A lot of states allowed gay marriage. Ellen wasn't the only gay one anymore—we had gotten Portia, too. If I had told them when I was sixteen, maybe they wouldn't have been okay with it then, either. The thought that really killed me was: maybe if I had waited and told Beth later, she would have accepted it, and I'd still have her in my life. But I couldn't let my mind go there. I told her when I told her, she reacted how she reacted, and that was reality.

Beth reached out to me one more time, before she got married. She actually picked up the phone and called, and I answered because despite all evidence to the contrary, I was still holding out hope.

"Mom and Dad probably told you I'm engaged." It was strange to hear her voice again after so long—it was higher than I remembered, almost like she had gotten younger instead of older.

"Yup. Congratulations."

"I've been thinking, and it just wouldn't feel right to get married without you there."

"That's not the same as *wanting* me there."

She sighed. "Of course I want you there. I wouldn't be calling if I didn't."

"You haven't wanted me in your life otherwise. Why suddenly now?"

"Because." Her voice became impatient. "A person's sister should be at her wedding."

"Why?"

"Because! That's what people do. Because we're *family*."

My heart blipped. "You know, people use that word like an excuse. 'But we're family!' I don't care if we share blood. I care how you treat me. Do you think you've treated me like family these past few years?"

"I know we've had our differences, but I think we can set them aside for the sake of this day." She huffed. "If you don't come, everyone will ask where you are. You'll be missing from all the photos."

"Oh!" I slapped my thigh. "So this is about appearances."

"That's not what I meant. God, you haven't changed at all."

"Clearly, neither have you." I hung up the phone, my hand shaking.

After that I blocked Beth but kept up with her life by hate-stalking her on Facebook, watching her climb the rungs of "the ladder": the close-up photo of her hand with the same diamond ring every other woman was given on bended knee; the "engagement photo shoot" where she and Brian put on their best sweaters and posed in front of fall foliage with her hand on his chest; when she and Brian stood in front of a small white shingled house next to a "Sold" sign; the 439048903543 pictures of their wedding like they were celebrities and the paparazzi were following them around; the Facebook pregnancy announcement "ad" where she took a photo of a bag of flour, a tin of baking soda, a few eggs, and a mixing bowl and wrote on a mini chalkboard "Bun in the oven"; the "pregnancy photo shoot" where she put on a flower crown and a long, sheer gown and cradled her belly next to a burbling brook; a Facebook memory of her wedding day, aka "the best day of her life"; the "over the moon" post about baby Dana being born; two years later another Facebook pregnancy announcement "ad" but this time with a photo of shoes lined up next to each other: Brian's Clarks, Beth's Hunter rain boots, Dana's Converse sneakers, and a pair of sewn booties for the "little sister"; another Facebook memory of Beth and Brian's wedding day; another pregnancy photo shoot but this time Dana kissed Beth's rounded stomach in the middle of a field; another "over the moon" post about baby Maggie being born; and from there you could literally fill in the blanks. Except for me—there was no way to fill in that blank space. It gaped open, a crevasse I had to be careful not to fall into every day.

5

"Do you want to cancel?" Aimee asked when I got home from therapy and she could see what a terrible mood I was in. Once a month we had friends over for a themed potluck party that was usually what I looked forward to more than anything else. This week the theme was herbs, and we were making a big pot of pesto pasta and a bourbon-and-grapefruit punch with chamomile-infused simple syrup. Aimee stopped stirring the syrup to hug me from behind and give me a string of soft, ticklish kisses up the back of my neck that made me giggle. She smelled like citrus and rosemary with a hint of cedar chest, and I leaned back into the comforting smell, craning my head to give her a kiss on the lips, then a kiss on the small mole above her lips, just to the right of the center of her

Cupid's bow. My eyes lingered on her face as I admired her winged eyeliner that was such a quintessential part of her that sometimes I swore she was born with it on. I also admired the white linen jumpsuit she was wearing that managed to look both very comfortable and very classy—most of her clothes fell into this genre.

"No, of course I don't want to cancel," I said, pressing another handful of basil into the food processor. "Maybe seeing everyone will make me feel better." I dropped a chunk of Parmesan on the floor for Bean, our little brown Chihuahua with an underbite and a tendency to pass very stinky gas. He picked it up between his teeth and trotted into the living room to chew it on the couch, pieces of it undoubtedly falling between the cushions. I would have chastised him if the couch was nicer, but it was already stained with coffee spills and lightly shredded on one side from an old cat. We wanted to buy a new couch. We wanted to buy new everything, really, but our bank accounts dictated otherwise.

Our apartment was an amalgamation of IKEA furniture in different faux-wood tones that was slowly being replaced by Actual Furniture, mostly mid-century modern items. We had recently splurged on a series of aerial photographs of US national parks taken from space, merging my love of parks and Aimee's love of space, and had them framed and mounted above the couch. But the rest of the walls were mostly bare, other than the mini shrine to Cate Blanchett above my desk, despite the fact that we had lived in the apartment for almost two years. We told ourselves we would commit to really decorating once we stopped moving every few years, but who knew when that would happen.

A heavy thud came from upstairs, then the wail of a child, then the raised voices of the two parents: our landlords, who lived above us in the long, narrow brownstone and fought constantly. South Slope, the neighborhood in Brooklyn where we lived, used to be known as a somewhat lesbian neighborhood until straight couples who generally had two scooter-riding toddlers came in and took it over. Aimee and I cemented our decision not to have children while living underneath this particular family, being woken up at 5:30 every morning by the drum-rolling feet and screeching cries of the kids and then kept up every night by the screaming matches of the parents. When we first moved in we'd mute the TV and eavesdrop on the fights, but we quickly realized the themes were boringly repetitious and mostly had to do with money, chores, and childcare.

Although I argued with countless people outside the house, Aimee and I rarely fought. We mostly loved the same things: Cate Blanchett (we had both given each other permission to sleep with her if we ever got the chance), reality TV (my favorite was *Bachelor in Paradise*; Aimee's was The Real Housewives of Anywhere), a hot fudge sundae from McDonald's, dog watching at the "beach" in Prospect Park, getting up early, and disco music like Donna Summer and ABBA. Most important, we hated the same things: Matt Damon, memoirs, The New Museum, concerts, baths, Bon Iver, and underwire bras. There were, of course, a few things that one of us loved and the other hated: hiking (it calmed my anxiety, whereas Aimee would choose a city walk any day), Ellen DeGeneres (Aimee worshipped her; I thought she was fake as fuck), bacon (Aimee loved it; I was vegan and thought people who ate pigs might as well eat puppies). With these things, we generally compromised—we'd go on a hike maybe every other month; Aimee would watch Ellen's talk show when I wasn't home; and she got bacon when we went out for brunch but wouldn't cook it at home.

When we did fight, it was usually about Aimee's dependent parents, who lived in Queens and visited almost every other weekend, playing endless games of Tong-its, a Filipino card game similar to gin rummy, and leaving stacks of Tupperware in the refrigerator full of pork adobo and chicken arroz caldo.

My parents weren't the traveling type, due to their limited resources and their belief that since I was the one who had moved away, it was up to me to come home. But as you know, they *were* the fighting type. I would sometimes get PTSD when listening to the landlords upstairs, a tight feeling forming in my chest and obstructing my breathing. When I told Aimee my parents had fought even worse than the landlords, Aimee said, "I can't imagine anything worse." When her parents had fought, she said they went into the bedroom and closed the door, talking quietly. I laughed out loud when Aimee told me this. "How considerate! How much like responsible parents!" It was a complete contrast to the fuck-laden brawls in my house that usually included thrown dishes and "I hate yous" and ended with one of them peeling out of the driveway.

Aimee sighed an extra-long sigh as she went back to stirring the pot of simple syrup.

"I'm sorry," I said. "I've been going on about my dissertation and my students but you probably had a terrible day, too." Aimee was an OB-GYN, and Fridays were when she performed abortions. Her clinic in New Jersey was one of three in the state that still provided them, and Aimee was one of twelve doctors, nationally, who would perform a termination up to twenty-four weeks, which sometimes involved seeing actual parts of the baby's body, like its tiny fingers or even a portion of its face. She never talked about it much, but she always came home looking paler than usual and would immediately pour herself a large glass of wine.

Aimee became an OB-GYN—specifically an OB-GYN who performed abortions—because her grandmother died of an infection from an illegal abortion in the Philippines, where it's still illegal but also extremely common. Aimee's mom was the first of five kids and by number six, her parents could barely afford to feed the ones they already had, so Aimee's grandmother found a man who would take care of it. She got sick shortly after, burning up with fever and cramping with intense pain. She refused to see a doctor because she was afraid they would know she had had an abortion. Two weeks later she was dead. Aimee's mom was only eight. When Aimee was little, her mom told her that her grandmother simply died of an infection after surgery, but when Aimee got her period her mom told her the truth in hopes of scaring her into abstinence. The story made Aimee want to become an OB-GYN, someone who might have been able to prevent her grandmother's death. She was now one of the most sought-after OB-GYNs in the area, since patients raved about her sympathetic bedside manner and how she took the time to both listen *and* explain things. She even had to stop accepting new patients because everyone at the clinic always wanted to see her.

"Oh, I'm fine," Aimee said, taking a drink of the whis-key that would be used in the punch. "Tiffany came in again today. Gave her another abortion, another lecture, and another prescription for birth control she'll never fill." She said this not in an annoyed tone, but a resigned one. Aimee was much better at letting things go than I was, which was one of the reasons we worked well together. When we first started dat-ing, she had a terrible roommate who would always put her dildo in the dishwasher and never paid rent on time, and one night this roommate fell asleep with a lit cigarette between her fingers and almost burned the entire place down. The landlord kicked them both out after that, but Aimee never said a harsh word to her roommate about it. "You should yell at her!" I had said, and Aimee had responded, "What would that accomplish?" It wasn't that she was a pushover; she sim-ply didn't see the point of expending energy and wasting time when the incident was over and her roommate likely wouldn't change. "Anger is usually an inefficient emotion," she would always say.

Everyone came over around eight, bringing herby dishes like Thai spring rolls and rosemary roasted potatoes and falafel with tabbouleh and salad with homemade green goddess dress-ing. We talked about the most recent school shooting, and the new Coen brothers movie about two assassins who were hired to kill each other but ended up getting married instead—the government had even gotten to *them*, probably paying them millions more than whatever movie they had really wanted to make—and all the foods that were giving us indigestion, and the clip of Sarah Hart (the Spouse Spotter founder) on Fox News saying that women who didn't get married and have kids served no function and should be deported.

"The other day my sister told me she was pregnant with baby number *four*, and apparently, I wasn't congratulatory enough," said Morgan, who was a year ahead of me in the feminist studies program at my university and who always had the best department gossip. "So then we got in a big fight that ended with her telling me I live in a liberal-queer bubble and don't know how to relate to anyone outside of it."

Van scoffed. "The only people who say the bubble is bad are people who feel completely safe outside of it, like your sister." Van was one of my closest friends from college, whom I had dated for a few brief months before we figured out we were better as friends and before he transitioned.

"Totally," said Jack. "But sometimes I do worry that we're like, one step away from starting a separatist commune where we all exclusively wear tie-dye and live in houses made out of recycled cans and worship a cardboard cutout of Laura Dern." Jack was so funny he probably could have been a stand-up comedian, but he was actually an accountant who did people's taxes.

I laughed. "Sign me up. I love my bubble, and I never want to leave it. Speaking of, I met up with Ellie last night and she told me her and the enema got engaged—" I paused to let everyone ugh or oy, because they had all met Kaivan "—and she wants me to be her maid of honor. I can't decide what to tell her. It's a complete catch-22. I'll regret it if I do it, and I'll regret it if I don't."

Ellie didn't exactly mix well with my core group of friends—she had previously told me they were "too intimidating."

"I always feel like I'm going to say the wrong thing around them, so I end up saying nothing," she told me once. I had to admit she was right about saying the wrong thing. Once Ellie asked Van if he had "fully transitioned," and I had to tell her that was kind of the number-one thing you shouldn't ask.

"I told Robin she should just say yes," said Aimee to the group. "It won't be the best time she's ever had, but at least she'll be a good friend." Aimee had recently been a bridesmaid for one of her friends from med school, and while she hadn't enjoyed it, she had barely complained.

"Is Ellie really that good of a friend to *you*, though?" said Van, who knew Ellie better than everyone else because of college. "She's always seemed so self-interested to me—expects a lot from you but never gives anything back."

"Do you know where Ellie, like, stands on wedding charms?" Leslie asked. She was a staff writer at the *New Yorker*, who was usually the smartest person in the room but fooled people into thinking she wasn't because she talked like a valley girl and smoked copious amounts of weed.

"She promised not to do any," I said. "Why?"

Leslie raised an eyebrow. "It just seems like she'd be totally into that kind of thing, based on her proclivity for crystals and tarot and witch spells. And you know that article I'm writing about the dark web? I did some exploring the other day and oh my God, I found all this creepy shit about new wedding charms. Like, one site mentioned brides getting period blood from an unmarried virgin and drinking it the day of the ceremony."

Everyone widened their eyes or made gagging noises or yelled "What?"

"Okay, I have so many questions," said Jack. "One, how are they supposed to *get* the period blood? Go to the mall and follow a pack of teen girls into the bathroom, then steal their used tampons out of the little metal box in the stall and wring them out over a glass? Or do they just so happen to have a young female cousin who uses a DivaCup and they toss her a twenty to dump it into a jar? Two, why does it have to be from an unmarried virgin? And three, what is drinking it even supposed to do?"

Leslie laughed. "They didn't mention exactly how you're supposed to get it, but it has to be from an unmarried virgin because, you know, *purity*, and drinking it will like, bring a clean slate to your union so you can stay together forever. Makes total sense, right?"

"Wow, the ladder climbers are not okay," said Jack. "They would do anything for the perfect wedding, and I mean *anything*."

I shivered. "That commune is seriously starting to sound like a good idea." I hugged my arms and looked at my friends, who at that point were most definitely my chosen family, people I wanted to be close to for my whole life. A warm feeling of safety spread through my body, like I was in a literal bubble. We had all known each other for at least a decade, some longer, through the insecurity and selfishness of our young twenties to the political wake-up of our midtwenties to the boredom of our late twenties to the digestive issues and midlife crises of our thirties, finding our opinions and voices along the way and somehow all landing on the same page. Maybe different words, but the same page nonetheless. Then there was Ellie, who was reading an entirely different book.

6

There was a time when Ellie and I weren't just on the same page but the same word, maybe even the same letter. By the end of junior year of high school, we were essentially sharing a body. We would spend half the week at my house, half at Ellie's, like each set of parents had shared custody. Ellie's mom would buy me the expensive snack foods my mom wouldn't, like pudding cups and string cheese. ("A box of JELL-O pudding is a quarter the price of those individual cups!" my mom would say. "Here's a block of mozzarella. Cut it up and it's string cheese.") Ellie would eat jars and jars of my mom's pickled vegetables, and my dad taught her how to shoot a BB gun, using George Bush's face as the target.

We would take showers together, at first wearing bathing suits, then eventually discarding them. We compared nipple hair, butthole hair, labia length and color, the amount of discharge left on our underwear at the end of the day, the blood clots clinging to the side of our tampons like red slugs. We would pop each other's bacne and pluck each other's chin hairs and hang out in the bathroom while the other one pooped. At night, curled up in each other's twin bed, we would try to make ourselves have identical dreams by picturing the same five images over and over: a small brown cottontail rabbit wearing a pale pink bow tie, a serrated steak knife with a wooden handle, a hot-air balloon covered in vertical rainbow stripes floating through a cloudless blue sky, a white porcelain toilet in the middle of a flat green field, a single red rose in a white teardrop-shaped vase. But we would wake up in the morning having dreamed completely different things.

When summer started, my parents told me I had to get a job, so Ellie decided she'd get one, too. We were hoping not only to get a job at the same place, but to work the same shifts. At the café on Main Street, we insisted on doing our interview together. "We're a package deal," we told the manager, a middle-aged man with a face like a chipmunk and mustard stains on his once-white button-down shirt. We smiled our most convincing smiles and batted our eyelashes and hugged each other like each of us was a life raft.

"Well, okay," he said, and we knew if we got the job we could convince him of almost anything. He led us to an office with a desk so stacked with papers and random junk that we had to peer over it to see his face. It reminded me of a *Where's Waldo* drawing: a stapler, a Tupperware with fuzzy mold in the bottom, a bottle of Windex, tangles of cords, a lightbulb, a plastic bag full of plastic bags, but no Waldo.

"So why do you girls want to work here?" he asked.

I had come up with the idea that it would be funny to answer questions by each of us speaking one word at a time and constructing a sentence together. Ellie said she would do it, but I wasn't sure if she would chicken out at the last minute.

"We," I said, looking at Ellie and raising my eyebrows.

She hesitated for a few seconds, her face filling with panic, before blurting out, "Really."

"Like."

"Sandwiches."

The manager chuckled, his eyes darting back and forth between us like a cat following a laser beam.

"And."

"People."

"Really."

"Like."

"Us."

Ellie and I beamed at each other—not bad!

"That's cute," he said. "But I don't think we can do the whole interview this way, do you?"

"Why," I said.

"Not?" Ellie said.

We grinned.

He pulled a piece of paper out of the middle of a foot-high stack and glanced at it, then set it on the top of the stack. "Okay, tell me why I should hire two high school girls who seem to have a penchant for mischief."

"Because we are hard workers who like to keep things interesting," we said, ping-ponging the words back and forth.

"You two remind me of my daughters," he said. "Maybe that's why I'll let you come in for a trial session tomorrow. If you do good, you can stay."

We squealed. We passed the trial session, and for the first few weeks we were on our best behavior, making sandwiches and coffee drinks and ringing up customers with no funny business. The manager, who we now knew as Rick, started letting us work the slower shifts alone. It wasn't long before I felt the mischievous itch. It began innocuously enough, thinking of gross smoothie combinations like lettuce and chocolate syrup, banana and onion, pickle and ice cream, then asking customers if they'd like to try the free smoothie of the day, which was always "mystery flavor." When someone said yes, we would silently shake with laughter as we watched them suck on the straw, then grimace as the liquid hit their mouth. Repeat customers learned not to try it again.

One day I was ringing up a customer who gave me exact change for their sandwich, and it occurred to me that if I hit the "cancel sale" button on the register, I could put all the money in the tip jar and no one would be the wiser. I held my breath as I pictured myself doing it, then I put the money in the register and slowly released the air from my lungs. For a few days I repeatedly pushed the thought away, then I told Ellie about it.

"That's stealing," she hissed, taking a step away from me like I was diseased.

"Yeah, and smoking pot is illegal," I said. "But you still do that." Since that night in the car with Chris Hatch, we had both started smoking pot and drinking occasionally, and we had worn our parents down until they finally said yes to getting our licenses. Now I was saving my pennies, literally, for the cheapest car I could find. So far I had two hundred and thirty-two dollars, after paying my parents back the three hundred for driver's ed. It was completely dispiriting how long it took to save money when working for minimum wage. It was like being dehydrated and filling a water glass by using a dropper. It felt unfair. I was the only kid I knew who had to pay for everything on my own—my whole life, I never had a friend whose family was less well-off than mine. I knew it got much worse than my situation, but it was hard to keep perspective as a selfish teenager who only saw people who had more. Ellie's parents had three cars, and had given her the extra one, a white Volvo with leather seats. Rather than be grateful, Ellie complained because she wanted a Volkswagen Beetle.

"Smoking pot is different," Ellie said. "That doesn't hurt anyone. Stealing hurts the owners of the café."

"Sandy and Jeff?" I said. "Have you *seen* their McMansion? I don't think they'd miss a few dollars here and there."

"Listen, if you're dying to do it, I won't stop you. I just don't want to be involved."

But after a few nights of me splitting the tips with her, she started to like having an extra twenty bucks at the end of the day. Once she started adding money to the tip jar, we were each taking home forty or fifty bucks. Then it at least felt like I was filling up the dropper before squeezing it into the glass.

A month went by, then one day Rick called us into his office. My stomach dropped.

He peered over his dump desk, moving a take-out container out of his sight line. "How are things? Are you girls liking the job?"

We nodded. I glanced at Ellie out of the corner of my eye. Her cheeks were already the color of red-hot lava.

"No problems?"

We shook our heads.

He leaned back in his chair and threaded his fingers in his lap. He looked up at the ceiling, then back down at us. "Well, for the past few weeks, we've noticed lower sales on the days you girls have been working. Would you know anything about that?"

We shook our heads again. I tried to open my mouth to say something, even the word *no*, but my jaw felt like it had been locked with a key.

"You're sure?"

We nodded. Ellie let out a small, almost imperceptible whimper and brought her hand to her mouth.

He sighed and put a tape into a VCR, then pressed Play. It was an overhead view of the café, and I was standing at the register. My stomach did an Olympic high dive. I watched myself take a ten-dollar bill from a customer, cancel the sale, and put the ten dollars in the tip jar. He fast-forwarded to Ellie doing the same thing with twelve dollars. He kept fast-forwarding to different scenes of us stuffing money in the tip jar until I blurted out, "It was my idea."

"Is that true?" he asked Ellie.

She stared at her lap. A perfectly round teardrop fell onto her jeans, then another.

"Ellie would never do something like this," I said. "It's not her fault. She just does whatever I tell her."

Ellie's head snapped toward me. Her eyes bored into the side of my face, but I wouldn't look at her.

After a few excruciating minutes of making us think he was going to call the police, Rick said we were lucky he had a soft spot for us because he was only going to fire us. "After you work for free until you earn back all the money you stole," he said. "Sound fair?"

We nodded.

"Hell, it's more than fair. You two should be kissing my feet. Now, get out of here."

Ellie stormed down the hallway and went out the back door that led to the parking lot, letting it slam behind her. I followed her out back, where she was kicking a loose chunk of pavement against the wall.

"It's my fault," I said, hovering in the doorway.

Ellie blew a hard breath of air out of her nose, then kicked the chunk of pavement, and as it hit the wall it split into two jagged pieces. "That's not what I'm mad about."

"Okay, what are you mad about?"

"You know what."

"No, I don't."

She crossed her arms and pressed the sole of her shoe against one of the pieces of pavement until it cracked again, forming two more pieces.

My stomach churned. "Is it what I said about you doing whatever I tell you? I only said that so you wouldn't get in trouble."

"Do you really think that? That I'm some fucking dog who just follows you around and follows orders?"

"No, I don't think that."

She quickly wiped a finger underneath her eye. "I think you do. I think that's like, *why* we're friends."

"That's not true. We're friends because—" I paused, breathing heavy. How could I articulate it? *Friends* didn't even feel like the right word. It felt like our DNA was tied up together in a mess of knots so complete that we wouldn't be able to untangle it even if we made it our life's work. At that point in our friendship, it didn't occur to me that the knots would loosen due to forces beyond our control. The thought of straying from Ellie, physically or emotionally, was so painful that I bent over and grabbed my stomach.

"Oh my God, are you going to fake an illness so you don't have to come up with a reason?" Ellie said.

"I was just thinking about if we weren't friends," I said. "It made me feel like I was going to die. I don't ever want us to not be friends."

"Well, me neither," said Ellie. "I just want you to be my friend because you like *me*, not because I'm like *you*."

I nodded, even though I couldn't quite see the difference. Everyone wanted friends who were like them, didn't they?

7

When I went to my office hours the following Monday, there was a sheet cake in the department lounge that said, "Congratulations Sandra!" Everyone milled around awkwardly the way they always did at department celebrations, hovering next to the stained '80s-print chairs but not actually sitting, scraping frosting off their slice of cake with a plastic fork and absently nodding as someone bemoaned how behind they were on grading—the most common topic of small talk in academia, at least for those of us who had to do our own grading. I saw Morgan in the corner and beelined for her, breathing a sigh of relief.

"What are we congratulating Sandra for?" I asked.

"She just got a book deal with Simon & Schuster based off her dissertation," said Morgan, shoving a large bite of cake into her mouth and giving me a direct-to-camera stare. Sandra's brand was "bad feminist," and not in the Roxane Gay way, but in the cishet-white-feminist-who-thinks-trans-women-and-minorities-are-distractions way. Her mother was the owner of a huge media conglomerate and had essentially handed Sandra her mouthpiece. She was accepted to the PhD program after one of her essays about modern feminists being "PC sheep" went particularly viral. She graduated the previous year and had promptly been given a full-time job at the university. I couldn't stand her, obviously, but had to admit she exuded a certain charisma.

Previously, I hadn't really thought about the fact that a dissertation could potentially become a book for a general audience, that it could have a life outside the bonds of academia, but I allowed myself a quick daydream in which I sold *The Plot to Save Marriage*, the acquiring editor calling it "genius" and "necessary" and "galvanizing." A publisher buying your book had to be one of the greatest forms of acceptance there was. They were essentially saying: *We agree with you. The thousands of people who will hopefully buy your book will agree with you, too. We're putting our money on it.* What if *The Plot to Save Marriage* could change the way people thought about marriage and weddings and thus society as a whole? My brain latched on to the idea like a leech supergluing itself to skin.

Sandra appeared beside us. She stood there with an expectant look and brushed her long blond hair out of her face. She had a horsey mouth and small eyes that looked even smaller due to the thick eyeliner ringed around them, but male students on Rate My Professors frequently gave her a chili pepper because of her blond hair and, I was convinced, her misogynistic opinions.

"Congratulations, Sandra," I said like a two-year-old being forced to say so by their mother.

"Oh, thanks," Sandra said, like I had just congratulated her on something as inconsequential as buying a new dish sponge.

"What's it about?" Morgan asked.

"Pop feminism," Sandra said, rolling her eyes slightly even though she was talking about her own book. "You know, whether it's a good or bad thing." She talked with this bored, flat affect that made everything sound sarcastic, so half the time I didn't know if she really believed what she was saying.

"And which is it, in your mind?" I asked. "Good or bad?"

"Oh, probably both," she said.

I tilted my head. "Probably?"

Sandra impatiently peered around the room like she was looking for a way out of the conversation, even though she had approached us. "We haven't exactly ironed out all the details yet."

"They bought your book without knowing its thesis?" Morgan said as she threw the rest of her cake in the trash.

Sandra sighed, twisting a section of hair around her pointer finger so tightly that the tip turned white. "I mean, *they* approached *me* about the book deal, saying they really liked my brand and that we could figure out how much the book would align with my dissertation later."

"Well," I said. "That's nice."

She slowly uncoiled the strand of hair from her finger. "How are your dissertations going," she said, no question mark.

"I met with Dr. Gaffney about my first draft last week. Went great." I hadn't meant it to sound sarcastic, but it came out that way.

Sandra put a hand on her hip. "Did she tell you it needed to be sexier?"

"Yeah, how'd you know?"

"She told me the same thing initially. When she says that she just means it needs to be sellable. Like, it has to have mass appeal. It's totally not the feedback you'd expect to get on a dissertation, but I guess it got me a book deal."

"Good to know," I said.

"Did she give you any concrete advice about what to change?"

"She wants me to interview some brides and go to some weddings. Overall make it more journalistic."

"That's good advice," Sandra said. "Do you know any brides?"

I groaned. "Yes, actually. My friend Ellie asked me to be her maid of honor the other night and I might have said no."

Sandra widened her eyes. "Eeeech, that's bold."

"Yeah, we're kind of in a fight now."

She shrugged. "Well, maybe you should say yes. For the sake of your dissertation slash future book, if not your friendship."

That night I couldn't fall asleep again—I hadn't gotten a decent night of sleep since the fight with Ellie because I kept going back and forth in my mind between saying yes or no. I was trapped between a rock and a wedding. I truly didn't know what was best for our friendship—if I kept my answer to no, it might actually *save* the friendship, since I wouldn't resent Ellie for all the expenses and judge her for all the heteronormative traditions and she wouldn't get mad at me for being up on my "queer high horse," something she frequently accused me of, which always made me laugh, picturing some horse with its mane chopped short and flopped across its forehead, a hole on the side of its nose where an adolescent nose ring used to be, wearing a gender-neutral romper and high-top Cons and saying, "haaaaaay girl."

I had heard of a lot of friendships that ended after someone was a maid of honor for their best friend, and they always blamed each other. I went online and read message boards about it: "the bride asked me to lose fifteen pounds—instead she lost my friendship"; "my MOH always had an excuse for why she couldn't help me with something and I realized she's totally toxic and self-absorbed"; "the bride told me the shower I threw for her was 'tacky' and that she no longer wanted my help with the wedding"; "my MOH called me a controlling bridezilla…" The lists went on and on. When I read the posts, I always internally sided with the maids of honor. *Yeah, she probably* was *being a controlling bridezilla*, I thought when I read the last one. A lot of brides used the word *toxic* to describe their maids of honor, a catch-all goopism they used to describe nonorganic food, shampoo with sulfites, and friends who didn't want to become unpaid wedding planners. I wondered if that was how Ellie was feeling about me right now—that I was toxic and self-absorbed because I hadn't said yes. Ellie wouldn't understand that it might be better for our friendship for me not to be involved in the wedding.

I tried to think of a reason it would actually be *good* for our friendship if I said I'd be her maid of honor. It would make Ellie happy—that was the number-one reason. In her world, it was important to have a big wedding and it was important for her best friend to be standing beside her. Why should my value system trump hers? And maybe I was jumping to negative conclusions about how the prewedding events and the wedding would go. Maybe Ellie wouldn't want to do all the super-traditional stuff; maybe that was *why* she had asked me to be her maid of honor—so I could help her choose things that subverted expectations. And once I got past the expense of flying to California, maybe I could look at it as a vacation. Aimee could come and we could spend a few extra days in town. Even though Los Angeles was full of vapid people, I could admit that it wasn't hard to look at, with all its palm tree–lined streets and bougainvillea spilling over fences and glass mansions perched on the edges of cliffs. Last, I had been thinking about what Sandra said. If I agreed to be Ellie's maid of honor, I could kill two birds with one stone: I could be a good friend *and* give my dissertation the best chance of becoming a book. Whenever I had to go to something terrible, like a family reunion or a conference in Florida or a baby shower, I tried to look at it as a sociological research opportunity—something to give me a new idea or breathe new life into a current project. And according to Dr. Gaffney, it was just what my dissertation needed.

I picked up my phone and sent Ellie a text.

Hey, I shouldn't have said what I said the other night. I thought you wanted to know what I really thought but regardless, I know I went too far. If Kaivan makes you happy then it doesn't matter what I think. Truly, I love you and just want you to be happy.

The ellipsis that meant Ellie was typing appeared immediately. I stared at it for a good thirty seconds, wondering if she was going to forgive me or not, until she wrote back, Really?

Of course.

Then be my maid of honor.

Oh, fuck, I thought. Hoisted by my own petard.

You really still want me to?

Yes. I meant what I said. I can't imagine doing it without you, despite your assholey tendencies.

Stop stalling. What do you say?

There was never going to be an answer I felt one hundred percent confident in. And I knew, deep down, that if I said no I would always feel guilty and wonder what would have happened if I had said yes.

Okay okay I'll be your maid of honor! Do you know who else you'll ask to be in the bridal party?

Mindy, Blair, Isabel, and Shaun.

Seeing his name sent a sad reverberation through my heart. Shaun was Ellie's friend from college, from The Time We Did Not Speak Of, aka our first big fight.

8

When it came time to apply to colleges, Ellie and I decided that we would apply to all the same ones, a smattering of liberal arts schools in the Northeast with a focus on Boston and New York. I chose schools that had strong gender studies programs, but Ellie wasn't sure what she wanted to major in.

"Well, what's your favorite class?" I asked as we sat in College Prep, supposedly working on our application essays on the computers. I was working on two essays: one I showed people, about how being in debate club had helped me prepare for life after high school, and another I showed no one, about how going to college wasn't just about education but about finally living authentically and meeting other people who were hopefully like me.

"Everyone's always asking that," Ellie said moodily. Her essay was about how living all over the world had made her adaptable to change. But she had given up on it for now, and instead she was doodling a series of long, curvy lines like octopus tentacles and filling them in with different designs. "What if I don't have a favorite?"

"You're really good at math and science."

"That's not the same as liking them."

"There must be a class you enjoy being in more than the others." The teacher, Mr. Rosen, got up from his desk and all the students closed their AIM chats and email and pulled their essays back up. He made a perfunctory lap around the class, glancing at everyone's screen, then sat back down.

"I guess I like photography," Ellie said.

"Okay, what do you like about it?"

She smiled, her neck flushing.

"Oh my God. Tell me it's not because Chris Hatch is in your class."

She rolled her eyes. "Okay, it's not because Chris Hatch is in my class."

"Jesus Christ. If there was a class called 'talking about boys,' it would be easy to pick your favorite."

Ellie crossed her arms defensively. "He's not *all* I like about photo class. I like that no one lectures me or asks me for answers."

"Do you like taking photos, though?"

"I don't know. Mrs. Horna told me I could be more thoughtful with my composition."

"You know college is like, all about lectures and answering questions. Maybe it's not for you, at least not yet. It's not for everyone."

She widened her eyes in alarm. "But then we'd be apart."

"We might be apart anyway. There's no guarantee we're both going to get into the same schools."

"We're bound to get into at least one of the same ones."

"But it might not be the best one for both of us. Like, if we both get into my fourth-choice school but then only I get into my top-choice school, I should probably go to my top choice. Right?" My top choice was an arts and communication school in the heart of Boston, and when I had visited, sitting in the dining hall watching people with purple hair wearing Doc Martens and spindly boys holding hands, a sense of belonging had washed over me. A feeling I was just starting to have—maybe at that very moment—was that it might be better to go to college without Ellie. If part of the reason I wanted to go was to leave my closeted life behind, how would Ellie fit into that? She didn't care that I was gay, but it wasn't like I was living a totally queer lifestyle. My identity was more hypothetical than anything else. What about when I found friends like me, or when I wanted to go to gay bars, or—the thought made my skin tingle—when I got a girlfriend? Would we still be best friends then?

She doodled more furiously, the ink getting darker. "So this only works if we both get into your top choice?"

"It's not just about me. You should go to your top choice, too."

Ellie's eyes filled up. She blinked and a teardrop fell onto her drawing, making the sharp lines of ink go blurry. "If you're changing your mind about us going to the same school, just say so."

I sighed. "I'm not changing my mind. I'm just trying to be realistic. We *are* two separate people."

She looked at me like I had slapped her in the face, then got up and ran to the bathroom.

When we both got into my top-choice school, my elation was quickly followed by a bitter aftertaste, not just about Ellie but also about money. My parents were, of course, unable to help with tuition or any other bills. The school had given me some financial aid, but the cost per year would still be around thirty thousand dollars, which would all have to be paid for with loans, and of course I'd get a job to cover my living expenses. I had also gotten into the University of Vermont, my safety school, and they were offering me a completely full ride. My parents sat me down and told me in very stern voices that the best choice was UVM, that otherwise I'd graduate with crippling debt and wouldn't ever be able to get out from underneath it, that I'd be paying back my loans for the literal rest of my life. But at least a third of our high school was going to UVM, and I thought of Burlington as a "city," with air quotes and an ironic tone of voice, whereas Boston was an actual city. For a few days I hemmed and hawed, chewing off all my nails, then I decided there was no way my queer dreams would be realized if I stayed in Vermont, so I sent my enrollment deposit to my top choice.

"You have to tell me if you don't want me to go, too," Ellie said. She had gotten into two other schools but had made it clear that my first choice was her first choice.

It wasn't fair of me to tell Ellie where or where not to go to college. I didn't even know what my honest answer was—I could have told her yes or no and they both felt true. I wanted the safety and familiarity of having her with me, but didn't know if her presence would hold me back. I tried to picture her there, and her not there. It was strange, the way life could play out any different number of ways. "Don't be stupid," I said. "Of course we're both going to go."

She squealed and locked me into a hug.

After just a few weeks at college, Ellie and I were already latched as a twosome in everyone's mind. No one ever said our names separately, or they called us the twins, and it felt like too true of a nickname. We might as well have been conjoined and sharing internal organs, unable to move or live independently. We were assigned to the same dorm (thank God the college gave us different roommates), took almost all the same classes, ate every meal together at the dining hall, and so far had all the same friends, zero of which were queer. The closeness that had felt so vital in high school now felt oppressive, and I didn't know what to do about it.

It all came to a head one day when our gender studies professor asked us to stay after class. She showed us the intro paragraph of both our most recent essays, with similar wording and an almost-identical thesis about abortion being a progressive economic issue. My heart hiccupped and I looked at Ellie, dumbfounded. She stared down at the paper, refusing to make eye contact. I had brought up the topic at lunch with her the week before, working the idea out in my head. Ellie had mostly listened and asked questions.

"You remember that talk we had about plagiarism on the first day," Dr. Azikiwe said. What I most remembered from the first day of class is how she had given a little speech about how important it was that we call her Dr. Azikiwe, since a) it was a title she had earned by getting her PhD, and b) it was gender neutral and therefore more inclusive while also avoiding the trappings of using "Ms." "Miss" or "Mrs.," since those titles were used to denote marital status, and men were only ever addressed as Mr. regardless of whether or not they were married. I had never thought about that. Every day I left her class feeling like my brain had been rewired, and I looked up to her probably more than anyone else I had met at that point in my life. I harbored fantasies about her inviting me and a few other choice students to her house for dinner, where we'd eat something fancy and meet her partner, whom she frequently and casually mentioned during lectures. It killed me that she might think I wasn't smart, that I had needed to steal an idea from someone else.

"The repercussions can be very serious," Dr. Azikiwe went on. "So I'd like to know how both of you came up with this idea." She threaded her fingers together and placed her hands on the table, waiting. The whites of her eyes cut through me.

I decided to go first, before Ellie could claim the narrative. "I was listening to the debate on TV the other week, where one of the candidates kept talking about how the Democratic Party's focus has to be on economics and not social issues like reproductive rights. But I didn't really understand how they could separate the two, since abortions are so often a financial decision. So the next day at lunch, I mentioned the idea to Ellie." I stopped myself there, waiting for Ellie to go on, for her to admit it.

"Yeah, we must have talked about it for at least an hour,"

said Ellie. "We bounced thoughts and opinions back and forth, so it would be really hard to say who had ownership of the idea. I don't know if you know this, but Robin and I are best friends, and we're so similar that sometimes it can be hard to tell like, who thought what first."

My eyes widened and my stomach lurched. Did she honestly think we had come up with the idea together, or was she just trying to save her ass? Was she stooping so low as to use our friendship as an excuse for stealing my idea? "But I brought it up first," I said.

"Yeah, but all that means is you happened to bring it up before me. It wasn't necessarily something I wasn't already thinking about."

A hostile laugh escaped me. "Was it? Had you ever thought to yourself, gee, abortion really seems like an economic issue?"

"Maybe not in those exact words."

I looked at Dr. Azikiwe, hoping she was reading the situation correctly. She sighed. "It's not a brand-new idea by any means. It's just strange to have two students in the same class turn in a paper about the same idea, phrased very similarly. In situations like this, where no one admits fault, you both are at risk for being dropped from the class with an F, or an even more severe sanction imposed by the Dean of Students. I'm required to report this to her and it will go in your file. So I'd like you both to think deeply about the personal genesis of this idea, and email me by the end of the day if anything has changed."

As soon as we left the classroom, I wheeled around and snarled, "We could be expelled, Ellie."

"No way," she said. "She'll probably just ask us to rewrite

the paper, which is still unfair. It sucks they can't acknowl-
edge that it's possible for two people to have the same idea."

I had never had the urge to punch someone in the face so intensely. "Would you stop saying that? You *know* it was my idea."

Ellie scoffed and walked faster. "That's so typical. We have
a conversation about something we *both* had thought about,
and you walk away thinking you have total ownership of it."

"No, what's typical is this carbon-copy routine of yours.
This is exactly what I was worried about when you followed
me to college. You need to get your own personality, your
own ideas, your own fucking *life*." I had finally said it. My
head felt wobbly on top of my neck, like it might topple over
and roll onto the floor.

Ellie stopped walking. We were standing in the middle of
the hallway, and people huffed by us, knocking our shoulders
with their backpacks. Ellie clasped her arms tightly around
her body, like she could make herself disappear. "That's what
you really think? That I follow you around? That I copy you?
Why are you friends with me, then?"

I didn't say anything.

She shook her head. Her face was the color of a freshly
boiled lobster. "I think you *like* that dynamic. You don't want
friends, you just want sycophants. You wouldn't know how
to have a relationship with someone who didn't act that way."

My fingers twitched. "That's not true."

"Okay," she said. "Well, in that case, I guess I'll get my
own fucking life." She turned on her heel and walked purposefully down the hallway, and that was the last time we
spoke for two years.

9

In mid-April, a month before the wedding, it was time for the bridal shower—the first occasion I should have realized that something was off. Initially, I had tried to convince Ellie not to have a shower at all, explaining that it was one of the invented customs from the 1950s-era wedding ad campaign, designed to increase income for businesses and reinforce traditional gender roles since the party was centered on gifts for either the kitchen or the bedroom.

"Oh my God, Robin, not everything has to be politicized," Ellie had said. "Sometimes a party can just be a party."

So then I tried to convince her to at least do something slightly unconventional, like a mixed-gender party with no gifts, or a charity bridal shower. I laughed remembering my efforts as I sat in a Pasadena rose garden drinking high tea while watching Ellie open gift after gift like Mr. and Mrs. coffee spoons with their wedding date engraved on them, a doormat that said "The Ellisons," and a Mrs. Ellison hanger for her wedding dress.

The hanger was from Mindy, a member of the bridal party who was Ellie's childhood friend and a stay-at-home mom of three boys who looked like they tortured cats for fun. The other bridal party members were Blair, Ellie's former "work wife" (a term I couldn't stand) who had been incessantly swiping right and left on various dating apps since she arrived, Isabel, a yoga instructor who kept ascribing everything to the new moon in Taurus, and Shaun, a lawyer at the ACLU who was the biggest ladder climber I had ever met—he wanted to climb it all the way to the top and be president someday. Blair's shower gift was a bunch of edible underwear and a "sexy dice game," Isabel's was a tarot deck for brides and a rose quartz wine stopper, and Shaun's was a red Le Creuset Dutch oven.

I didn't want to see Ellie's disappointed face when she opened my set of *Golden Girls* candles, so I got up and wandered around the rose garden, which I had to admit was pretty stunning—as far as you could see, row after row of roses bloomed in practically every color imaginable: brilliant magenta and golden yellow and ballet-slipper pink and dusky purple and creamy apricot, my favorite. There were roses for every gradation on a paint swatch. Some of these gradations were even encompassed within a single flower. A few roses had the classic sweet, perfumey scent I was used to, and others smelled like citrus or clove, and others were strangely scentless.

Since the garden was in LA, many of the roses were named for celebrities: Marilyn Monroe was platinum blond with big buxom blooms, and next to her, with a wink from the rose curator, was John F. Kennedy, a rather plain white rose. Julia Child was the color of butter and Neil Diamond was a striped rose of burgundy red splattered with blushing pink.

The focal point of the garden was an arbored walkway, where roses spiraled their way to the top before spilling over in abundant mounds. Two towering willows bookended the walkway, and farther down a stone sculpture sat on top of a long, sloping hill. The statue was titled "Love, the Captive of Youth," and it depicted Cupid and his captor, a fair maiden, encircled by Grecian columns.

I wound my way through each row, passing Japanese tourists in bucket hats and New Balance sneakers who wielded selfie sticks, and mothers with bleary eyes pushing strollers draped in gauzy white blankets, and young handholding couples with visiting parents who marveled at the weather. I marveled at it, too: high sixties with full sun, accompanied by a breeze so cool that it felt air-conditioned in the shade. It was hard to believe that back home it was still bitterly cold, probably raining or snowing or some combination of the two. It was a shame I was here for a bridal shower and not just to enjoy the weather and the roses and the larger botanical garden that surrounded the roses.

When I got back to the patio area, all the women in long, floral-print dresses were slinging purses over their shoulders and hugging Ellie goodbye. I breathed a sigh of relief and started packing up my things, until Blair put a hand on my arm and said Ellie wanted the bridal party to stay. *Probably to help clean up*, I thought, surveying the damage and trying to estimate how long we'd be held hostage.

After everyone outside the bridal party had left, Ellie clapped her hands and smiled at us excitedly. "It's time to play a game," she announced.

Jesus, one of those idiotic games like newlywed trivia or designing a wedding dress out of toilet paper—was that better or worse than having to clean up? Ellie hadn't mentioned any games when we were planning the party.

"Or maybe a game isn't exactly the right word," Ellie went on. "More like a trust exercise."

I glanced at the other bridal party members, trying to figure out if they knew what Ellie was talking about, but they looked just as clueless as me.

She put on a weird, rehearsed voice like she was giving a speech. "It probably goes without saying that you all are the people I trust most in the world. It means so much to me that you've agreed to stand by me and support me during this time." Her eyes went teary, and she wiped a pinky underneath the corner of her eye.

"Aww," Mindy said, tearing up right back.

Ellie smoothed her hands on her long, white, floral-print dress, took a deep breath, and continued. "For this wedding to be the best it can possibly be, we have to trust each other so deeply, so innately, that if we stumble or fall, we know someone will be there to catch us. So I thought what better way to practice than with a trust fall?" She dragged a chair onto an empty patch of grass, then removed its cushion and placed it on the ground in front of the chair. She collected a few more cushions and lined them up behind the first one until they were the length of a body lying on the ground. "Just in case," she said, grinning. "Now, who wants to go first?"

We all looked at each other and forced out a few uncomfortable laughs when no one immediately volunteered. I didn't even like standing on the stepladder to get the serving platter from the highest shelf in the kitchen, so I wasn't about to go first. I didn't know if I would go at all—sure, everyone *meant* to catch you, but what if you fell at a weird angle or their hands slipped or something else went wrong? There were probably a slew of YouTube videos with titles like "Trust Fall Gone Wrong" or "Trust Fall Epic Fail," the person on the chair closing their eyes and falling backward only for their head to crack against the floor.

"How about you go first, Ellie?" I said.

"Oh, no," she said. "It's meant to be a game for the bridal party. The bride doesn't participate."

"But trust is a two-way street," I said. "Don't you need to trust *us* to catch *you*?"

"I trust you by *you* falling," Ellie said.

I put a hand on my hip. "That doesn't make sense."

Mindy stepped forward. "It's okay, I'll go." She kicked off her platform wedges, the kind with woven rope covering the platform part, and stepped onto the chair facing backward. It wobbled slightly and she moved her feet farther apart, steadying herself. Her toenails were long and unmanicured, and she had huge, scaly calluses on the outside of both her big toes. It was reassuring to see that she had a physical imperfection— Mindy looked like Angelina Jolie's *prettier* sister: a prominent square jaw, cheekbones you could see from about a mile away, full lips and wide gray-blue eyes, and thick dark brown hair. It was hard to believe she had three kids.

"Everyone gather around her and link arms," said Ellie. We lined up with two of us on either side, and Ellie stood at the end. Shaun was directly across from me, and as I reached my hands to his, I widened my eyes as if to say, *This is a little kooky, isn't it?* He shrugged back as if to say, *Sure, but what can ya do?*

"Mindy, I trust you to do anything and everything to help me make my wedding day dreams come true," said Ellie. "If you trust me and your fellow bridal party members, close your eyes and fall."

Mindy shook her hands at the wrists. "I think the last time I did this was summer camp when I was ten years old. I didn't have quite as far to fall then." Mindy didn't have just the looks of a supermodel but also the height—she must have been at least six feet tall. "Okay, okay, okay, here I go." She took a deep breath, folded her arms over her chest, and leaned back until her body smacked into our arms, almost forcing my hands apart from Shaun's. A gust of perfume that smelled like gummy bears trailed her falling body. We lowered her down onto the cushions and she *whooped.* "That was a rush," she said.

Isabel went next, followed by Blair and Shaun. No epic fails. Everyone turned to me.

"I think I'll pass," I said. "I kind of have a thing about heights."

A chorus of protest.

Isabel tsked her tongue. "So Aquarius. Afraid to let go of control." The first time we met, Isabel hadn't even released the handshake before she asked me what my sign was, and after that, everything I said and did was just *so* Aquarius.

"It really wasn't scary," said Blair, who loved roller coasters and horror movies.

"Would these arms *not* catch you?" said Shaun, kissing each of his formidable biceps. Shaun looked like a Black version of Mr. Clean: shaved head, clean-shaven face, thick brows, wide facial features, a jawline so strong it could probably support the weight of his whole body. The only thing that deviated were his Dumbo ears, which I thought were his most endearing feature.

"You wouldn't do it for *me*, Rob?" said Ellie, taking my hand and squeezing it. "It would mean so much to me. Like, so much." She looked at me like a kid asking their parent for a puppy.

"You can do it, Robin!" said Mindy, then she started chanting my name, and everyone joined in. Their eyes glinted and their hands pressed my back, pushing me toward the chair until before I knew it, I was standing on top of it. My bowels surged. The willow tree's long branches waved in the wind and I tried to breathe in rhythm with their lazy back and forth. Everyone else had done it and they were fine. I was much smaller than Shaun and Mindy, much easier to catch. They wouldn't leave me alone until I did it.

"Okay," I said, swallowing a mouthful of spit. The smell of roses was suddenly incredibly strong. I shifted my weight to my heels and leaned back until my feet left the chair. My stomach slid into my throat and the sun zoomed through the sky and then my back thudded into the five pairs of arms waiting for me. Everyone cheered. My whole body shook like

Bean's did in the waiting room at the vet. Hot tears leaked out the corners of my eyes and crept into my hair. But it was over—I had done it. We all stood up and started to head back to the table where our things were.

"Who's hungry?" said Blair. "I read about this great sushi place—"

Ellie cleared her throat. We all turned around. "We're not quite finished," she said.

We dragged our feet back to where she was standing.

She put on the rehearsed voice like she was reading from a speech again. "We've established who I can trust when things are easy. But what about when things are a little harder?" She picked up the cushions and moved them to the side, then stood there with her hands folded over her stomach, expectant.

"So you want us to do it again, but without the cushions?" asked Blair.

"Yes," Ellie said.

We all stood there with slumped shoulders and glassy, bloodshot eyes. "Wasn't once enough?" I said. "It's been a long day and I think everyone is exhausted. Plus, it's more dangerous without any padding."

Ellie frowned. "Sorry, I thought the purpose of today was for me to feel *showered* with love and support, but if you're all too tired..." She threw her hands up. "I guess we can just leave."

Isabel sighed and turned to the bridal party. "It'll just take a few minutes for us to do it again." She stepped back up onto the chair. So we did it again. Isabel, then Mindy, then Blair, then Shaun. When it was my turn, I wasn't even scared anymore, just annoyed and anxious to leave, so I went ahead and got it over with.

"Now can we go home?" I said to Ellie.

She bit her lip. "Just *one* more thing, then I promise we can go." From a nearby table, she gathered a bunch of champagne flutes between her fingers then turned and abruptly dropped them on the cement tiles that covered the dining area. As they shattered, we all rushed over, thinking it had been an accident, but there was no shock on Ellie's face. "It's okay, I meant to drop them," she said, kneeling down to collect the biggest shards and deposit them in a white cloth napkin. We all watched uneasily as she carried the full napkin to the trust-fall chair, then she started methodically stabbing the sharp pieces of glass into the grass, leaving each piercing triangular top exposed by a few inches. "This will show me who I can trust when I'm at my breaking point," she said. *Breaking* as a pun for the glass shards that would puncture our tender skin if we failed to be caught, I assumed.

I crossed my arms and waited for someone else to say this was too far as Ellie kept driving daggers into the ground. A plane flew by overhead, the jet stream cutting a sharp white diagonal line into the blue sky. "Someone could get really hurt," I finally said. "Someone could die."

"It's just a *metaphor*," said Ellie. "No one is actually going to fall on them."

I scoffed. "A metaphor is a figure of speech, Ellie. These shards of glass are real, and could cause real injuries."

Ellie's bottom lip started to quiver. Her voice came out high and choked. "This is really important to me, and if you, my best friends, can't see why..." She pulled her mouth into a deep frown, sniffed shakily, wailed, and wiped at her eyes, but I didn't see any actual tears falling.

Blair knelt down and rubbed her shoulder, then pulled her into a hug. She said something I couldn't hear, then Ellie said something back. Blair stood up and addressed the rest of us. "We've caught everyone so far, so there's no reason we won't this time." She stepped onto the chair.

Shaun wrapped his hands around my forearms.

"I'm not comfortable with this," I said, and tried to pull away, but Shaun's thick fingers were locked around my arms and everyone was already counting down from three. Then Blair's bony back hit my arms.

I watched like I was in a bizarre dream as everyone else climbed onto the chair and fell backward. Time either whizzed by or crawled, I couldn't tell which. When it was my turn, I shook my head back and forth vehemently. "Nope. You're all nuts. I'm not doing that."

"We'll catch you, we promise," said Shaun. "Right, guys?"

"Yeah, we promise, we promise," everyone chirped like a nest full of baby birds who believe they'll fly on faith.

"Nope," I said again.

"Trust means nothing unless there are stakes," said Ellie.

I laughed, pointing at the bed of broken champagne flutes. "*Literal* stakes!" I kept laughing because my body didn't know what else to do. It was a manic, hyena-esque noise. As the laughs turned into something more like a wail, the group of bridesmaids closed in around me. They smiled at me with their gleaming teeth and cooed that everything was okay. Their gentle hands pet my head, stroked my arms, then suddenly gripped my midsection. My feet left the ground only to be placed on the chair. My legs wobbled like JELL-O, and my head swam like I was drunk or had a bad flu. It felt like a magnetic force was pulling me backward, and I didn't have the strength to resist it. As my body began to tilt, I wondered if I would even feel the shards of glass the moment they stabbed through my skin, or if it would be such a shock that the pain would be delayed. A tiny, dark part of me wanted to find out what would happen if I did fall on them. But then the arms of the bridal party encircled me and I recognized, disdainfully, that I did feel closer to them, that I felt I could trust them more than before. Ellie, though, I wasn't sure.

10

If you were to chart my trust for Ellie over the years, it would look like those jagged seesawing lines on a lie detector test. After our fight about the paper, Ellie really did get her own life, which allowed me to get mine. I let her take the mutual friends we had made, and for the first few weeks after our breakup I had no one. I was too embarrassed to sit by myself in the dining hall, so I'd eat Pop-Tarts and easy macs in my dorm room. I didn't want to go to parties where I knew I'd see Ellie, so I stayed in and watched DVD box sets of *Seinfeld* and rigorously did my homework. Even my socially challenged roommate from Iowa went out more than I did.

Then the unthinkable happened—Dr. Azikiwe asked me

to stay after class, and it wasn't because I was in trouble but because she wanted me to come over for a small dinner party. She had never kicked Ellie and me out of the class, but instead, just made both of us rewrite the paper. She must have noticed that after that, Ellie and I no longer spoke and sat on opposite sides of the room. The dinner party fulfilled my fantasy and was one of the most exciting nights of my life. I met Dr. Azikiwe's partner, who was a chef at a very fancy restaurant, and cooked us red curry—something I had never eaten before. I also met Alice, one of Dr. Azikiwe's students from a different class who was a year ahead of me, and who I started dating not long after. I became friends with all her friends, and since they were mostly queer and all a year ahead, I almost never had to worry about running into Ellie anymore outside class.

From what I could tell, she flitted from one social group to another, from the too-cool-for-school film buffs to the social justice warriors to the indie rockers, trying them on like outfits. Once I passed her on the street walking next to a friend. They were dressed like twins, the same outfit of boho dresses over jeans with cowboy boots, just in slightly different styles and colors. Ellie and I passed within a few inches of each other, our hands almost touching, and made charged eye contact for a blink of a second. It might have been a trick of the light, but I was wearing all red and I swear I saw her skin flare, like a chameleon matching color, as I passed by.

A year and a half passed, then one day Ellie posted on Facebook that her dad, who had had ALS since our junior year of high school, passed away. He and Ellie's mom had gotten divorced right after she left for college, and she said it was the worst thing that had ever happened to her. Now there was this. Without thinking, like it was a knee-jerk reaction or something even deeper than that, like a cellular reaction, I immediately picked up the phone and called her. I didn't expect her to answer—I was already planning what I'd say in my voice mail—but then I heard her voice.

"Wow," she said coldly. "Weird to see your number on my phone's screen. I guess you're guilt-calling because you saw the post about my dad."

A jolt went through my heart. I hadn't anticipated that she'd still be mad. I had assumed she'd be glad, even thankful, to hear from me. That it would be all forgiveness on both sides. "I don't really know why I called. It felt like the right thing to do."

She sniffed, even though it didn't sound like she was crying. "So you didn't call because you wanted to, but because you felt obligated. Great."

"No, that's not it." I wished I had emailed or texted instead. Given us both some time to figure out how we wanted this to go. I cast around for something to say. "I still remember in high school, when he'd—"

"No, stop," she hissed. "You don't get to do that. You don't get to disappear from my life and then reminisce about the good old days like you've been there for me. These past few months were hell, Robin." Her voice broke then. "I really needed someone like you around."

"I had no idea, Ellie. You could have called me. I wish you would have called me."

"And said what?" She hiccupped the way people do when

they're crying. "My dad is dying so please be my friend again?"

"Essentially, yeah."

"And you would've? Been my friend again?"

"Of course."

She blew her nose. "So that's what it would take? For you to be my friend, someone had to be dying?"

"Ellie, that's not it at all."

"Then why didn't you ever call?" She raised her voice. "Didn't you miss me at all?"

The thing was, I had missed her. I had found other friends and the life I had always so desperately wanted, but I never felt the way I did with Ellie again. That mind–meld, synchronized-swimming, harmonizing-like-the-Indigo-Girls closeness. Looking back, I wondered if the closeness was real or if she had just faked it, matching herself to me in an imitation of intimacy. I wondered if it mattered. "Why are you pinning all this on me?" I said. "*You* could've called."

She scoffed. "*I* wasn't the one who ended the friendship."

"It seemed pretty mutual to me."

"You told me to get my own personality and my own fucking life. I still remember your exact words."

"I shouldn't have said that. I was afraid I was going to be kicked out of school, and I was mad at you." Even at that moment I thought Ellie might finally admit she had stolen my idea.

"Yeah, mad at me for something I didn't do."

So she had been waiting for an admittance, too. We had both been living in our own subjective reality, with our own subjective truth. Maybe all those years when I thought we were thinking the same thing, we weren't at all. "Let's not rehash all that," I said.

"Okay." I could practically hear her crossing her arms over the phone.

"So when's the funeral?"

"Next week. Wednesday."

"Can I come?"

"I don't know. I don't know if you'd come because you want to or you feel guilty."

I wasn't sure, either. "Listen, I know we wouldn't be talking right now if your dad hadn't died, but it feels right that we're talking. I want to come if you want me to come."

"Okay," she said. "Come, then."

When I walked into the service, I slid into the second-to-last pew without realizing that I had seated myself next to Ellie's best friend since we had stopped being friends, Shaun— or as I thought of him, Ellie's Replacement Gay. All I knew about him was that he was a political science major, and student government president, and I had once seen him in the dining hall slicing a banana onto a piece of pizza. Since being friends with him, Ellie had started volunteering for John Kerry and going to protests in support of gay marriage, racial justice, and women's rights. The Ellie I had known before was pretty *apolitical*—she said reading the news was "too depressing" and feminists were "too angry." So when I heard she was running around town brandishing signs and clipboards, I wasn't sure if Ellie actually cared about the issues or if she just liked the way it made her look, like wearing the latest fashion.

"You're Shaun, right?" I said when he glanced at me.

"Yeah, and you must be Robin," he said, giving me a firm handshake. "I've heard a lot about you." He gave me a fake political smile, the kind he had probably been practicing his whole life.

Instead of going down that conversational road, I asked if he ever met Ellie's dad.

"No, I didn't." He fished around for something else to say. "But he sounded like a great guy."

"He was," I said. "It's nice of you to come, considering you didn't know him."

He raised an eyebrow. "It's nice of *you* to come, too, considering you haven't spoken to Ellie in two years." He said it in the same cheery manner he had said everything else.

I laughed, liking this version of Shaun. I recrossed my feet and knocked them against a gray gift bag with white tissue splaying out of the top. "Did you bring Ellie something?"

"A book of poems about grief and healing called *The Art of Losing*." He made a self-satisfied face like he was about to receive an award for Best Grief Gift.

"Ellie hates poetry." It plummeted out of my mouth. Ellie had once called poetry "a whole lot of words to avoid using the one adjective that could sum up your emotional state."

Shaun shrugged. "For someone who hates it, she reads a lot of it. Especially these past few months. Grief can really change an unsentimental person."

I thought about the gifts I had waiting in the car: *Clueless* on DVD, Mario Kart, a box of Sleepytime tea, and two batches of homemade blueberry muffins with loads of blueberries— Ellie's favorite things from high school, but maybe not anymore. I suddenly felt ridiculously out of place in the church, ridiculously out of place in Ellie's life. It had been the wrong move to come when so much time had passed, when what Ellie needed was people who had been there for her, not someone who had seen the news on Facebook and then guiltily called her after two years of silence.

At the reception the feeling intensified. I busied myself washing dishes, pushing Ellie's Polish aunts out of the way and scraping sour cream and half-eaten pierogies off plates, or else building LEGOs with her cousins who were too little to understand what had happened, happily revved up on all the babka and cheesecake and apple tart that no one else wanted to eat.

Ellie came into the kitchen when I was on my third round of dishes. Her eyes were so swollen they looked like slits and her face was the splotchy color of pink tie-dye. "You've been avoiding me," she said.

I scrubbed at a fork with coagulated cheese stuck between the tines. "I know this must be the worst day of your life, and I just don't want to make it any harder."

She leaned against the countertop like it was the one sustaining thing left in her life. "Why would you make it harder?"

"Because I wasn't there for you," I said. "I don't even know what it's been like these past few months. Shaun told me you like *poetry* now."

Ellie snorted and slumped even farther onto the countertop. "I'm *trying* to like poetry, does that count? I've been trying a lot of things."

I gave up on the fork, letting it soak some more as I switched to spoons. "Like what?"

She rolled her eyes playfully. "Like healing crystals and death metal and MDMA."

I widened mine. Ellie and I had always been too scared to try anything stronger than pot. "How was MDMA?"

"I became really obsessed with my armpits and listened to SexyBack probably two hundred times. It was fun, but the next day I felt like it probably wasn't worth it."

"Wow," I said. "Maybe you should have tried reading poetry while you were on MDMA. Bet you would have liked it then."

Ellie laughed and pushed herself up from the countertop. "Yeah, maybe. There was this one poem I really liked. It was by Edna St. Vincent Millay, and it went something like, 'I know what my life is like, since I lost you. It's like a little pool, left by the tide, drying from the outside.' But you know, more beautifully worded than that. It made me cry buckets."

"That's really sad and lovely," I said. "Did you know Edna St. Vincent Millay was queer?"

Ellie clucked her tongue. "Of course you know that. Maybe that's why it made me cry."

"Why?"

"Because it made me miss you. When I read it, I wasn't sure if I was crying about my dad, or you." She sighed and pulled me into a tight hug. "At least I didn't lose both of you."

11

The day after the bridal shower, we all flew to Vegas for the bachelorette—we combined the two parties into one weekend so those of us who lived on the east coast wouldn't have to fly across the country two separate times. Just like the shower, I had tried to convince Ellie not to have the standard Vegas bachelorette, and she had said if there was any time to embrace your inner basic bitch, this was it. So Blair, who frequently cried while watching the backstory segments on *America's Got Talent* and who always did a thirty-day countdown to PSL (Pumpkin Spice Latte) season on her social media, planned it. Thus how we found ourselves on a party bus with a stripper pole and disco ball, dancing half-heartedly to eardrum-

rupturingly loud R&B from the early 2000s, drinking vodka
Red Bulls out of penis bottles, wearing "I do crew" sashes
while Ellie wore one that said "I do," on our way to a club
that would be indistinguishable from the one we were just at,
where we would continue playing "Drink and Dare Bachelorette Bingo," which included dares like getting a man to
give you his underwear or having a stranger show you their
favorite sex position.

The driver said he had to use the bathroom and pulled into
a gas station. Blair came around and refilled our vodka Red
Bulls. I passed out waters and reminded everyone to stay hydrated. Once we got to the next club, my plan was to go to
the bathroom, tell everyone I puked, then take a cab back to
the hotel. The driver had left the door open and the sewer
smell that permeated the whole city invaded the bus. Combined with the chemically saccharine smell of Red Bull, it
made me feel like I really might puke. I closed my eyes and
took a few deep breaths through my mouth. Everyone on
the bus other than me sang along to "Hey Ma" by Cam'ron
at the top of their lungs, until they suddenly stopped at the
line about "dome."

I opened my eyes to a stocky man in a black ski mask
standing at the front of the bus, pointing an assault rifle in
our direction.

I blinked, trying to take in the reality of the situation, then
I dropped to the floor of the bus, trying to get out of the rifle's sight line. What the fuck was happening? If his intention
was to simply rob us, he would've had some kind of hand-
gun. But the assault rifle seemed to signal something more
sinister, like a mass murder. My stomach went cold. I exam-

ined everyone else's face for signs of how to react, but their expressions were strangely numb.

Two other men in ski masks ran onto our bus—one slid into the driver's seat and closed the door before peeling out of the gas station, and the other came around snatching our bags and phones. That was when I went from terrified to petrified. My heartbeat rose into my throat like bile. If it was just a robbery, we wouldn't have left the parking lot. So what was it? Kidnapping? Human trafficking? I forced my darting brain to focus on what I could possibly do. There was no rear exit to run to, no windows to jump out of, and no way to get to my phone.

The driver took the first turn off the strip, then another turn down a dark alley. I desperately sucked at the sewer-scented air, but it could barely make its way to my panicked lungs. The Cam'ron song stopped, and "I'm Real" by J.Lo came on. Halfway down the alley, the bus screeched to a stop. The guy who had taken our stuff took a roll of duct tape out of a bag and ripped off a piece with his teeth, then smacked it over Ellie's mouth. Next, he snapped a pair of handcuffs over her wrists and yanked her to the front of the bus. She didn't resist him, and her eyes appeared curiously calm. The driver opened the door and the man who handcuffed her dragged Ellie down the steps and through a graffitied door at the back of a building. The other two men followed and bizarrely, we were left alone on the bus.

Isabel, who was sitting closest to the control panel, reached up a shaky hand to turn the music off. "What the fuck?" she said. "What do we do?"

"Why would they take just Ellie?" I said.

"Do we go after her?" said Mindy.

Shaun stood up. "One of us needs to find someone with a phone and call 911."

"On it," said Blair, and she raced off the bus.

"Shouldn't we all be getting the fuck out of here?" I said.

"We can't just leave Ellie," said Mindy. "What if they took *you*? You wouldn't want the rest of us to abandon you." Mindy was always talking about loyalty, and I figured anyone who talked about it that much must have been the opposite of the word, but if she was willing to go after Ellie, her money must have been where her mouth was.

"I wouldn't want you to die for me, either," I said. "The only people who have a chance at saving Ellie are trained professionals. That's why we should all be out looking for someone with a phone."

Mindy scoffed. "Some maid of honor you are."

"Now isn't the time for your jealousy," Isabel said to Mindy.

"I *wish* you were the maid of honor," I said to Mindy. "It's the last thing I wanted."

Shaun clapped his hands once, loudly. "We're wasting time! Let's just take a vote. Who's for going after Ellie?"

Shaun and Mindy raised their hands immediately, then Isabel raised hers.

"Right, I guess I'm the only asshole," I said.

"You can do whatever you want," Shaun said. "But if you come with us, it's four against three."

"I should probably mention I have this." Mindy leaned over and rolled up her jeans, then unzipped her boot and pulled out a tiny silver pistol with a pink rubber handle. "I wasn't about to come to a big city like Vegas without protection." Mindy lived in a small town in North Carolina and was all over the place politically—she loved the second amendment but also LGBTQIA+ rights (because her brother was gay) and abortion (because she had had one, as she would happily tell anyone).

"That doesn't make me feel better, Mindy," I said.

She put a hand on her hip. "I can shoot a Coke can dead center from thirty yards away, but okay."

"According to the new moon in Taurus—" Isabel started, but Shaun interrupted her.

"We've got to move," he said. "Now."

Mindy grabbed my hand. "If you stay out here, you'll feel like shit the rest of your life no matter what happens. You know it's true."

She was probably right. People who survived things like this always talked about the guilt eating them up—they were alive, but at what cost? I tried not to think about what would happen as Mindy pulled me down the stairs of the bus and through the graffitied door that enclosed us in total darkness. None of us had our cell phones, thus no flashlights. We stood still for a minute, holding our breath, straining our ears for a noise that might indicate where Ellie was. Muffled bass pounded from the front of the building, maybe, and a pipe above our heads creaked. Then, men laughed from somewhere below us. The fucking sickos, laughing at Ellie and whatever they were going to do to her. It occurred to me, suddenly, that they would probably rape her unless we got to her soon.

"We have to hurry," I said.

"I'm going to try to find the stairs to the basement," whispered Mindy. Her feet shuffled across the floor. She made a small noise of surprise, like when you trip, then said, "Found them."

Someone took my hand—I assumed Isabel, because it was delicate and soft, and we shuffled in a handholding chain, Mindy then Shaun then Isabel then me, to the first step. *If we don't die at the hands of the kidnappers, we'll probably die going down these stairs*, I thought as my foot inched along, waiting to feel the edge of the stair. I had expected my eyes to adjust after a minute, to at least distinguish vague shapes, but the darkness was still complete. Isabel pulled at my hand, trying to get me to go faster to stay connected to the chain, and my foot slipped off the edge of the stairs, making me fall onto my butt.

"Are you okay?" Isabel whispered.

"Yeah," I said. "I'm going to stay here and scoot down on my butt. Seems safer."

"Good idea," said Isabel, and she passed it down the chain until we were all scooting. I would have laughed if it wasn't for what we were scooting toward. Instead, I forced myself to take a calming breath in through my nose, and for a second I swore I smelled pizza. As we descended, the male voices got louder. I thought I even heard a woman's voice. Could it be Ellie? No one was yelling. It sounded like they were chatting casually, with intermittent laughter. They wouldn't be hurting her while talking like this, would they? Finally, my butt hit a step that ended up being the floor. A strip of yellow light shone from underneath a door at the end of the hallway, and that light finally allowed me to make out the shapes of Mindy and Shaun and Isabel. Mindy took slow, soundless steps toward the door like a cat stalking a bird, her tiny gun raised in front of her. When she reached the door, she kicked it open in one fell swoop. Light flooded the hallway and the men yelled, "Don't shoot! Don't shoot!"

Mindy lowered her gun. "What the fuck is going on?"

We all crowded into the doorway. Ellie was sitting at a folding table with the three men who took her, and they were all eating pizza. My brain struggled to connect the dots.

"Oh my God, you came for me!" Ellie said through a mouthful of pizza. "That's *so* sweet!"

"Are you okay?" Mindy said. "What's happening?"

"These guys work for the party bus company," said Ellie. "One of their new packages is called 'Body Snatch Bachelorette' and all the girls on the wedding charm forums were talking about it, then my mom even said it was something they used to do in Poland way back in the day, so I just had to try it."

My legs started to shake so violently that I collapsed onto the ground. "It didn't occur to you that that was really fucked up?"

"Aw, I'm sorry if it scared you, but that's kind of the point. It's supposed to be scary in a fun way, like a horror movie."

Shaun shook his head. "The difference is people *consent* to watching a horror movie. We didn't consent to this. It's honestly a lawsuit waiting to happen."

"You all signed the release of liability forms," said the stocky guy.

"We assumed that referred to pole-related injuries," said Shaun. "Not traumatizing kidnappings."

"We should sue *Ellie*," I snarled. "You almost gave us heart attacks, and for what?"

"You guys were willing to potentially sacrifice your lives

for me," Ellie said, putting her hand over her heart. "Do you know how much that means? Do you know how completely I trust you now?"

"Yeah, and in the process we completely lost our trust in *you*," Mindy said.

We all left the next day without speaking to Ellie, and we continued not speaking to her for weeks, until she sent us a text the length of a CVS receipt apologizing profusely, saying it was hands-down the most messed up thing she had ever done and she understood if we didn't want to be part of the wedding anymore. I seriously considered it, but once everyone else decided they were still going to go, I felt pressured— just like I had felt pressured to do the trust fall and to try to save Ellie after her "kidnapping." If Ellie herself had tried to pressure me I probably would have ended up bowing out, but she just kept telling me that she only had herself to blame and that there would be no hard feelings whatever I decided. Aimee told me I should still go, that Ellie had clearly learned her lesson, that she was my oldest friend—the closest thing I had to a sister after Beth abandoned me—and that really meant something. Plus, I had had another meeting about my dissertation with Dr. Gaffney, and she liked my new edits to *The Plot to Save Marriage*; said it was getting "sexier," but she still wanted me to attend a wedding to add the journalistic angle that would make it "orgasmic."

A week before the wedding, when I was still technically undecided about going, Facebook served me a "memory": a photo Ellie had posted exactly eight years earlier of the two of us in our empty Brooklyn apartment after we had signed the lease. The landlord took the photo for us—we were doing one of those jumping poses and I had barely made it off the ground but Ellie was like two full feet in the air, her legs akimbo. We both looked exhilarated, like we had just won the lottery. We were only able to get the apartment because Ellie fronted me the money for the security deposit and the last month of rent—without telling me first, because she knew I wouldn't have let her otherwise. It took me two whole years to pay her back, and she never asked about it, even when I knew she really could have used the money.

Fuck you, Facebook, I thought, and I texted Ellie that I'd still be her maid of honor.

12

The lease-signing photo was from the first and only time Ellie and I lived together. It was a couple years after college, and I got bedbugs at the same exact time that Ellie's lease was about to be up, and her current roommate was going to move in with her boyfriend. We knew it was risky, best friends living together, but we promised not to eat each other's food and to communicate about stuff that bothered us, like hair on the bathroom floor (my pet peeve) or the dish sponge not being thoroughly squeezed out after each use (Ellie's pet peeve). We found a two-bedroom above a barbershop in the neighborhood between Bed-Stuy and Bushwick, which we called BushStuy. My bedroom (the smaller, less-expensive

one) didn't have a window and the J train thundered by Ellie's window every twenty minutes, but it didn't matter when
you combined it with all the other noise. The two-bedroom
apartment above us housed about ten people who sounded
like they spent all night rearranging the furniture and dropping bowling balls on the floor, and the barbershop below
us started blasting music promptly at 8 a.m. when it opened.
We got maybe five hours of sleep a night if we were lucky,
but we didn't mind—we were twenty-three, broke, and un-
discriminating.

Our "decorating" consisted of unframed motivational
posters above the couch, the kind that said "Believe & Suc-
ceed" below a picture of a rocky ocean shoreline, or "Excel-
lence" below a picture of a lion. We put them up ironically,
obviously. On the opposite wall we installed a shelf above our
TV and filled it with tchotchkes from the dollar store: a Hello
Kitty piggy bank, a ceramic rooster-shaped jar, a figurine of a
golden Labrador retriever, and our prized find, a model ship.

We were both receptionists at the time, the only job we
could get with our fancy college degrees after months of ap-
plying to the entry-level positions our professors promised
were waiting for us. We decided that if the world wouldn't
take us seriously, we wouldn't take ourselves seriously, either.
Whatever professional goals we had were eschewed for going
out to bars until 3 a.m. most nights, and the nights we didn't
go out, we cooked two boxes of macaroni and cheese and
blew through DVDs of addicting TV like *The Wire*, *Lost*, or
Battlestar Gallactica. We watched them on Ellie's laptop, in my
bed for the windowless movie theater–esque darkness, and we
usually fell asleep at some point during the fifth episode. In

the middle of the night I'd close the laptop and put it on the floor, then Ellie would scooch over and spoon me.

It felt like we were in high school again, merging back into the same body. We started showering together because the hot water always ran out otherwise, comparing our vulvas to make sure we didn't have STIs, and sharing all our clothes to double our meager wardrobe. It reached a point where we couldn't even remember whose underwear was whose, and when we went to the laundromat, we'd just divide it evenly. The whole day while we were at work we G-chatted each other about the men who constantly came up and flirted with us, how bored we were, how we had to poop but there was someone squatting in the bathroom, about the people from college who we hated but still stalked on Facebook, how no one ever said thank-you, how we couldn't wait to get home and watch more TV.

Neither of us was really dating. Sometimes we'd make out with someone at the bar, but that was about it. One night we went out to a lesbian bar, a huge, two-floor building in South Slope that always attracted a diverse crowd. On the first floor, dubbed the "meat market," they played house and hip-hop and there was a stage with a pole that was sometimes utilized. A massive butch was usually sitting on a stool in the corner, rocking her head back and forth and getting danced up on by the high femmes. On the second floor they played '80s pop, and small groups of women tended to dance only with their group of friends. Ellie and I usually started the night on the second floor, then moved down to the first when we were a few drinks in.

As we shimmied around, I noticed a woman near me with

long black hair and flawless winged eyeliner underneath oversize, old-fashioned glasses. She was wearing a neon yellow tank top with a graphic hamburger printed on it, skinny jeans, and high-top Cons. Her dancing was half-sensual, half-hilarious as she planted her hands on the floor and popped her small ass to the beat of Janet Jackson's "If." When she went to the bar to get a drink, I followed her.

"You've got some good moves," I said.

"I guess that's why Beyoncé hired me for her next tour," she said, putting her hand on her hip and striking a pose.

My mouth fell open. "Really?"

She laughed and pushed her glasses up her nose with her pointer finger. "No, I'm just fucking with you."

"That's *my* thing!" I yelled, smacking her shoulder.

"Being Beyoncé's backup dancer or fucking with people?"

She was a quick one. I laughed and held out my hand. "I'm Robin."

"Aimee," she said, giving me a sweaty shake. "But isn't that your girlfriend over there?" She let go of my hand and pointed to Ellie, swaying in the middle of the dance floor by herself.

"Oh, that's just my best friend," I said.

Aimee pursed her lips. "You sure you're not fucking with me? You two looked pretty up close and personal on the dance floor."

"I swear," I said. "I wouldn't be talking to you if I had a girlfriend." As I said it, it felt like the tiniest lie. Ellie and I weren't a couple, we both knew that, but our compact intimacy prevented us from letting anyone else get too close. It felt like a form of betrayal, to think about forging that kind of connection with someone else.

When Aimee slept over for the first time a few weeks later, it was also the first time Ellie hadn't slept in my bed since we moved in. When I got up to go to the bathroom, Ellie was already in there with the door shut, which she must have done because Aimee was there. Otherwise, we never shut it.

I knocked. "It's me," I said softly before going in, the door hitting Ellie's knees as she sat on the toilet.

She made an accusatory face at me. "It feels so claustrophobic in here with the door shut."

"Sorry," I said, squeezing by her to inspect my face in the mirror. "Do you care? That Aimee's here?" There was a tiny whitehead on my chin and I worried about how visible it had been before popping it.

"No." She wiped and stood up. "Maybe a little."

"I would probably care if you had someone sleeping over, too." I pointed to her bright yellow urine in the toilet. "You're dehydrated. Drink a glass of water before bed, okay?"

Ellie rolled her eyes like she always did when I told her to drink water. "I guess I'll...see you in the morning?" she said as she scooted out of the bathroom.

"Yeah, see you in the morning," I said, and we both made a sad face at each other before Ellie disappeared down the hallway to her room.

By the time I met Kaivan, seven years later, Ellie and I had drifted apart again, due to me becoming even more radical while I was in my grad program and Ellie becoming even more desperate to get married as she inched closer to being "rotten." But we still got together once a month or so, and generally tried to steer clear of any hot-button issues, which ended up resulting in activities where we didn't really have to converse: exercise classes, comedy shows, museum exhibits where we would wander the rooms separately.

Ellie had been talking about Kaivan for months before Aimee and I were allowed to meet him. Prior to Kaivan, Ellie had had a few years of really bad dating luck, or maybe just bad dating *choices*—there was the guy with a gambling addiction whom she was always lending money to, the mysterious guy whom Ellie found out was married after a full year of dating, the verbally abusive guy who once kicked her cat, the guy who had sexually assaulted his coworker and Ellie only found out after the coworker sent her a Facebook message, the "perfect" guy who told her on their fifth date that he had stage-four lymphoma and his doctors had given him six months to live... The list went on and on.

After every breakup she would say dramatic, semisuicidal stuff like, "I want to fling myself off a cliff," or "I don't see the point in living if this is just going to keep happening," or the more literal "If I don't find someone soon, I'm going to kill myself." After a particularly bad breakup with a guy who told Ellie he "couldn't picture her as anyone's wife," she actually called me, wasted, from the roof of her ten-story apartment building, saying she was going to jump. I eventually talked her down, but it scared the shit out of me, the depths of her desperation for a partner. By the time she met Kaivan, I figured she was ready to settle for anyone remotely decent and normal.

Ellie only wanted me to meet him when she was reasonably sure that it would last. Once she was feeling confident enough, she texted me about a thousand options for what we should do: drinks at a bar (would it be too loud?), dinner (was that too formal?), a picnic in the park (picnics were better with a big group of people but a big group might be overwhelming), a movie (not a lot of talking time, which could be a good or a bad thing), etc., etc., etc.

She finally settled on an early Sunday dinner at the brick-oven pizza place in South Slope down the street from my and Aimee's apartment—Sundays were relaxed, so no one would have to rush there from work; the pizza place was casual but delicious, and going early would ensure it wasn't crowded.

Go easy on him, okay? Ellie texted beforehand.

You realize that's like telling a dog not to bark, right? I texted back.

I'm serious. I really like him and I don't want you to scare him off.

He's not dating ME.

But you're my best friend, which is an extension of me. If your partner doesn't like your friends, you've got way less of a chance of making it.

Well what if *I* don't like *him*?

That's a given. You've never liked anyone I've dated.

Hey, I liked Jeremy!

Ugh, the guy who always reminded me to pee after "making love" so I wouldn't get a UTI.

Yeah, he was nice. The reason I usually don't like your boyfriends is because they're usually not nice.

Listen, sex with nice guys always sucks.

Sigh. Heterosexuality is so flawed.

See, that's a perfect example of something you shouldn't say tonight.

When Aimee and I got there, Ellie and Kaivan were already sitting outside—on the *same* side of the table. They had their arms linked together but they were both on their phones. When Kaivan stood up to greet us, he towered over me at probably at least six feet, and shook my hand with a strong grip. I couldn't tell if he was attractive or unattractive. He had a long face with wide-set eyes, a Roman nose, and a gigantic mouth full of Chiclet-style teeth—when he smiled I swear it took up a third of his face.

"Is it pronounced Kay-vahn or Kevin?" I asked as we sat down.

"I told you it's Kevin," Ellie said with a tight smile.

I held my hands up. "I just wanted to make sure."

"Don't worry, it confuses everyone," he said to me.

We all sat there for a second in uncomfortable, smiling silence before Aimee said, "How did you two meet, anyway?"

"Ellie won't tell me," I said.

Kaivan looked at her; cocked an eye. "Really, babe? Why not?"

Ellie put her hands over her face. "It's embarrassing! Aimee would probably be nice about it, but Robin would give me all kinds of shit."

A group of people went inside and the smell of pizza wafted through the open door.

"You met on Spouse Spotter, didn't you?" I said.

They turned to each other and grimaced.

I smacked the table. "Oh my God, you did!"

"A dating app so regressive even people from the Middle Ages, who shat on the street and who only bathed once or twice a year, wouldn't use it," Ellie said, mocking me.

"I mean, you have to tell them your bra size," I said. "That's fucked up."

A car drove by blaring "Single Ladies" by Beyoncé. "It's the only app for people who are fully ready for marriage, though," said Kaivan. "Even on Match and eHarmony I kept meeting women who didn't want to get married, or who wanted to date for a few years first—"

"And you think that's unreasonable?" I asked.

"Not at all," he said. "I'm just ready to get married like, now." He laughed and gave Ellie a dopey look like he was about to propose right then. Red splotches appeared on her neck as she batted her eyelashes at him.

"It's a good thing you met Ellie," I said. "She's about as hot to trot down the aisle as they come."

Ellie shot me a wide-eyed look.

Aimee took the opportunity to translate my comment into nice-speak. "It's good you're both at the same place in your life, and you seem really happy together. Who cares how you met?"

"Clearly, Robin does," Ellie said sulkily.

"Don't listen to her," said Aimee, knocking her shoulder against mine. "She could have an opinion about a blank piece of white paper."

They all laughed, then Ellie asked what we did over the weekend.

"Oh, we finally saw *Jane Bond!*" I said. "I was really skeptical it was going to be like, faux-feminist, but you were right. It was actually really good."

Kaivan pulled his brows together and looked at Ellie. "Who was right? I thought you said you didn't like it."

"I had mixed feelings," Ellie said, picking at her split ends. A kid at a nearby table started wailing when his mother wouldn't let him throw crust at a pigeon on the street.

"You texted me that it was 'totally badass and fun,'" I said, scrolling through my phone for evidence.

"We talked about how it was clunky and a little man-hating, didn't we?" Kaivan said.

"When we walked out of the theater I agreed with you," Ellie said to Kaivan. "But after I thought about it some more I decided there were parts of it I liked," she said to me, blushing.

"Ellie, you can say what you really think," Kaivan said.

"I am saying what I really think," she said defensively. "There were good and bad parts, like with most movies."

"You didn't think it was a little man-hating?" Kaivan asked me and Aimee.

A waitress came to take our order, then backed away when she sensed the mood at the table. The kid was still screaming his head off and the parents were just letting him.

"I'd say it was critical of some men, which isn't the same thing," I said.

"Hashtag not all men," Aimee said in a jokey voice, and the two of us laughed.

"It's really just semantics," said Ellie.

"But did you *like* that it was critical of men or whatever, or didn't you?" Kaivan asked her, his tone purposefully light-hearted in that way that's a little scary.

She looked from me to Kaivan, then up at the sky like God might beam down and save her. "I guess if there was a *gun* to my head," she said accusatorily, then lowered her voice, "I didn't like it." Then she turned to the family near us and yelled, "Can you do something about your fucking kid?"

PART II

13

If you've been wondering when we're going to get to the part where Ellie and I try to kill each other, we're getting close. After another cross-country flight, a two-hour wait in line at the rental car place, then an hour and a half drive, I arrived at a Malibu mansion turned country club, where everyone was staying and where the ceremony would take place the next day. It belonged to Ellie's family, and had since the 1970s when her grandmother bought it—I had always vaguely known that Ellie's mom came from money, but I hadn't known quite how much. Once you stepped inside, though, the mansion was decidedly less impressive. At one time it was probably richly ornate, but now it just seemed shabbily ornate. Think faded paisley wallpaper, flaking gilded crown molding, dusty chandeliers, Baroque furniture, and doors cut out of walls that were no longer actual doors. But everyone booked it for their wedding because it was right on the water, with the best uninterrupted view of the Pacific.

A sign near the front desk listed all the wedding charms the venue offered: sage-and-garlic bouquets, on-site witch for marriage spells, basement room for kidnapping of the bride, train lengtheners up to one hundred feet, dove blood for sacrifice rituals, and the list went on with at least ten more items. *Ask us about our top-secret charms ;)*, the sign said at the bottom. I jumped when someone put their hand on my shoulder, but when I turned around it was just Ellie.

"I'm so glad you're here," she said, and pulled me into a hug that I tried to escape from after a few seconds, but she locked her arms around my back. I wasn't sure how I felt about her—if I had forgiven her for the terror of the bachelorette, if I trusted her not to do something similar this weekend, if we would keep in touch after the wedding or if this was the final scene of our friendship and the following distance, both physical and emotional, would give us permission to finally let go.

After everyone had checked in, Ellie gave us a tour and recounted the history of the place. In the early twentieth century it was initially the home of a gold-rush heiress (which would explain all the gilding), who hung herself at thirty years old due to mental illness. The family believed the property was cursed after that, so in an act of either charity or cruelty, they turned it into an insane asylum. In the late 1960s, California passed an act that effectively ended all involuntary hospitalization for mentally ill people, so the asylum was shut down. It sat empty for a span of years, then it was bought by

Ellie's grandmother Lena, a former patient who had extreme agoraphobia. While she feared the outside world, she still enjoyed being around people and loved entertaining, so she decided to turn the property into a wedding venue. Planning and hosting the weddings was her only outlet, so she became obsessed with making everything perfect and living vicariously through the brides—so much so that rumor had it she tried to murder one of the brides and take her place (which Ellie's family always vehemently denied), but instead the bride ended up murdering *her*. Specifically, stabbing her twenty times. Ellie's mom was only sixteen when it happened, and it was a big news story at the time. *Bride Stabs Wedding Planner in the Back—Literally!*

After Ellie's grandmother was murdered, her great-aunt ran the place. For a number of years, no one wanted to get married there, but after a while everyone either forgot or moved on. By the time Ellie's great-aunt died (of natural causes), Ellie had gone to college, so Ellie's mom moved out to take over.

As an homage to Lena, a painted portrait of her hung over the mantel. She was wearing a satiny white dress that could or could not have been a wedding dress, with a black cloak over it. Her chin was tilted down toward her long neck, so she was looking up at the painter, her brown irises bobbing at the top left of her eyes. It gave her a darkly mischievous look—a look like you knew why she had been in an asylum. Her tiny mouth was twisted to the side in either a grin or a scowl, or a cross between both.

"I can't believe you never told me about your grandma," I said to Ellie after the tour. "You only ever said she died when your mom was a teenager."

She grimaced. "My family doesn't like to talk about it, for obvious reasons. Honestly, I didn't even want to get married here—the place kind of creeps me out—but my mom insisted. Tradition, saving money, et cetera."

"It kind of feels like we're at the beginning of a darkly comic horror movie," I said, before affecting a deep male tone akin to the voiceover of a movie trailer. "A young couple plans the wedding of their dreams, but the venue has a dark past of suicide, insanity, and murder. Will the wedding of their dreams become the wedding of their nightmares? Mua-hahahahaha," I laughed exaggeratedly.

"Shut up!" said Ellie, slapping my arm. "Now I'm even more creeped out."

After the tour we gathered for breakfast on the terrace, which overlooked a shockingly green lawn striped with mower marks, where the ceremony would take place, and beyond that, cliffs lined with leaning palm trees and the unbroken teal expanse of the Pacific. It was a nice view, something you'd never see in Brooklyn, and I told myself I should try to enjoy it.

"I think he's going to pick Casey L.," said Blair. We were talking about *Wild for Love*, a reality show that was like a blend of *The Bachelor* and *Survivor*, stranding a group of conventionally attractive men and women in a dangerous, desolate location and making them compete for each other's affection. The winners were the man and woman who survived and, of course, got engaged. The show was one of those rare bridges between groups of different people—liberal or conservative, highbrow or lowbrow; I didn't know anyone who didn't watch it. People like me tended to tune in jokingly, critically, like it was a ridiculous societal case study. Aimee and I would yell at the TV about the show being objectifying, regressive, and racist, relieved that our lives looked nothing like it.

Then there were people who watched it more earnestly, either oblivious or unbothered by the gender stereotypes because their own lives were too close to distinguish the difference—women who said things like "he better put a ring on it by next year," or who described themselves as "Wife. Mother. Coffee lover." on social media, or who wrote braggy Facebook posts when their "best hubby ever" did the dishes. Blair seemed somewhere in the middle, critical of the construct even while it reflected her reality of dating douchey guys and hoping they'd propose despite clear evidence to the contrary.

"Casey L.?" I said. "She's like an AI amalgamation of every *Wild for Love* contestant ever. Actual robots could have a more scintillating conversation than her."

"If I've learned anything from watching the show, it's that men only want women who don't talk and always look like they're two seconds away from puking," said Blair.

I laughed. "RPF, resting puke face. Casey totally has that."

"It's like she finds existence distasteful," Isabel said.

"I think she's just scared of being hurt," said Mindy. "It makes sense, considering how her last fiancé left her."

I frowned. "That's a nice way to look at it. But it's no fun talking about *Wild for Love* if we're going to be nice."

Mindy grinned conspiratorially. "Okay, you know who I don't like? Grace, the kindergarten teacher who always calls

her students 'my kids.' I know she's the fan favorite or whatever but it's like she's *trying* to be. I mean, who *gives away* an
adventure card?"

"Yes!" I said, surprised that Grace wasn't Mindy's favorite.
"I just said that to Aimee last week."

"The one I can't stand is Frank," said Shaun. "He's like a
beige pashmina with limbs. Like, you know there's a human
underneath there *somewhere*, you just can't distinguish any of
his facial features or personality traits."

"They're *all* beige pashminas," said Isabel. "I think that's
kind of the point."

Mindy's phone rang and she answered it without getting
up from the table. "How much diarrhea? What color is it?
A wet or dry cough? What color is the phlegm? All right,
take them to the doctor and let me know what she says."
She hung up and blew air out from between her lips, making a noise like a horse. "Bill thinks the kids have whooping cough. Why is it that disaster always strikes the minute a
mother takes a vacation?"

Aimee texted me a picture of Bean curled up on our bed
with his trademark sad eyes. Bean wants you to come home,
she wrote. Aimee couldn't make it to the wedding because
she had to go to a medical conference to present a paper about
the sharp decrease in abortion accessibility—yet another government method to push people back toward marriage. It was
happening all over the country—Texas was down to one abortion clinic for the entire state, and even New York, which
used to have almost a hundred, only had twelve. I knew it
was more important for Aimee to be presenting her paper,
but it made the wedding weekend seem that much more un-

bearable to be there alone. As a member of the bridal party I wouldn't have been able to spend much time with Aimee anyway, but I would have loved to go back to the room at night and commiserate with her while watching reality TV.

Trust me, I'd rather be home with you two, I texted back. Three more days!

A server came by and placed another pitcher of mimosas on the table. I waved him away from my glass and chugged some water instead. "Is everyone staying hydrated?" I asked. "Remember, one glass of water for each mimosa."

"Here she goes," said Ellie. "Robin thinks drinking water is the answer to all our problems. Depressed? Drink some water. Have whooping cough? Have some water. Speaking of, your kids might have whooping cough?" Ellie said to Mindy. "Isn't that like, an old-timey disease?"

"Yeah, they invented a vaccine for it in the 1940s," said Shaun, whose knowledge of random factoids rivaled a contestant on *Who Wants to Be a Millionaire*.

Mindy rolled her eyes. "I'm not putting any of those toxic chemicals in *my* children's bodies."

"Wait. Your kids aren't vaccinated?" I said. Mindy's politics were like a box of chocolates: you never knew what you were going to get. The more I learned about them, though, the more they seemed to funnel into the same idea: freedom of choice, almost like she was a libertarian, although she had previously said she was registered as an independent but rarely voted.

"Hell no," said Mindy. "I didn't want them getting autism or something worse."

Ellie gave me a narrow-eyed *please don't go there* look. Mindy was Ellie's oldest friend, from when Ellie's dad was stationed in North Carolina while she was in elementary school. Ellie was bullied a lot because she was the new kid, and Mindy, already taller than most of the boys, took on the position of Ellie's protector. Ellie loved to tell the story about how Mindy punched a boy who wouldn't stop making fun of her and Mindy was suspended from school because of it. Ellie never forgot Mindy's intense loyalty, and forgave a lot of Mindy's opinions due to her nostalgia for those young, vulnerable days when Mindy watched over her.

I pressed my lips together and took a few deep breaths, trying to push back the urge to set Mindy right, but it was like trying to halt the leviathan waves that curled toward us. I looked around the table, thinking someone had to jump in and correct Mindy, but everyone stared at their plate of eggs and fruit.

"You know the link between vaccines and autism was disproven, right?" I said, my heartbeat tripping over itself.

"That's what the vaccine-makers *want* us to think," Mindy said.

Ellie's phone rang. "It's Debra, the wedding planner," she told us before answering. "What?" She shot out of her chair and started pacing around the deck. "*All* the flowers?" she yelled.

"The doctor who wrote that study lost his medical license," I said to Mindy.

"Which study?" Mindy said.

"The one that claimed a possible link between vaccines and autism."

She shrugged flippantly. "I didn't know there was any study."

Ellie threw herself back in her chair. "There was some kind of blight at the flower farm, and it's too late to book another florist. So I guess we're doing sage-and-garlic bouquets." She blinked, tears glossing her eyes. "I won't know if I'm getting married or preparing a fucking roast."

As part of her apology re: the bachelorette, Ellie had promised not to do any more wedding charms. Had she forgotten, or did she just not care? "Aren't sage-and-garlic bouquets a wedding charm?" I said. "Didn't you say you wouldn't do any more of those?"

Ellie's mouth contorted in a cry as two tears rolled down each cheek simultaneously. "There's literally no other choice. It's not like sage-and-garlic bouquets will affect you, and it's not like I even *want* to use them." She was sobbing dramatically now.

Isabel rubbed Ellie's shoulder, a stack of bangles on her wrist clanking together. "Sage-and-garlic bouquets have some great benefits. The garlic wards off evil spirits and sage brings wisdom to your marriage." In addition to being a yogi, Isabel was also an herbalist. She had been releasing droppers full of various tinctures into her mimosas all morning.

Shaun nodded. "They're all the rage. Queer couples are even using them now."

I rolled my eyes. Shaun had had a traditional, million-dollar wedding two years before, then he and his husband bought a four-bedroom house in New Rochelle and got a puggle. They were currently in the process of planning for baby number one.

Blair looked up from her phone. "Isn't the color of our bridesmaid dresses called sage? It's like, kiss-met."

"You mean kismet?" I said.

"Yeah, that's what I said," said Blair.

So no one else had a problem with the sage and garlic. I stabbed three pieces of honeydew and shoved them into my mouth, then opened a new note in my phone and titled it "The Plot to Save Marriage," adding a bullet for the sage-and-garlic bouquets. Ellie noisily blew her nose into a napkin, then dabbed at her eyes with it, apparently done with her crying fit. On the patio below, an employee in a white polo shirt scrubbed a rust-colored stain on the stones, the wire brush grating against the stone surface. Mindy was eating her fifth piece of bacon—I guess she wasn't concerned about actual health threats like clogging her arteries. "So I'm just curious—if you didn't know about the study, how did you think this whole autism theory came about?" I asked her.

"From mothers whose kids have autism," she said. "Most of them had been vaccinated."

"Yeah, most children *are* vaccinated. That's what protects us against diseases like whooping cough. But it only works if we all do it."

"This is *America*," said Mindy, widening her eyes. "I have the right to choose."

My heart walloped against my chest, making my breath catch in my throat. "If everyone chose not to vaccinate, we'd go back to being sick with polio, hepatitis, and the measles."

"Well, maybe that's natural," she said.

"You know what else is natural?" I said. "Death."

14

When everyone went back to their room to shower and get ready for their mani-pedi appointments, I sneaked out to my rental car and drove to a local bookstore with the intention of buying Mindy a book about vaccines. Despite what Alonzo had said about the backfire effect, if she was presented with all the information, from a credible source with a credible publisher, she would have to change her mind, wouldn't she? It was more than ideological, and it was more than personal— it was putting the health of the general population at risk. That had to merit an intervention. In the medicine section, I found a book written by a doctor called *Deadly Choices: How the Anti-Vaccine Movement Threatens Us All*, then in the children's section I found one called *You Wouldn't Want to Live Without Vaccinations!*

As I stood in the checkout line, I shuffled past a flyer taped to a support beam for a missing woman named Stephanie Bennett. In the slightly grainy photo, she had dark hair in a chunky pixie cut, a wide nose, and a full red-lipsticked mouth. Her smile looked forced, like she had been holding it for a long time. The photo was cropped close to her face, cutting out someone next to her, but their hand reached around her shoulder, covering up half of a hummingbird tattoo. She was last seen about a week ago, wearing a long strapless peach-colored gown, at the Malibu Palms Country Club—where Ellie was getting married. I wondered if she had been there for a wedding. Before I could read any more details, the cashier yelled, "Next!" and I went up with my two books.

"How are you doing today, ma'am?" the cashier asked with an exaggerated smile like she was in a fierce competition for Employee of the Month. She had blond, shoulder-length hair that curled under and disconcertingly symmetrical teeth, like they were veneers.

"All right, I guess," I said.

"Just all right?" She made a pouty face as she scanned my books.

"I'm here for a wedding, so…"

Her face lit up. "Then you should be doing fantastic! Weddings are so much fun. That'll be thirty-five seventy-two."

I lowered my eyes at the cashier as I handed over my credit card. "Have you ever been a bridesmaid?"

She smiled proudly. "Seven times."

"Seven? God, I would die."

She tilted her head in annoyed confusion. "Being a brides-maid is the biggest honor a friend can give you."

I leaned in conspiratorially and lowered my voice. "But if you're being honest, wouldn't you also call it the biggest pain in the ass?"

She straightened up and ripped the receipt from the machine with a flourish. "I certainly would not." She pressed her lips together and slid my bag across the counter. "Good day, ma'am."

I almost laughed, but my cheeks burned as I walked out of the store.

When I got to the nail salon, the rest of the bridal party was sitting in pink leather massage chairs with their feet in bubbling water. The air reeked of chemicals and multiple competing perfumes, and cheesy spa music came through the speakers. On the back wall, there was a large mural of a stone patio with ornate fountains and Grecian columns wrapped in ivy. The patio overlooked a sprawling green yard edged with cypress trees, and beyond that, a mountain-rimmed lake.

"Where have you been?" Ellie said, frantic. "You're twenty minutes late!"

"I was doing something important." I walked up to Mindy and held out the books. "Some reading for you, based on our earlier conversation."

Mindy glanced at the titles and scoffed. "You can keep those."

My heart jerked.

"Robin," Ellie said. "They had to give your appointment

to someone else because you were so late. We need to figure out what to do about your nails."

I set the books in Mindy's lap, wishing she was one of my students and she had to read them, or else she would fail the quiz. "Please. Just read them. This one was written by a doctor. It's full of referenced facts from reputable sources."

"If someone handed you some books about why vaccines are dangerous, would *you* read them?" Mindy said.

I crossed my arms, squeezing them against my body. "You can't just flip the situation. Facts support my position. They don't support yours."

Mindy picked up the books and glanced at them for a second. Then she held them over her steaming footbath and dropped them in. "Whoops. There go your facts." Water splashed out of the tiny tub as the books fell in, floating on top like rafts in a pool. Mindy pressed them down with her feet.

"Wow," I said. "Really mature."

"You know what's mature?" said Mindy. "Accepting that people have different opinions than you."

"Robin!" Ellie yelled. "Can we focus? Your nails. I don't know when they'll be able to fit you in, and we have a lunch reservation at one o'clock. Maybe you should just skip it. But it'll be really obvious if your nails look different than everyone else's in the wedding photos."

"I don't think anyone will notice my nails in a photo," I said. "Unless I'm supposed to be a hand model."

"Excuse me," said the woman in the massage chair next to Ellie. Her face had the puffy, pulled-back look of too much plastic surgery, and she had a diamond ring even bigger than

Ellie's. "I couldn't help but overhear. You girls are getting your nails done for your wedding?"

Ellie nodded.

"You can take my appointment, dear," the woman said to me. "I remember how stressful my wedding weekend was. Anything I can do to make it easier for a fellow bride," she said to Ellie, standing up from her chair.

Ellie put a hand to her heart and looked at the woman like she had just rescued Ellie's future child from falling down a well. "Thank you so much," Ellie said. "You're an absolute lifesaver. Let us pay for your mani-pedi as a thank-you."

"I wouldn't dream of it," the woman said.

Ellie looked at me and cocked her head toward the register. For the bachelorette, the bridal shower, and the wedding combined I had already paid for two round-trip flights across the country, three gifts, accommodations for each trip, all of Ellie's food/drinks/activities, and another bridesmaid dress I planned to throw directly into the trash after the wedding. I seethed—now after paying for not only my and Ellie's nails, I had to pay for some stranger's? The unexpected expenses hadn't stopped sprouting up like weeds since I landed, but I didn't want to send Ellie into another fit, so I ground my teeth together and walked to the register. After I doled out an extra sixty dollars, I came back and sat next to Ellie, rolling up my jeans before putting my feet in the vat of warm water.

Ellie's eyes zeroed in on my calves. I had stopped shaving my body hair sometime in my early twenties, which Ellie knew. But her pupils might as well have been shooting red laser beams onto the long, fluffy hair I had stopped noticing ages ago. "You know the bridesmaid dresses are knee-length, right?"

"Of course I know that," I said. "Why?"

Ellie shrugged. "No reason."

A nail technician wearing a ruffly floral blouse came up to Ellie. "I checked in back. We're all out of the Ballet Slipper color."

"That's impossible," said Ellie. "I called a few days ago to confirm you had it, and someone told me you did."

The technician shrugged and handed Ellie three bottles of light pink polish. "This is what we have. They're all very similar to Ballet Slipper."

"I don't want something *similar*," Ellie said, stomping her feet in the footbath and sending water over the edge. "First the flowers, now this?"

"What's wrong with those other colors?" I asked. "They all look ballet slipper-y."

Ellie looked at me like I had just asked what was wrong with genocide. "This one is too shimmery, this one is too pink, and this one isn't pink enough."

"Okay, Goldilocks," I said. "Here, drink some water." I handed her my Hydro Flask.

"Water won't fix this, Robin." She turned away and consulted with Shaun as the nail technicians sat down and began massaging our calves. I took out my phone and added another bullet to the *Plot to Save Marriage* note.

"Right, this pink is a little creamier," Shaun said, and I wanted to explode into laughter or a scream. "This one has just the right opacity. A beige-toned pink will look really natural."

A few minutes later Ellie turned back and took a deep breath. "Crisis averted."

"Thank God," I said. "Which color are you going with? The light pink, the light pink, or the light pink?"

Ellie held out one of the bottles. "It's called Rosy Future, which seems apropos."

Too bad they didn't have one called Divorced in a Year, I thought. "I'm glad you're happy."

"I'm not happy," Ellie shot back. "I'm just making it work."

As my nail technician ran a thumb up and down my shin, Ellie stared at my hairy legs, her cheeks going from Ballet Slipper to a deeper pink. "Had you…" She picked at a thread coming loose from the wrist of her cardigan. "Had you thought about maybe shaving for the wedding tomorrow?"

I could practically feel my heart flexing its metaphorical biceps muscle. Mindy made an amused wide-eyed face at Shaun. Isabel pretended not to listen. The technician lifted my right foot out of the water and dried it with a towel before buffing the calluses on my heels with a pumice stone. I took a deep breath. "Yeah, I haven't shaved in a decade, but I was thinking about it for tomorrow."

Ellie sighed. "It'll grow back, you know."

The fine white dust of my dead heel skin drifted toward the floor. I focused on it, pretending I was in a snow globe, and tried to slow my breathing. "So you're actually asking me?"

"I don't see why it's such a big deal."

"You just had a meltdown about identical shades of nail polish and you can't understand why asking me to shave is asking me to change an intrinsic part of myself?"

Ellie guffawed. "*Leg hair* is an intrinsic part of yourself?"

"See, this is why I told you I shouldn't be your maid of honor." I stood up and stepped out of the footbath. "We value completely different things."

"Yeah, I guess we do," Ellie said.

15

After I stormed out of the nail salon, one heel smooth as a wave-lapped pebble, the other like someone had taken a grater to it, I got in my rental car and slammed the door. I pictured driving to the airport and getting on a plane home, flying over the sharp peaks of the Rockies and the circular green fields of the Midwest while half-heartedly grading papers but really watching subpar movies, opening the door to the apartment and Bean wiggling his butt off and jumping into my arms—always the same level of excitement whether I ran out to the bodega or was on a long trip—giving Aimee a hug that was like a battery charge for my heart and going out for drinks with friends who didn't care what other people did with their body hair.

If I couldn't go to my friends, maybe I could bring a version of them to me. I typed "gay bar Malibu" into Google Maps and waited as the blue circle rotated. The service was terrible. A few seconds later the map shifted east and dropped red pins all over West Hollywood. There were no pins in Malibu. It would take an hour and five minutes to drive there, which meant I would miss lunch at the expensive seaside farm-to-table place Ellie had reserved for us. What a shame. I decided on a place described as "casual with a diverse crowd" and started the car.

The bar was dark and cavernous. I blinked, waiting for my eyes to adjust. It smelled like hot sauce and yeasty, sour beer. My sneakers confirmed the smell, catching on various sticky patches. In a booth near the back, two men wearing sunglasses despite the dim interior were devouring a basket of chicken wings. A butch in her fifties wearing a black T-shirt covered in white dog hair sat at the bar, drinking what looked like vodka on the rocks. I sat down next to her, leaving one stool between us.

The bartender, who had at least four different facial piercings (lip, nose, eyebrow, faux Cindy Crawford mole), looked up from cutting lime wedges to ask what I wanted.

I glanced at the beers on tap. "I'll just have a Stella. And a big glass of water, please."

"You don't come into a bar like this in the middle of the day for a beer," the woman said, still facing forward, so I wasn't sure if she was talking to me or making snide commentary to the bartender. "Sam, give this kid a double vodka on the rocks."

"Okay, boss," Sam said.

"You own this place?" I said to her.

"Boss is his nickname for me," she said. "Adorable, isn't it?"

"She spends so much time and money here, she might as well own the place," Sam said, placing a water and what had to be at least a triple vodka on the rocks in front of me.

"Jesus," I said. "Thank you, but I don't know if I can finish this. I have to drive back to Malibu soon."

"Malibu," said the woman in a haughty tone, holding her pinky up as she took a drink.

"I know," I said. "My best friend, or someone who used to be my best friend, is getting married there tomorrow."

The woman raised an unruly eyebrow. "Uh-oh. Someone who *used* to be your best friend?"

"Yeah, we've kind of grown apart over the years, and now she's turned into this total bridezilla." I took a drink and grimaced, the astringent taste making my tongue contract. I thought about asking for some soda and lime, but for some reason I didn't want this woman to think I was a wimp. Instead, I guzzled my glass of water.

"Is she having one of those paint-by-number weddings?"

"What do you mean, *paint-by-number*?"

"So formulaic all you have to do is follow the steps." She started counting on her fingers. "A long white gown like she's a virgin going to the Oscars, bridesmaids wearing something so unmemorable it'll give you temporary dementia, the bride given away by the father like she's a used car, a wedding band that plays a mix of soulful oldies and current hits, a registry full of a bunch of fancy kitchen shit they'll never use—"

"Don't forget the Mason jars full of flowers and the photo booth full of zany props."

"Mason jars?" She scrunched her nose. "In my day those were for pickled vegetables."

"They're really trendy now," I said. "Really *rustic*." A word Ellie had repeatedly used to describe her wedding even though there was nothing rustic about it that I could see. "Do you think people who have these kinds of weddings actually think they're original?"

"They probably think the tiny changes they make set them apart. Like having pie instead of cake, or having their friend be the officiant."

"Or having a gay man as one of the bridesmaids."

She huffed. "Exactly."

I forced myself to take a swig of vodka. "So I take it you're not married."

"Kid, that wasn't even an option when my lover was alive. And if she was still here, I don't think we'd be rushing down the aisle just because the government finally told us it's okay." She grabbed a peanut from a bowl and cracked open the shell. "What about you?"

I shook my head. "I think my partner and I are the last few holdouts."

"It must be different, coming of age now that it's legal. You must feel some pressure."

"Everyone's just turning into straight people," I said. "Buying into the whole homogenized kit and caboodle."

The woman pulled her lips down. "You sound nostalgic for the bad old days."

"I guess I am, in a way. I know that's fucked up."

She shrugged, tossing a handful of peanuts into her mouth. "Being an outcast comes with a lot of bad shit, like having to protest in the streets for basic human rights or getting fired from your job, but it sure as hell forces you to question the status quo."

"Cheers to that," I said, knocking my glass against the woman's.

The woman signaled the bartender for a refill, then pointed to my glass, too, even though I wasn't even halfway done. "What's your name, kid?"

"Robin. Yours?"

"Kyle. And my parents were surprised when I turned out to be a raging dyke." She barked a laugh. "How old are you, Robin?"

"Thirty-four."

"Aha." She gave me a knowing look. "That was the age I fell out with someone who used to be my best friend, too. Any common ground we had went to hell after the wedding and the house in the suburbs and the babies. She'd invite me over for dinner, because after you have kids you're basically on house arrest, and none of us would complete a single sentence the whole night what with the little fuckers screaming and crying and interrupting to say things the parents thought were just so darn cute. You don't want kids, do you?"

"God, no."

"Cheers to that, too," said Kyle, and we crashed our glasses together again. "Things really came to a head with Carol— the ex–best friend—when she caught her husband cheating on her and then *didn't leave him*. She kept saying it was her life, why should I care if she left him or not, but I was the one who had to listen to her complain about him all the time. So finally I said, 'Either you leave him or you stop talking about him, one or the other,' and she said, 'I guess I'll just stop talking to *you*,' and that was that." She shook her drink, the ice compressing, and drank the last gulp.

"Wow," I said. "So you still don't talk?"

"No siree, bob. I found out she died last year. Ovarian cancer." She stared into the distance, her eyes faraway.

"Do you regret it? Not speaking for all those years?"

Her eyes snapped back into focus. "Hell no. Fuck her." She spat out the words, then tapped her glass against the bar as a signal for a refill.

I imagined myself fifteen years in the future, hearing Ellie had died and not caring, not lamenting the years we had spent in silence. It sent a cold jolt through my heart. A few minutes ago I thought Kyle was my new best friend. Now I was starting to understand why she spent her days drinking alone in this bar. "I should get going," I said, checking the time on my cell phone.

"Oh, come on!" Kyle said, raising her voice. "Fuck your friend, too. Fuck 'em all!" She slammed her drink down and gave me a seething stare that sent a shiver down my spine. The pulled-down mouth, the clenched fist, the eyes lit up with rage—it was like looking into a mirror. I asked myself if this is where I would be in twenty years if I kept being so uncompromising. If I kept never letting anything go. The thought was sobering enough that I blinked and actually felt the vodka leave my system. I placed a twenty on the bar and quickly walked out.

As I was searching for a place to eat, my phone vibrated— Ellie, probably calling to berate me for missing lunch. I debated letting it go to voice mail, then picked up. "Hi."

Ellie sniffed. "Rob, I'm really sorry," she said, her voice wobbly. "I never should have asked you to shave. It's just that

I have this picture in my head of my perfect wedding, and things keep going wrong, and when I brought up your legs, I was just trying to stay in control of whatever I could."

"Okay," I said, waiting for her to go a little further.

"I didn't realize what I was asking. How selfish I was being. Is there any way you could forgive me and come back? I honestly can't imagine doing this without you."

I took a deep breath. It was a good apology—another one to add to the list, and I wondered how many more I would hear before the end of the weekend. But I was inclined to accept it after that cautionary encounter with the woman at the bar. A small nagging part of me wondered if Ellie was just apologizing to get me back to the wedding and thus align with the picture-perfect day. (How would the photos look with five groomsmen and four bridesmaids? Who would take my place and give the maid of honor speech? Et cetera.) Or maybe Ellie really was as sorry as she sounded, and she wanted me there simply for my friendship. "I guess I could forgive you," I said.

"Really?"

"Yeah, I haven't been the best, either. I could be more understanding. This weekend is about you, not me."

"Are you drunk?"

"Just a little bit."

"Where are you, anyway?"

"West Hollywood."

She laughed. "I should have known. The surf lesson is in two hours, if you want to come back. But only if you want to. I don't want to force you to do things."

"Sure," I said. "You know how much I love life-threatening activities."

★ ★ ★

When Ellie and Kaivan moved to LA, he took up surfing, prompting me to raise his enema score by ten points.
They were going to Hawaii for their honeymoon, and Ellie
wanted to learn some basic moves and surprise him. So she
had booked a lesson for all of us as "a fun bonding activity."
I refused to even ride a bike in my day-to-day life because I
found it unnatural and scary, perched up there on two wheels
the width of a bagel, but because Ellie had apologized and I
was newly committed to being a good maid of honor, I returned to Malibu in time for the lesson.

I picked my way down a steep, rickety staircase that led to a
beach below cliffs topped with mansions. The water was pure
aquamarine blue, dappled darker where rocks threatened the
surface. A cool breeze carried the coconutty scent of sunscreen
and the brininess of salt water and seaweed. When I stepped
onto the warm sand, Ellie ran over, looking distraught.

"I think this wedding is cursed," she said between quick,
choppy breaths. "Debra just called. The lead singer of the wedding band has bronchitis. We chose her because she sounded
just like Etta James, and our first dance is to 'At Last.' They're
replacing her with someone who sounds like Katy Perry. I
can't *stand* Katy Perry." She put her hands on her knees and
leaned over like she had just finished running a marathon.

"Could they find someone whose voice you might like
better?"

"Debra played me samples from five different people," she
said from underneath her hair. "At least Katy Perry can sing
on key."

"Is Debra going to keep looking for other singers?"

"She said everyone is booked, that she searched 'heaven and earth' just for these five." Ellie covered her face with her hands and sank onto the sand.

"Let's try to keep some perspective. It's just a wedding singer, not the end of the world." I pet the top of Ellie's head with one hand, and with the other I handed her my Hydro Flask. "Have some water."

Ellie ducked away from my hand and swatted the Hydro Flask so hard it went flying. She clenched her fists until they shook. *"Just a wedding singer?"* With each word her voice climbed in pitch until she screeched the word *singer*. It sounded like one of those flat-faced owls that scream bloody murder in the middle of the night. Her voice pealed across the beach and people looked over, concerned.

I reached out to put a hand on her shoulder, then thought better of it. "Jesus, Ellie. You have to calm down."

She took a shaky breath and looked at me with narrowed, bloodshot eyes. She spoke in a carefully controlled croak. "I know you think none of this matters, but to me it does. I've been picturing this day since I was little, and I spent so much time choosing every detail, and spent so much money to get things just right, and now it's crumbling before my eyes. I don't know what I'll do if another thing goes wrong." The control left her voice, climbing toward deranged again. "I really don't." She squeezed handfuls of sand like she was trying to squeeze the life out of them.

I wished someone else would come deal with her, someone who knew how to placate her. I felt disgusted by her, and a little scared. "I know it's frustrating when things don't go the way you planned. All I'm saying is, the wedding singer has nothing to do with the big picture. You're marrying Kaivan tomorrow. Isn't that ultimately all that matters?"

Ellie scoffed. "You really don't get it."

I pressed my lips together.

In the ocean surfers sat straddling their boards, looking completely calm as they waited for the right wave to ride in. Saving me from having to say anything else, the surf instructor strutted over and introduced himself. He was like a surfer avatar: his name was Brent, he had shaggy bleached-blond hair, was wearing knee-length Billabong board shorts, and greeted everyone with the hang loose hand motion. His eyes were the translucent blue-green of a wave right before it breaks, and it made me think of how flamingos are bright pink because of the shrimp they eat. Were his eyes that color because his body had somehow absorbed the ocean? After he taught us where to lie on the board, how to pop up, and how to "turtle roll" underneath the oncoming waves, he handed out wetsuits and brought us out into the water so we could "catch a whitewash," which meant riding a baby wave.

By the time I was just calf-deep in the ice-cold water, the powerful undertow pulled sand from underneath my feet, making my head swirl. My stomach flipped as I pictured being pulled under, my head smashing against a sharp rock, tendrils of my blood feathering the water. In contrast, Ellie's face looked semicalm again—Ellie was the type of person who would go for a run or take a yoga class during a crisis, since the physical activity always brought her back to baseline.

When we were waist-deep, it took me at least five tries to even get onto the board. A big wave approached and Brent yelled, "Time to practice those turtle rolls!" The vodka from earlier crawled up my throat as I grasped the rails of the board, which felt like trying to grasp a stick of butter, and tilted my weight to the side until I rolled underneath it. The wave rushed over and the board slid from my fingers. The rope connecting my foot to the board tugged me backward and I tumbled like laundry in a washing machine until I emerged, gasping. Everyone else had made it through the wave except Mindy. We exchanged defeated looks, bonding for a moment despite our earlier argument. Mindy gritted her teeth and paddled forward, and I was just about to head back to shore when Ellie turned around and paddled toward me.

"I'm still mad at you, but I'm going to take pity on you since I know how terrified you must be."

"Thanks." I grimace-smiled. "How did everyone else make it through that massive wave?"

"It wasn't easy," Ellie said. "I didn't think I was going to be able to roll back over."

Before we could say anything else, another wave came at us. An ominous, curling wall. I had no choice but to go through it.

"Bend your arms and hold on tight," Ellie said. "Try not to fight it."

I took a deep breath and repeated the steps: grasped my board, tilted my weight, rolled under. This time I held the board closer to my body and kept my arms bent. I tried not to fight it, to move with the water. The wave gushed past, and as the water stilled, I tried to roll back on top of the board, but it felt like it was weighted. Was I that weak? Was the board that heavy? I moved my head to the edge of the board, but something was pushing my head down. It felt like a hand, fingertips pressing into the sides of my skull.

Looking back it sounds ridiculous, but it honestly didn't occur to me that it could be Ellie. She had been reckless with the bachelorette kidnapping, but she hadn't purposefully hurt us. That didn't even enter my mind as a possibility. So instead, I wondered if it was Mindy, getting revenge for the vaccination altercation? Or a baby octopus, the tentacles feeling like fingers? Maybe even a severed hand, like Thing from the Addams Family? The most likely option, I told myself, was that it was a phantom sensation and I was actually just having a panic attack. My breath was running out. I opened my eyes, but the salt water burned them and blurred what was above the surface. I flailed around, trying to grab whatever was holding me under and when that failed I paddled my arms down into the water and tilted my head back, trying to raise my face enough that just my nose could break through the surface to take a gasp of sweet, sweet air, air my lungs craved so badly they burned, a craving that made me claw at my throat and chest as I told myself to keep holding my breath and wondered if it had been around thirty seconds or more like a minute because the pressure in my chest felt like it was about to explode, and as hard as I tried not to my lungs finally gave out and I took a deep, deep inhale.

But of course the inhale was water and it was like when a drink goes down the wrong tube and you can't stop coughing, but a million times worse. My throat spasmed and darkness began seeping in the edges of my vision and I thought *this is it*. Through the darkness Aimee's face appeared, her deep brown eyes and her apple cheeks and the small perfect mole above her lips, just to the right of the center of the Cupid's bow, that I loved to kiss. Beth's face appeared next, but her face from high school, because I had no idea what she looked like now. I wondered if she would regret all the years of not speaking to me when she heard I'd died. Then, just when I was starting to give in to it, a gigantic wave came, bowling me over and finally releasing me from whatever had held me under.

When I came up, choking and coughing, both Mindy and Ellie were ahead of me by at least fifteen feet, and the wave had carried me in close enough that my feet could touch. No one else was nearby. I stood there gasping and coughing for what felt like minutes, hacking up water until I finally puked, then I felt better. I touched the top of my head: no octopus, no severed hand. I turned around and paddled toward the shore. What my brain refused to accept, my body already knew: my teeth clacked together in a convulsive shiver even though the wetsuit had kept me perfectly warm. On the beach I sat on my towel, taking deep breaths, trying to still my heart that was blipping like the buildup of an EDM song before the drop.

I calmed down as I people watched. A fellow ginger kid who was probably around ten years old repeatedly rehearsed a dance routine for his grandma, who was sitting in a beach chair. The dance involved a lot of sexy hip swivels and humping motions, and I was curious what the grandma thought of it—she was sitting in front of me so I could only see the back of her white-haired head. Did she think the dance was funny? Or was she embarrassed and wished he'd stop? Did she worry he was gay or would she accept him no matter what? A middle-aged guy in a Hawaiian shirt walked down the beach with a metal detector and a tiny black terrier that wasn't on a leash. Whenever the detector beeped, the terrier would run over and start furiously digging in the sand, like it was helping. I wondered if the man had trained the terrier to do this, or if it was something the dog did of its own volition.

After the lesson, when everyone was high-fiving each other and Blair was giving the surf instructor her number, I approached Ellie. "You looked good out there," I said, trying to seem nonchalant instead of completely fucking freaked. "I can't believe you caught a wave. Kaivan will be impressed."

"Let's hope I can do it again in Hawaii," Ellie said. "What happened to you? Why'd you go back?"

"This is going to sound really weird," I said. "But after that second wave, I swore I felt something...or someone...pushing my head under." I forced myself to laugh, like I knew what I was saying was bonkers. "I think I like, almost drowned."

"Almost drowned?" Ellie made an incredulous face and twisted a section of her wetsuit, wringing out water. "That's bizarre. How many drinks did you have at that bar?"

I crossed my arms. "I made sure I was sober by the time I drove back."

"Huh," Ellie said. "Maybe you were having a little panic attack, then. I know sporty stuff like surfing is scary for you, but I really appreciate you trying." She pulled her vibrating phone out of her purse and showed me the screen—Debra calling again. "Anyways, don't worry. Surfing should be the only life-threatening activity of the weekend," she said before picking up.

16

"Welcome to our emotional sanctuary," said Kaivan's dad, Bruce, when everyone arrived at their ultra-modern house for the rehearsal dinner. They lived in Topanga, a mountainous hippie enclave thirty minutes from Malibu, and from far away their house looked like a game of Jenga, paneled redwood jutting out here and there between wide expanses of glass. The house was built directly into a steep cliff, and from the front you couldn't tell just how massive it was.

"What do his parents do?" Isabel whispered to me as we walked in.

"His dad is a life coach, and his mom has a sculpture at LACMA right now," I said. "But I think they both come from money."

The inside of the house was all low benches covered in throw pillows, Hindu goddess sculptures, abstract paintings by artists I didn't recognize but felt like I should, and African face masks. Ellie and Kaivan stood in front of a large stone fireplace greeting guests. Ellie was wearing a knee-length white dress and beige flats to try to make up for the fact that she was taller than Kaivan. Dark makeup surrounded her eyes and she had curled her stick-straight hair with a curling iron. As she talked to someone, she twirled a wineglass between her fingers, the tendons that connected to her knuckles flexing. I blinked and felt the weight of a palm on the top of my head, the soft pads of fingertips pressed into the sides of my skull, then I shoved the memory away.

Kaivan was holding his phone in front of someone's face, probably showing them his latest idea. I hadn't seen him since he and Ellie moved to LA six months before, and he looked different. He was growing out his hair to try to compensate for the fact that it was thinning on top, and he now had a weird kind of man bob. In jarring contrast to that, he had gotten *jacked*. Like, pectorals the size of B-cups jacked. I remembered Ellie saying something about him getting into CrossFit.

"Robin!" said Kaivan with false enthusiasm as I approached them. "It's been a while. How's…" I saw him sifting through his mind for my job or any specific tidbit about my life and coming up blank. "Things?"

"*Things* are good," I said. "My job is going really well— you know how I'm a fashion blogger?"

He started to nod like when you can't hear someone in a crowded room and are just going along, hoping you're not making an ass out of yourself.

Ellie crossed her arms and sighed. "She's fucking with you."

"Yeah, I know, I was fucking with her right back," he said unconvincingly.

I told myself I'd give him three minutes of small talk before escaping. "How's your app doing?"

"Pretty tight," Kaivan said. "I actually just sold this new filter to FaceApp, you know the one that lets you gender swap and see how you'll look when you're old?"

A panicked look spread across Ellie's face. "Babe, no business talk. Robin doesn't want to hear about that."

"Sure I do," I said. "What's the filter?"

Kaivan smiled proudly. "It lets you see what you'd look like as a different race. So like, if you wanted to know what you'd look like as an Asian person—"

Ellie bit her lip and grabbed his arm. "I think I see your grandma across the room. We should go say hi."

"Yeah, in a minute," Kaivan said, then continued on, holding his phone in front of my face to show me what he'd look like as an Asian person. "Look at all these fun props you can add, like one of those long Fu Manchu mustaches or chopsticks in your hair." He laughed as he added each item.

Ellie gave me a pleading look.

"Wow," I said. "You're not worried that'll come across as just a tad racist?"

"Nah, man," said Kaivan. "The opposite! It helps people see themselves as someone else, so they can imagine what it would be like to be different. It's actually like, a great tool for empathy."

I gave an exaggerated nod. "Impressive. What do you think of it, Ellie?"

She spoke through clenched teeth. "It is my wedding weekend, and I don't want to be talking about this right now." Her voice rose to a shout. "Doesn't anyone care what I want?" Then she stormed out of the room.

Kaivan gave me a weary look, then followed Ellie. I figured I should give them some time to cool off, so I walked through the house to the back, where there was a Japanese garden complete with a red torii gate that Bruce told me "marks the transition from the profane to the sacred." To the side of the garden was a patio area where the caterers lined up silver trays of steaming food and bartenders poured drinks.

I ordered a water and two glasses of white wine, telling the bartender one was for a friend, and guzzled the first one while in the bathroom. Normally, I wasn't a big drinker, but I wasn't normally a maid of honor, either. After we walked through the ceremony, we got in line for the buffet, which included rabbit tagine (rabbit seemed like a strange choice, but I figured it had something to do with Kaivan's hippy parents), spiced couscous, and roasted vegetables. Resigned to my vegan fate, I loaded a plate with couscous and vegetables, until a server came to my table to drop off a bowl of chickpea tagine.

"The bride had the chef make this for you," the server said, setting the steaming bowl in front of me. The aroma of cumin, turmeric, and cinnamon wafted into my nose and my stomach gurgled hungrily in response. I was touched, and surprised—I thought Ellie was furious with me, but instead she had given me a special vegan meal. She had probably planned it before I pissed her off, but still, it was unexpectedly considerate of her to think of me in the midst of all the wedding craziness. I looked over at her table and caught her eye, mouthing "thank you" as I pointed to the tagine. She mouthed back "you're welcome, bitch" while tilting her head and playfully rolling her eyes, to let me know she was joking about the "bitch" part, or at least mostly joking.

I scooped out a spoonful of the tagine and blew on it for two seconds, then ate the too-hot bite, scalding my mouth. I breathed air around the food and chewed cautiously. The tagine had a deep flavor that was equally savory and sweet— it was probably one of the best ones I had ever had. I gobbled it down, not even caring that I was repeatedly burning my mouth.

As soon as everyone had their food, Bruce stood up and tapped a glass with a knife.

"Twenty bucks he makes a joke about the wife always being right," I said to Shaun, leaning over to him.

"He seems a little more out-of-the-box than that," said Shaun, using a toothpick to extract a piece of rabbit from between his blindingly white teeth.

"*Fifty* bucks if he makes a joke about when he can expect grandkids."

Shaun shook his head. "You think everyone is so predictable."

"Thank you all so much for coming to our humble abode," said Bruce, laughing at his joke about the abode being humble. He was wearing a flowy silk tunic and his feet were bare. "I hope you're enjoying your tagine. We chose rabbit because they symbolize prosperity, good luck, and of course, abundant fertility. So I assume I won't have to wait too long for grandkids, right?" he said, winking at Ellie and Kaivan. The crowd laughed.

I looked at Shaun and held out my palm. He rolled his eyes. A server came by and filled up my empty wineglass. After I took a drink, my tongue prickled with a small itch. I scraped my teeth across my tongue and the feeling intensified. This was usually the way an allergic reaction started—I was allergic to nuts—but tagines didn't typically have nuts in them, so I swished some water around in my mouth and hoped it was nothing.

"Speaking of," I said. "How's the baby-making going for you and your husband?" We were sitting at a table near the back of the patio, far away from Bruce, and I figured talking to Shaun about babies would be slightly more interesting than listening to a list of dad clichés.

"There's a lot of hoops to jump through," he said. "But we know it'll be worth it."

I waited for him to expand, but he took a bite of tagine as if to punctuate the sentence. "What kind of hoops?" I asked.

"You know, just bureaucratic bullshit."

"Like, related to…adoption? Or surrogacy? Or…" I took a gulp of wine, followed by a gulp of water.

He twisted around in his chair. "You *do* know asking about that is kind of intrusive, right?"

"Oh, really?" My heart tripped as the wine in my stomach churned, hot and acidic. "Why?"

He sighed. "Would you ask a straight couple what sex position they used to conceive their kid?"

"That seems like sort of a false comparison. There's one way most straight, reproductively compatible couples have a baby, so there's no need to ask. There are all kinds of ways for queer people to have one. Is it wrong to be curious?"

He huffed. "It would be one thing if it was just about curiosity. It's usually about judgment, too."

I crossed my heart with my pointer finger. "If you want to tell me, I promise not to judge."

He gave me a dead stare. "That's like a Kardashian promising not to start drama."

I shrugged. "Fine. Don't tell me, then." Kaivan's dad was now telling a story about how when Kaivan was little, he never got in a bad mood when his baseball team lost. I didn't understand how it thematically connected to Ellie and Kaivan's relationship; he might have been drunk and rambling.

Shaun turned back to me. "If I told you we were using a surrogate, you wouldn't judge?"

I pressed my lips together and shook my head.

"I know the question you're dying to ask."

I kept my lips pressed together; kept shaking my head.

He took a bite of tagine; chewed it methodically. Then he took a long drink of wine. "You want to know why we're not adopting."

I held my hands up. "I haven't said a word." The itchy feeling had now spread to my lips. I rubbed a cloth napkin back and forth across them, then texted Ellie, hoping she had her phone nearby.

Did you happen to ask the chef if there were any nuts in the tagine? Kinda feel like I'm having an allergic reaction.

I watched her to see if she would notice the text. When she looked down at her phone, the right side of her mouth flinched in either a twitch or a smirk. She wrote back right away.

Yup, they told me everything was nut-free.

Huh. Ok thanks.

I swished some more water around my mouth and tried to ignore the sensation. "It feels like you *want* to tell me why you're not adopting," I said to Shaun.

He laughed. "I didn't *want* to talk about this at all, but now that you've backed me into a conversational corner…" He pressed his hands into the table as if to steel himself. "All you white feminists think you're so intersectional, but I bet you've never thought about the race component. It's important to us that the baby reflect our particular background, and you can't really specify that you want a baby with both Dominican and Indian heritage at the adoption agency."

My cheeks flared as I scratched at my mouth with my barely existent fingernails. "Okay, that's a pretty good reason."

He widened his eyes and pulled his neck back. "Did I just… convince you, Robin Hawkins, to concede?"

I laughed and held up a finger. "Technically, I never voiced my opinion."

He tutted his tongue, then leaned in closer to me and narrowed his eyes. "Hey, are you okay? The skin around your mouth looks a little red. Or maybe really red."

"Really?" My stomach twisted in a cramp as I took out my phone and tried to use the front camera to get a look, but it was too dark, so I speed walked to the bathroom, hoping it was nothing.

17

The line for the main bathroom was halfway down the hall, and after standing there for a few minutes, my mouth getting itchier and stress sweat dampening my temples and armpits, I tiptoed up the stairs and hoped Kaivan's parents wouldn't mind. I peeked into various rooms—a bedroom, an entertainment room, another bedroom, a library, until I found what could only be the master bedroom. It was about the size of my entire apartment in Brooklyn, with a California King in the center sprawled underneath a skylight. To the right, the promised land: a master bathroom with not one but two Japanese toilets.

I flicked on the light, then closed and locked the door before regarding myself in one of the large, round mirrors. I looked like a kid who had drunk too much fruit punch at a party, with a ring of red skin enveloping my mouth. My face also seemed swollen, my ballooning cheeks subsuming my shrinking eyes. Before I could assess any further, another stomach cramp hit—this time like a kick—and I hunched over the closest toilet just in time to empty the contents of my stomach. It was the most violent vomit I could remember having—like an unstoppable geyser spewing forth from the depths of the earth. I had never puked from an allergic reaction before. It had been a long time since I had drunk five glasses of wine, but my body's reaction seemed extreme even for that. I leaned back from the toilet and tried to take a deep breath but it felt like half the air couldn't make it to my lungs—my throat must have been swelling, too. I felt amazingly tired all of a sudden. I lay my head on the toilet lid, appreciating the cool plastic on my cheek. The wall I faced was entirely glass, looking out onto the dark undulations of mountains. The moon was a crescent but from the bottom instead of the side, like someone was shining a very bright flashlight on it from below. The faintest outline of the top was still visible.

As I was trying to remember if this was called a waxing or waning moon, a door clicked beyond the bathroom and I heard someone moving around. Fuck. It was probably really rude to be using the private bathroom attached to the bedroom. I didn't know if I should make some noise, signaling to whoever was in the bedroom that I was there, or sit still and try to wait them out. After a few seconds my stomach decided for me—I heaved again, mostly bile this time. The liquid fought to get past my enlarged throat tissue, some of the acidic bile getting trapped there.

"Hello? Are you okay in there?" a familiar-sounding male voice asked.

"I'm not sure," I answered, realizing it was hard to talk. I took a shallow, wheezy breath. "Who is it?"

"It's Kaivan."

I felt mildly relieved it wasn't his parents, but still embarrassed. I flushed the toilet and crawled to the door, opening it. My nose was immediately hit with a skunky, herbaceous, smoky smell. Kaivan, who had been sitting on the bed, jumped up when I appeared, a joint curling smoke between his fingers. "Holy shit, you look like death," he said. "What happened?"

"I don't know," I croaked. "Maybe I drank too much wine, or maybe I'm having an allergic reaction—I'm allergic to nuts, but Ellie said the chefs told her there weren't nuts in the food."

Kaivan scoffed. "Never trust a chef when they tell you something's not in the food. Do you have an EpiPen with you?"

"Yeah, in my bag, but you really think I need it?"

"If you're having symptoms, which you definitely are, it's always better to just use it." Kavain stamped out the joint and rifled through my bag until he found the pen.

"Ready?" He removed the blue safety cap and held the pen in the air, poised.

I nodded and pulled up the hem of my dress to my upper thigh, slightly self-conscious but also not really caring because of the direness of the situation.

Kaivan counted down from three, then with a swift motion, he swung the pen and stabbed it into my thigh with a click.

I gasped as the medicine coursed through my body, making my heart race. After just a few moments I took a deep breath, my mouth stopped itching, and my nausea dissipated.

"You okay?" he asked.

I nodded. "Thank you. You really took charge of that situation."

He smiled. "Ellie always says I'm good in a crisis. I'm deathly allergic to shellfish, so I've learned the hard way that you've got to take action right away."

"I don't know why I didn't use the pen sooner. I wasn't thinking straight. All the wine, I guess."

"Our head gets cloudy when our body is having a gnarly reaction like that. I'm just glad I was here to help."

I shook my hands like they were wet and I was trying to dry them. "The one thing I hate about the EpiPen is how anxious it makes me feel."

"Oh, man, I know. You know what I do?" He reached onto the dresser and retrieved the joint. He smiled, placing it between his lips and flicking the lighter, then he took a long inhale. The tip of the joint burned orangey red.

"You don't think it'll interact with the EpiPen in a bad way?" I asked.

He blew out a long stream of smoke. "Nah, I've done it a bunch of times."

"I haven't smoked in years," I said. "But maybe a hit would do me good."

Kaivan passed me the joint. "I think your nerves, and your stomach, will thank you."

I brought it to my lips and inhaled tentatively, but didn't feel anything coming through.

"I rolled it a little tight," he said. "You've gotta pull harder."

I sucked on the joint like it was a straw full of air and I was drowning. The smoke hit my throat and burned. I tried to hold it in but barked a cough almost immediately, the kind where you can't even pull in enough air between coughs to keep coughing.

"Oh, shit," said Kaivan. "You're gonna be so high."

I ran back into the bathroom and drank from the faucet. In the mirror, my face had almost gone back to normal. When I came out I knew I was high by the feeling of my brain floating just above my head to the right. My head was so light without a brain in it, weighing it down.

"Will you do me a favor?" Kaivan asked, looking sheepish. "Don't tell Ellie about us smoking?"

"Why not? You think she'd care?"

"Ellie doesn't like when I smoke," he said, taking another hit. He held it in and kept talking in a croak. "And on top of that, this is her *perfect wedding weekend*. Anyone who does anything to compromise it better watch out."

I smacked my lips. My mouth was so dry it felt like it was made of gum, everything sticking together. "So I'm not the only one who's been feeling the wrath of Ellie?"

"My boys told me this happened with all their wives, too," he said. "They became a totally different person near the wedding. Almost like they were possessed."

I laughed. "So you don't care about the flowers or Ellie's nails or the wedding singer?"

"Nah, man. I care about Ellie. It kind of makes me wonder, like…does she care more about this wedding than she does about me?"

Maybe it was the weed or his vulnerability, but for the first time I felt a warmness toward Kaivan. Maybe he did love Ellie more than she loved him and that was why he was constantly trying to prove himself. Bravado as a synonym for insecurity. Maybe he wouldn't go down on Ellie not because he was a jerk but because he worried he wasn't good at it. "I'm sure that's not it," I said. "Women are bonkers about their weddings. My cousin got married a few years ago, and when she found out the cake had strawberry filling instead of raspberry, an ambulance had to come."

He shook his head, staring out the window at the moon. "It's weird to see the crescent on the bottom like that. Makes me feel like we're living in some trippy alternate reality. Or maybe it's because you and I are like, bonding. I don't think we've ever done that." When I didn't immediately reply, he looked down at his hands, rubbing them in circles like he was washing them. "That was a dumb thing to say. You probably don't think we're bonding."

"Sure I do," I said. "It's nice."

"I wish we would have done it sooner."

"Well, we've got a whole lifetime," I said. "You're about to marry my best friend."

When Kaivan and I returned to the back patio, people were gathered around in a loose circle with uneasy looks on their faces.

"What's going on?" I asked Blair, who was reapplying her trademark red lipstick with a compact mirror. Blair had a carefully cultivated pinup girl look, with red lipstick I swore she wore while she slept, thick winged eyeliner, lots of bandannas in her hair, and '50s-style high-waisted dresses. She said people always told her she looked like Joan Crawford, but I wondered if they would think so without all the adornment.

She put her lipstick back in her purse and traded it for her phone, opening up Spouse Spotter. "Apparently, they're going to sacrifice a rabbit." She said it without looking up and with no audible emotion, like she was relaying any simple fact.

I turned toward her. It felt like my head was moving in slow motion. "What? *Why?*"

"I think it's one of those wedding charm things."

"Jesus, it wasn't enough that people had to eat rabbit for dinner? Now they have to kill another one for no reason? I've never heard of a wedding charm that extreme."

"Apparently, it's something Ellie's Polish ancestors used to do?"

"Yeah, probably back when the only way to feed all those wedding guests was to slaughter something." There was a tight feeling in my chest, like a burp was stuck in there but it wouldn't come out. It made it hard to breathe. "Once people start killing animals for sport or whatever this is, we can agree it's gone too far, right?"

Blair shrugged. "I'd kill a rabbit if it meant I didn't have to spend any more time on these fucking apps." She held up her phone that displayed a dick pic—a veiny one that curved to the left. "I'd kill a whole bunch of rabbits if it would help me hang on to someone I wanted to be with for life. I know people think I'm just a slut or whatever, but what if a *'slut'* is just a woman who's really committed to finding lasting love? Who hasn't given up on the idea that her person is out there even though sometimes giving up would seem like the very logical thing to do? So she dates a lot and tests out the sexual chemistry even though ninety-seven percent of guys end up being jerks who don't understand the clitoris, but she wouldn't know that if she didn't go on the dates and try. It's a shitty, necessary pathway to the end goal."

The first time I met Blair, I barely spoke the entire time. She never asked me a single question, and instead regaled me with a drawn-out tale about how she ended up having to keep her ex's cat. Eventually, I had to put a moratorium on hanging out with Ellie and Blair because it was always dick this, dick that, what do you think he's thinking, he's a musician, he's in finance, he told me I was pretty, why hasn't he kissed me, why hasn't he texted, he'll be lucky if I'm still around when he realizes he made a mistake, how do I get him to brush his teeth/wax his brows/trim his fingernails/shave his beard, how long should I wait before texting him back, he's a good guy but I'm not attracted to him, I didn't have an orgasm but it was still fun, tonight I have a date with Jeff/Mark/Chris/Sam/John/David/Paul/Brian. It was like an episode of *Sex and the City* on crystal meth. After Ellie met Kaivan, she would sometimes admit to me that Blair's dating escapades had become "a bit much," "but you've got to admire her tenacity," she'd say.

"I always tell women never to use the word *slut*," I said. "But that definition is kind of beautiful. Sad, but beautiful."

"Just feels sad to me," Blair said.

I thought about going back inside and pretending the whole rabbit thing wasn't happening, but I wanted to see what Ellie

would do. There was no way she would go through with it.
She wouldn't even watch shows like *Grey's Anatomy* or *True
Blood* because she didn't like seeing fake blood, and if she saw
blood in real life, she'd faint. I pushed my way through the
crowd to the front. Ellie had changed into jeans and a T-shirt,
and was sitting on a tarp feeding a brown-and-white mot-
tled rabbit some lettuce while tears streamed down her face.

"I can't do it," she said to her mom, who was kneeling
next to her tying slipknots around the rabbit's hind legs. I had
talked to her mom briefly earlier in the night—or more like
I had stood there while she talked *at* me, as usual, about how
she was on a new diet where you didn't eat any sugar but she
was going to make an exception for the cake tomorrow and
how impressive Kaivan's parents' house was and how relieved
she was that Ellie was finally getting married because she had
been starting to worry Ellie was cursed.

Ever since we were little, Ellie's mom was obsessed with
Ellie's romantic life, constantly asking about boyfriends and
giving Ellie tips to keep them happy and setting her up with
guys from church or even the grocery store. It got worse after
she and Ellie's dad divorced, then even worse after he died.
She kept saying Ellie needed a man in her life to take care of
her. Whenever Ellie would break up with someone, her mom
would get more upset about it than she would, crying about
how she thought they were "the one" and how the older Ellie
got, the fewer men would be available and the less desirable
she'd be. By the time Ellie was in her midtwenties her mom
switched the focus to grandkids, and since Ellie was an only
child it was her responsibility to give her mom "little El-
lies." Every year on Ellie's birthday, her mom would remind

Ellie that she only had however many childbearing years left. When I thought about all that, it was easier to see why Ellie was the way she was.

"Honey, it has to be you," said Ellie's mom. "Remember, you're doing this for the strength of your marriage." She picked up the rabbit by the rope around its legs, then tied the rope to a tree branch so the animal hung a few feet from the ground, upside down. The rabbit squirmed and kicked its legs, then let out a piercing scream that sounded eerily close to a terrified child's scream. No joke, the hairs on my arms stood up.

Ellie whined and shook her hands frenetically. "Mom, listen to it! I can't, I can't."

Ellie's mom grabbed her chin and forced Ellie to look at her. She spoke in a hard, stern voice. "Listen to me, Ellie Bellie. You are thirty-four years old and this is your last chance. Do you want this marriage to work?"

Ellie nodded as more tears cascaded down her cheeks.

"Okay, then. Be a big girl and do it." Her mom passed her a sledgehammer for one hand and a butcher's knife for the other. The rabbit had gone completely still, like it had either accepted its fate or was trying to trick them into thinking it had already died. Ellie's mom sprinkled some water on its head and mumbled something that sounded like a prayer before turning to Ellie and giving her a decisive nod.

Ellie raised the sledgehammer a few inches, then lowered it. She put the back of her hand to her mouth and leaned over. Her back rose and fell as she took deep breaths. She stayed like that for a few seconds, and when she stood back up, there was a resigned, determined look in her eyes. Before I could even take in the reality of the situation, Ellie had thunked the rabbit on the back of its head with the sledgehammer hard enough that it convulsed a few times, then went limp. She set down the sledgehammer and immediately used the butcher's knife to slice a quick, fast line through the rabbit's throat. The blood gurgled out like someone had squeezed an almost-empty ketchup bottle, the noise making my throat constrict. Ellie seemed completely fine, a concentrated yet unbothered look on her face.

I turned away, the tightness in my chest intensifying. I took out my phone and frantically typed another bullet into the *Plot to Save Marriage* note, then almost texted Aimee before remembering it was the middle of the night on the east coast, and she'd be asleep. I sat under the red torii gate, waiting to feel the transition from the profane to the sacred, but it never came. Instead, I felt like I was on the verge of a panic attack, and cursed myself for smoking weed and agreeing to be involved in this whole horrifying situation.

When it was time to leave, we piled into the van that would take us back to the country club and waited for Ellie, who was washing up. We sat in silence, minus Mindy's drunk hiccups, Meat Loaf's "I'd Do Anything for Love" playing softly on the classics station.

"So no one's going to talk about what just happened back there?" I said. "None of you are a little weirded out?"

"In some cultures they still sacrifice animals," said Isabel. "Like Hasidic Jews who sacrifice chickens after Rosh Hashanah to transfer their sins to the bird."

"But this wasn't a chicken!" I said. "It was an adorable little bunny rabbit. And it wasn't for any kind of religious ritual. It was for a *wedding*." I looked at Shaun. "Come on, you can't think this is normal."

"It's not my place to judge other people's decisions," he said.

"Jesus, Shaun, you're not running for president yet. There aren't any reporters in the car. Stop being so fucking diplomatic."

"I'm not trying to be diplomatic," he said. "I actually mean it. Would I sacrifice a rabbit during my wedding weekend? Probably not. But it's not my wedding, so why should I care?"

Just then the van door slid open and Ellie got in, sitting in the empty seat next to me. Kaivan was staying with his parents in customary fashion. The tradition not to see each other until the wedding dated back to when marriages were arranged as business transactions. The bride and groom weren't allowed to meet until the ceremony in case the bride's looks weren't exactly what the groom was expecting, so it would be too late for him to back out. That was why brides wore veils, too, so the grooms couldn't see their face until the last possible second, when they had already been pronounced husband and wife. No returns or exchanges. Apparently, it didn't matter what the brides thought of the grooms' looks.

The driver started the car and turned up the radio, Meat Loaf singing, *no one else can save me now but you.*

"Are you feeling okay?" Ellie asked. "You had texted me something about having an allergic reaction?"

"I'm better now, but I had a bad one. Had to use my EpiPen and everything, so there must have been nuts in something I ate."

"Huh. That's so weird." Ellie shook her head. "I definitely asked the chef, and he definitely said no nuts. I'm sorry. You're feeling better now, though?"

I nodded, then leaned toward Ellie and lowered my voice. "Are *you* feeling okay?"

She nonchalantly picked blood out from under her fingernails. "Why wouldn't I be?"

"Um, maybe because you just killed a rabbit."

"People kill animals all the time."

"Like what people?"

"Farmers."

I rolled my eyes. "Ellie, you're not a farmer. I'm worried about you. It seems like you're dangerously close to losing it."

Ellie swung her head around to face me. Her eyes felt like they could bore a hole into my head. "*You're* dangerously close," she snarled.

I leaned away from her. "To what?"

She looked out the window and muttered something that sounded like "You'll see."

A chill spread through my heart. "What?"

She went back to scraping her fingernails for blood. "Nothing."

18

As I lay in my hotel bed with a cupcake competition show on TV, I scrolled through Facebook on my phone, past "thrilled to announce" posts and pet pictures and recipe videos for things like mac 'n' cheese–stuffed garlic bread that always managed to suck me in, and I was about to scroll past a picture of a woman when I stopped. She looked familiar, with a pixie cut, red lipstick, and a hummingbird tattoo—it was the woman from the missing poster in the bookstore. The post was from Sarah, one of my friends who lived in LA. "Please share," it said. "Stephanie has been missing for a week now. She was last seen around 10 p.m. the night of her friend's wedding at the Malibu Palms Country Club. We're very concerned for her well-being. Please call the Malibu Police if you have any information."

I messaged Sarah.

Hey, just saw your post about that missing woman. Get this: I'm at the Malibu Palms right now.

That's crazy! Are you there for a wedding?

Yup, an old friend from high school and college.

Let me ask you something. Are there still posters up around the country club?

No. The only one I saw was at a bookstore nearby.

Those fuckers. I knew they would take them down.

Who? The country club?

Yeah. They've been really unhelpful.

That's terrible. Is there anything I can do?

Do me a favor and just ask someone about her tomorrow. See how they react.

Will do. Do you know anything else about the night she disappeared?

Everyone said she was really out of it. Like, on drugs or something. Which seems weird to me—she wasn't really into that. But I know she was really stressed because she was the maid of honor and her friend was being a total bridezilla.

Wait. I'm the maid of honor for a bridezilla this weekend! Fingers crossed I don't go missing...

Oh, shit! No, I really think Stephanie's fine. I just want to hear from her. She's kind of a free spirit who will just spontaneously book trips around the world, so I'm hoping that's what's happened.

Okay, well, I'll let you know if I find out anything tomorrow.

Thanks! Good luck with your bridezilla. ☺

I thought about all the missing women on posters and wondered what percentage of them were ever found alive. I resisted the urge to google it and go down a disturbing rabbit hole, instead setting my phone down beside the clock on the bedside table. 11:52. I needed to get to sleep since I had to wake up before 7 a.m. for wedding-day yoga then rush to an 8:00 hair and makeup appointment, another expense to add to the jar. A 4 p.m. wedding, and I was getting my makeup done at 8 a.m. because there was only one makeup artist/hair stylist for all five bridesmaids plus Ellie. It was going to be a long day. I could practically feel my pores clogging at the thought of wearing a thick layer of foundation for over twelve hours, my feet throbbing from the gold heels Ellie insisted we all wear. Then my stomach flipped when I remembered I had to give a speech.

On the flight from New York, I had googled "maid of honor example speeches," and all I would have had to do was change the names; the speeches were so one-size-fits-all. *The first time I met [the bride] was... [The bride] and I have laughed together, cried together, and laughed until we cried. We have sooo many inside jokes that no one else would understand! I'm so glad she gets to marry the man of her dreams. Remember, [groom], a happy wife makes for a happy life. [Pause for laughter] Let's raise a glass to the beautiful bride and handsome groom and their happily-ever-after!* I wondered if so many maids of honor gave carbon-copy speeches because they lacked imagination or because they didn't think the bride and groom were a good match. I told myself that regardless of my feelings about Ellie and Kaivan's relationship, I was going to write something completely original and specific.

Just to get it out of my system, I wrote a brutally honest version. *The first time I met Ellie I thought she seemed super boring. We've laughed together, cried together, and there have been times I've wanted to strangle her. Now we're so different we can barely have a conversation! I'm so glad she's settling for the dictionary's definition of toxic masculinity because she's dying to get married to anyone. Let's raise a glass to the bride who looks like every blonde woman before her and the groom who is significantly less attractive and their completely expected, subpar year(s) of marriage that will most likely end in divorce!*

But when it came to writing a version I could actually say out loud, it was like one of those movie montages where a writer sits at a desk, crossing out sentence after sentence and a wastebasket eventually fills with balled-up paper. When the wheels touched down in LA, I had something pretty close to those example speeches online. I told myself it didn't matter, that Ellie probably *wanted* something that was sweetly generic, so I was actually doing her a favor by giving a speech that was less "Robin."

Around the third mental rewrite of my speech I must have fallen asleep, because at some point I opened my eyes and Ellie was standing over me, staring at me. Reflexively, I sat up and darted out the other side of the bed. Ellie was wearing a white tank top that said "bride" in chunky pink cursive with matching pink polka-dot pajama pants. The clock read 3:17.

"Ellie? How did you get in here?"

She didn't answer, but just kept standing there. Her body was rigid, her eyes staring through me with huge pupils. Her feet were bare, tiny blades of grass stuck between her toes. She must have been sleepwalking, something she used to do when we had sleepovers in high school and that I remembered as more entertaining and less creepy.

"Ellie," I said loudly. "You're asleep."

She abruptly pulled her tank top away from her body and looked down at her breasts. "What are these raspberries doing on my nipples? I need them for the wedding cake." She sounded genuinely distressed. She stuffed a hand in her shirt and proceeded to try to yank off her left nipple.

I came around the side of the bed, grabbing Ellie's arm to make her stop. "It's okay, I have plenty of raspberries."

Ellie tilted her head, narrowing her blank eyes at me. "Don't lie."

"I'm not lying, I really have a bunch of raspberries."

"Don't lie," she said again, more sternly.

"Ellie? Wake up. You're creeping me out." I put my hands on her shoulders and shook her back and forth.

Ellie's body went rigid, bracing against me. "Please stop that."

"Okay, but you have to wake up, because you're really creeping me out. Wake up!" I yelled, waving a hand in front of her vacant pupils.

"I am awake," Ellie said, giggling.

The hairs on my arms stood up. I pulled my hand back and whacked my palm across Ellie's cheek. "Wake up!" I yelled again, louder this time. "Wake up, wake up, wake up!"

"Be quiet!" Ellie whisper-yelled before clamping her palm across my mouth. I was so surprised that I just stood there. Ellie's eyes darted around the room as she tilted her head like she was trying to hear a faraway noise. Her hand was warm and slightly moist, and smelled faintly of the cocoa butter hand lotion she always kept in her purse.

I made a questioning "mmmm?" noise from under Ellie's palm, and she sharply shushed me before going back to listening for whatever noise she was trying to hear. All I could make out were the waves outside and the whir of air blowing through a vent in the ceiling. After a few moments Ellie let out a deep sigh, her body relaxing—like the noise, or the threat of the noise, had passed.

"There, there," she said. "See how nice it is when you're quiet?"

I tried to pull away from her palm against my mouth but she brought her other hand to the back of my head, trapping me. I made another "mmmm" noise in protest.

She pressed her palm even more firmly against my mouth. "Shhhhhhh," she said like she was trying to soothe a crying baby. Then her thumb and pointer finger slowly closed around my nostrils, so gradually that I wasn't sure if Ellie— sleepwalking Ellie—had meant to do it.

I tried to make another noise but it was nearly impossible with all my air cut off. I grasped at Ellie's forearm, trying to pull it away from my face, but it was like a steel bar. I whipped my head back and forth and squirmed my body this way and that, but her hands stayed robotically locked in place. Her glazed eyes stared straight ahead like her whole body was frozen in some kind of muscle spasm. My breath was running out. I needed to try something else. Leaning back, I fell on the bed and pulled my legs to my chest before shooting them out and kicking Ellie square in the chest. Her hands finally released as she fell back, stumbling until she hit the wall and sank to the floor.

I writhed on the bed, sucking deep, shaky breaths as air finally entered my lungs.

"Robin? Why am I in your room?" Ellie said, standing up. Her eyes were finally in focus again.

I backed away from her. "Get out," I tried to say, but it came out as just a breathless whisper.

"What?" Ellie walked toward me.

I held up my hands like a crazed crossing guard. "Don't come near me," I wheezed.

"Why? What's going on?" Ellie said.

I pointed to the door. "Get out," I said again, this time my voice creaking through.

Ellie gave me a confused look, but complied. I rushed to

close the door behind her, swinging the U-bar over the circular knob and clicking the dead bolt.

"Robin?" Ellie said from behind the door. "Did something happen? Was I sleepwalking?"

I peered through the peephole, but couldn't make out Ellie's facial expression because of the fish-eye effect. I leaned my forehead against the door. "You were suffocating me," I said quietly, trailing my fingers from my nose to my mouth. The skin there still smelled ever so slightly of cocoa butter.

"I what? Why?"

"I don't know why. Do *you*?"

"Of course not. I wasn't awake."

She *had* seemed like she was asleep, but why would even an unconscious Ellie try to suffocate me? Had she been dreaming that I was someone else, an attacker she needed to vanquish? Was it just her body doing something her brain wasn't even aware of? I ran my fingertip along the molding of the door until it was coated in fuzzy gray dust. "Go back to your room and get some sleep. We can talk tomorrow."

I watched through the peephole until Ellie disappeared around the corner, then pushed a chair underneath the doorknob before getting into bed and lying there, feeling my heartbeat shake the entire room.

19

When my alarm went off at 6:45 for Isabel's yoga session, it woke me from a recurring dream in which Beth and I were in our childhood house looking out the window at a dilapidated white Bronco approaching up the long dirt driveway. The car was occupied by men with guns hanging out the windows, and it was playing music so loud that I could feel the bass vibrating my heart. Our parents weren't home, and the men were coming to kill us. I ran to the front door to try to lock it—but no matter how many times I tried, the door wouldn't latch. I heard the car's engine turn off and doors slam. Beth tried locking the door, but she couldn't do it, either. We looked at each other, fear filling our eyes, and then, in a divergence from the usual dream, Beth became Ellie. She gave me an eerie, calm smile, then turned to face the door. Before it opened, I woke up. I had this dream, or a variation of this dream, multiple times a month, and I dreamed of Beth almost every single night in various situations. I had asked Alonzo why I constantly dreamed of someone who was no longer in my life, and he had said, "Maybe it's your way of *keeping* her in your life."

I considered turning off the alarm and getting another hour of sleep before my makeup appointment. I also considered sleeping through my makeup appointment and my maid of honor duties and the wedding itself, staying locked in my room until my flight home. I had probably only slept for an hour or two total—it took forever to fall back asleep after Ellie had sleep-busted into my room. But she had previously stressed how important it was to her that we all go to yoga and "get centered" with her before the big day, so I threw some water on my face, brushed my teeth, and went down to the expansive green lawn, where the sun was just starting to rise above the mountains, tinting the clouds a creamy orange.

Isabel sat cross-legged on a purple yoga mat, her long black hair waving in the wind. She smiled and waved when she saw me approaching, like she was genuinely glad to see me. Isabel had one of those faces where you knew exactly what she must have looked like as a kid—wide eyes, round cheeks, button nose, short chin—and she seemed to have held on to a child-like sense of wonder and kindness, too. I wasn't sure if it was because of the yoga or if it was just her natural disposition.

Isabel was Ellie's newest friend within the bridal party. They had met a few years ago when Ellie took a yoga class and Isabel was the instructor. After that, Ellie exclusively attended Isabel's classes. "I have such a friend crush on my yoga teacher," she'd tell me. "She has this super warm, calming energy, and after I leave her class I feel like I've done a magical drug." Ellie would hang around after class, chatting with Isabel, and eventually they went out for coffee, then Isabel started tagging along on weekend brunches, then I was dragged to her yoga classes, which I had to admit were pretty good even though I wasn't a yoga person.

One day Ellie told me she was going to start yoga teacher training in the evenings after work. Ellie had ended up majoring in psychology in college, and still didn't know what she wanted to do after she graduated so she got a job in HR, which probably couldn't qualify as anyone's passion. "I think this might finally be it," she told me. When she finished her training, she and Isabel went to a yoga teachers' retreat in Tulum, Mexico, where they did ayahuasca and discovered their purpose for being on earth, which was apparently teaching yoga. They were pretty insufferable for the few weeks after they got back from that trip, going on and on about their spiritual rebirth and the true nature of the universe. Ellie's plan was to quit her job as soon as she had lined up enough yoga clients, but I went to a few of her classes and they just felt like a cheap knockoff of Isabel's classes. After a few months of standing at the front of near-empty yoga rooms, Ellie decided it wasn't her calling after all, and stopped talking about quitting her job.

When it was five minutes past seven, everyone but Ellie was seated on their purple mat in front of Isabel.

"Should I go get her?" Mindy asked.

"I don't think she had the most restful night," I said. "She sleepwalked into my room around 3 a.m."

"Huh, that's weird," said Isabel. "Let's go ahead get started. If she shows up, great. If she doesn't, then she probably needed the rest." Isabel instructed us to come to a comfortable seated position, close our eyes, and take three deep breaths. "Clear your mind and focus on what you feel inside and outside of your body. Where are you feeling pain or discomfort? What is your inner voice saying? What do you feel and hear in the environment?"

I took a deep breath and tried to do what Isabel said. My right temple throbbed from all the wine at the rehearsal dinner and the lack of sleep. My stomach bubbled from the puking and the alcohol and because I had yet to take my morning poop. My inner voice was saying fuck Ellie for making all of us wake up for yoga while she was still sleeping, fuck Ellie for keeping me up half the night and creeping me the hell out, and fuck Ellie for asking me to be her maid of honor when she knew it would be misery for me.

If Isabel could read my thoughts, she would probably say "fuck Ellie" thoughts weren't the best kind to be having during yoga. She would tell me to release my anger and focus on my surroundings. So I took another deep breath and tried to home in on the hint of sun warming my forehead, the breeze blowing across my shoulders, the smell of bubblegum coming from the small white flowers shaped like miniature pinwheels, the birds chirping like they were ecstatic another morning had arrived. I wondered if there was such a thing as a bird who wasn't a morning person, who grumpily hunkered in the nest with a wing over its head until past 10 a.m., wishing everyone else would just shut up.

Isabel led us through a class focused on the belly, with lots of stomach-pumping breaths and twists and forward bends, since she figured Ellie might have a case of "nervous stomach" on her wedding day. But Ellie never showed up. As we lay in Savasana at the end of the class, Isabel told us that after the brain, the place in the body with the highest level of neurotransmitters was the gut: the very center of the energy system. "There's a reason we talk about gut instinct," she said. "Our belly's brain responds on the intuitive, nonverbal, instinctual level. I want you all to listen to what your stomach is saying right now. Is it tight? Churning? Fluttering? Bloated? Acidic? What do you think is making it feel this way?"

My stomach kind of felt like every symptom Isabel had described. I sent my brain to my intestines and trudged through the mucky coils, peering around each bend. Suddenly, it felt hard to breathe, and the taste of cinnamon and ginger and cumin flooded my tongue. Then goose bumps covered my skin and I was once again in the frigid ocean, waves violently pulling me back and forth, my head submerged and my breath running out, fingers pressed into the sides of my skull. I gasped—a gasp like I had just come back from the dead—and opened my eyes. Isabel was crouched above me, giving me a scalp massage.

"Are you okay?" she said. "Had you fallen asleep?"

"No, you just startled me," I said.

"Where were you just now, in your mind?"

I shuddered. "Nowhere."

After everyone else had rolled up their yoga mats and gone

back inside, Isabel softly laid a hand on my shoulder. "I just wanted to check in," she said. "You've seemed really on edge this weekend."

I feigned nonchalance. "Have I?"

Isabel tilted her head and widened her already-wide eyes at me.

I let out a tight laugh. "Okay, yeah, I've been on edge."

"Why, do you think?"

"Weddings just aren't really my thing. I feel like I've been disagreeing with everyone about everything." Two humming-birds buzzed by our heads, diving and circling before landing on the small white flowers that smelled like bubblegum.

"And disagreeing with people makes you angry?"

I gave Isabel a *duh squared* face.

"How many hours a day would you say you're angry?"

I shrugged. "A lot."

"It's not healthy to hold on to so much anger, Robin. Anger releases adrenaline, which in turn raises your heart rate and elevates your blood pressure, and it also releases cortisol, a stress hormone that alters immune system responses and suppresses the digestive system. You mentioned your heart palpitations the other day, and you've complained about your stomach at least five times since we've been here. I know it might not all seem connected, but it is. The mind, body, and spirit are all one. The bottom line is, you're hurting yourself."

You're hurting yourself. The statement slammed into my chest. Outwardly, though, I rolled my eyes, noticing a crow that had been perched on a nearby palm tree swooping down and landing on a bush by the bubblegum flowers. As soon as the crow's feet touched down, one of the hummingbirds jumped into action, frantically thumping the crow on its head until it flew away. "You're not a doctor," I finally said.

"No, but I'm a licensed acupuncturist and herbalist, which I think allows me to see things that traditional doctors don't. Most of them don't recognize the mind/body connection, which I think is detrimental to patients' health. Wouldn't you like to feel better? Wouldn't you rather *not* be angry?"

I sighed and put a hand on my hip. "No, I don't think I would." I said it as a knee-jerk reaction, but as the words settled over me, I recognized it was true. What would I be, if not angry? *Who* would I be? "It's sort of like, my whole personality," I added in a jokey tone.

"That's interesting. So you feel like you'd be giving up your sense of self if you gave up your anger?"

"Kind of."

"I'd investigate that, if I were you. Instead of trying to change everyone else, maybe look inward and try to change yourself." She pushed her hair out of her face. "You know, I used to be really angry, too. It was a problem."

I scoffed. "So angry that you didn't say namaste to someone after yoga?"

Isabel looked me straight in the eyes and crossed her arms. "So angry that I almost beat a girl to death outside a bar one night."

I huffed a surprised laugh, not sure if she was serious. "Um, what?"

"Yeah. I used to get into a lot of fights."

"Jesus, that's out of left field," I said. "I can't picture you punching someone like, at all."

Isabel looked out over the ocean, squinting. "I was a foster kid growing up, and I had to learn how to protect myself pretty early. Then protecting myself turned into...something else." Her face clouded over, and underneath the kid-like innocence, I saw a hard-edged layer of pain. "Just anger, constantly taking over."

"Wow." I shook my head. "So how did you get from that to Zen yogi Isabel?"

"After that really bad fight I was put into court-mandated therapy. It helped me understand how my childhood was connected to a lot of my behavior, and my therapist taught me how to meditate, and recommended yoga, and it was a really long process to get to where I am today."

"I'm in therapy, too," I said.

"For how long?" Isabel asked.

"About a year."

Isabel let out a small laugh. "So you've barely scratched the surface."

20

When I knocked on the door of Ellie's suite for my makeup and hair appointment, a woman with one side of her head shaved and a full sleeve tattoo opened it.

"I'm Mia, the makeup artist," she whispered. "Ellie let me in and then went back to bed." Mia gestured at the closed bedroom door. "She said she took a sleeping pill last night and didn't feel fully functional yet."

Sleeping pill—that would explain the sleepwalking, even though I still got a chill up my back when I thought about it. Five "getting-ready robes" with a watercolory azalea print and each of our names stitched above the right breast were laid out on the couch. I put mine on, then sat in the chair opposite the vanity covered in cases and cases of makeup.

"So what has Ellie instructed you to do to my face?" I asked.

"Let's see." Mia counted on her fingers. "Champagne eye with false lashes, full brows, rose gold lip, contoured face, waterproof everything."

"Oh God, I'm going to look like a clown. No offense. I'm sure you're really good at makeup. It's just not my style." Mia's own face looked barely made up, and I wondered if that was the case or if she had just perfected the non-makeup makeup look.

"If it were up to me I'd do a much more natural look, but I've learned not to make suggestions to brides."

I flicked my eyes toward the ceiling. "Tell me about it."

Mia squeezed a dollop of light green cream into her palm, then spread it over my face. "It's funny, I used to think I wanted to get married. But after doing this job for a few years, I think I'll pass."

"Yeah, you must've seen some stuff."

Mia pumped foundation onto something that looked like a contraception sponge, then patted the sponge across my face. "In a wedding I did last weekend, the maid of honor told me she had to give the bride a Brazilian wax herself because the bride forgot to schedule an appointment. Another maid of honor told me the bride weighed her as soon as she showed up for the wedding weekend, to make sure she had lost the required ten pounds. And this one is the kicker. One woman was going through chemo at the time of the wedding, so her hair had started falling out. The bride made her get three-hundred-dollar extensions."

"Damn," I said. "That's ice-cold." Then I thought I

wouldn't put it above Ellie, either, and my heart sank into my stomach.

Mia picked up a pair of super-pointy tweezers and plucked a stray eyebrow hair from below my arch. "I've heard even worse than that through the grapevine. Bizarre, scary stuff."

My heart sped up and thumped through my intestines. "Like what?"

The standard iPhone alarm went off in Ellie's room, then Ellie groaned and the bedsheets rustled.

"Like what?" I asked again.

"I'll tell you later," Mia whispered quickly, before Ellie's door flung open and she stood there rubbing her eyes.

"I had the weirdest dreams," she muttered.

"They might not have been just dreams," I said.

"What?"

"You sleepwalked into my room last night. You don't remember?" I searched Ellie's face for any sense of memory, but she stared down at her phone, distractedly scrolling.

"I sleepwalked? I haven't done that in so long. It must have been the pill I took."

"So you don't remember anything at all?" I asked.

"No, I never do when I sleepwalk. Did I do something funny?"

"You could say that." Mia took a light reddish-brown pencil out of a bag and started tracing the shape of my eyebrows. "How did you even get into my room?" It finally occurred to me to ask. "Did you have a key?"

"How would I know? I wasn't awake." Ellie eyed the window suspiciously, then walked over and pulled the curtains open with a hooked pointer finger. "What the fuck! Did you see how cloudy it is?" She took her phone out of her pocket and frantically swiped at it. "There's a fifty percent chance of rain today. Perfect. One of the three days a year it rains in LA and it had to be today."

Mia and I made eye contact in the mirror, trading tiny eye rolls.

"There's a fifty percent chance," I said. "That just means it might."

"Please," Ellie said. "You've seen the way my luck is going."

"Well, *if* it rains, which it might not, I'm sure they have tents," I said.

"Yeah, everyone wants to stand under a plastic tarp on their wedding day." Ellie squinted at my face. "Make her brows fuller, would you?" she said to Mia.

Ellie's phone rang, the customized "red alert" sound effect that meant it was Debra, the wedding planner. The noise was starting to give even me PTSD. "I swear to God," Ellie said before picking up. "Oh," she said in a voice that didn't sound like the apocalypse was coming. "Well, I'll take it." She took a deep breath and plopped down on the couch. "My second choice for the wedding-band singer just became available again, thanks to some other bride's cold feet."

"That's good news," I said. "Maybe your luck is turning around."

Ellie harrumphed. "What's that they say? It ain't over until the second-choice wedding singer sings."

By the time Mindy arrived for her ten o'clock makeup appointment, the room service breakfast we had ordered at nine still hadn't arrived, so Ellie sent me downstairs to check on it.

The concierge, a blonde woman with cakey foundation, was on the phone and refused to make eye contact.

"Yes, ma'am, of course the room will have a bed," she said. Every thirty seconds or so, she lifted a large bottle of cranberry juice to her mouth and took a swig. I wondered if she just really liked cranberry juice or if she thought she had a UTI.

"Yes, the room has a window."

Clearly, this was going to be a long one. I waited while looking at the wedding-themed art behind the desk. I recognized one as *La Mariée (The Bride)* by Marc Chagall, widely regarded as an ode to young love but to me it seemed creepier than that. The main image of the piece was a woman in a red gown and a long white veil, holding a bouquet of flowers. A man, presumably her soon-to-be husband, hovered next to her like he was flying. He held his face close to hers and watched her intently while pulling back her veil. He seemed like an overbearing presence, like she could feel him mouth-breathing on her cheek and was tolerating it but she wasn't enamored by any means. Her facial features were indistinct, two round black dots for eyes, a shadow of a nose, and a flat smudge for a mouth—she kind of looked like she was in a trance, like Ellie did when she was sleepwalking. Behind her, a bunch of weird shit was happening: a goat played a violin, a man played a flute, a fish with arms held a candle and a chair, and a church floated far in the background. The colors were mostly shades of midnight blue and purple, which made it feel nightmarish.

When the concierge finally hung up with the person who had probably inquired about every amenity, I asked about the room service and she called the kitchen to check on it, even though I knew the answer would be "any minute" regardless of whether the food would arrive in five minutes or twenty minutes.

"They said it should be there any minute," the woman said.

"Thanks." I started to walk away before turning back. "Hey, does the name Stephanie Bennett mean anything to you?"

She had just taken a big gulp of cranberry juice, and she swallowed audibly. "I don't think so."

I pulled up Sarah's Facebook post on my phone. "What about this photo? Do you recognize her?"

The woman glanced at it and her mouth twitched. "No, sorry. Who is she?"

"She was the maid of honor at a wedding here last weekend, and now she's missing. My friend said they put posters up here, but I don't see any now."

"I wasn't working last weekend, so I haven't heard anything about that, or seen any posters."

"Can you check your records and see if Stephanie stayed here?"

"I'm sorry, that's against our policy," she said, giving me a tight smile.

"All right, thanks anyway," I said, and walked away, but instead of going back to the suite I waited around the corner of the hallway. I figured the concierge would have to leave her post at some point, probably to pee—the bottle of cranberry juice was almost gone. It only took about fifteen minutes before she glanced around the empty lobby and disappeared behind a door. I made a run for it.

The computer system looked like something from the nineties with a bunch of small text fields that weren't easily scan-nable. My heart thumped as I Where's Waldo'd for anything akin to a search bar. After what felt like thirty full seconds, I found a button that said "RSV Search" with a microscope icon, so I clicked it and typed in Stephanie Bennett's name. A rainbow circle in the middle of the screen rotated. I ground my teeth and glanced at the door the concierge had gone through. When I looked back at the screen, a listing had appeared showing Stephanie Bennett's reservation from the weekend before. Her room was listed as #113. When I saw the number, a jolt went through my stomach. 113 was the room I was staying in. Instead of listening to my gut, as Isa-bel would recommend, I quickly shoved the feeling away—it was just a coincidence, of course. Maybe it was common prac-tice to put the maids of honor in that room for some reason. And the mansion only had about twenty rooms total, so the chance of staying in the same room as *anyone* was pretty high.

I darted out from behind the desk and let out a sigh of relief that cranberry juice lady hadn't caught me. When I got back to my room, I found myself searching for clues, although clues for what I wasn't exactly sure—just something I could share with my friend Sarah that might help them find Stephanie. If she had been missing for a week, I wondered if the police had searched the room, or if I was the first one to do it. I slid my hand between the mattress and the box spring, opened all the dresser drawers, and shined my phone flashlight under the bed. Then, in the back corner of the closet, I found a smooth marbled black-and-white stone the size of a quail egg. It was a worry stone, with a worn groove for a thumb to rub back and forth. I felt something rough on the underside of the stone

and turned it over, where in very tiny font a sentence was engraved. I held my phone's flashlight above it while squinting.
"Don't let the brides grind you down." Why did that sound
familiar? I googled it and most results showed a Latin phrase
"Nolite te bastardes carborundorum," which roughly translated
to "Don't let the bastards grind you down." Then I remembered it was from *The Handmaid's Tale*. Offred finds the sentence carved into the closet of the commander's house and
uses it as a prayer of sorts to keep her going. But then at the
end of the book, when she thinks the Eyes might be coming for her, she realizes the bastards *have* worn her down and
she's tired of resisting.

Could the stone have been a joke of sorts, a gift a group
of literary bridesmaids distributed amongst themselves as a
way to keep them sane over the wedding weekend? It might
not even have been Stephanie's—who knew how long the
stone had been sitting in the corner of the closet. Was it left
there by accident or on purpose? If it was left by accident, it
was certainly a coincidence that it was in the closet, the same
place as *The Handmaid's Tale*. I snapped a picture of it and
sent it to Sarah.

Not sure if this will help, but I found it in the room Stephanie
was staying in.

I held the stone in my hand, rubbing my thumb back and
forth across the dip while wondering what I should do with
it. Something told me to put it back where I found it, so I
placed it in the corner of the closet and closed the door.

My phone buzzed with a missed call from Aimee even

though I hadn't seen or heard a call. When I tried dialing her back, my phone made those three annoying beeps that meant the call wouldn't go through, so when I got back to Ellie's suite, I asked if I could use her phone.

"I've been telling you to get Verizon for years," Ellie said before begrudgingly handing over her phone. "Just let me know if Debra calls."

I went out to the hallway and was about to dial Aimee when, of course, a text from Debra came through. On a reflex, I opened it. "The photographer's house was broken into last night. All his equipment stolen. Try not to freak out. Making calls now." I didn't want to go back into the suite and deliver the bad news, so I sat down in the hallway, delaying the inevitable. After I read Debra's text, I hit the back arrow that took me to the main message screen.

I told myself I shouldn't look, but I had always been a snoop. When I was little and would have sleepovers with my friends, I would search their room in the middle of the night for their diary, trying to find out if they had ever written anything bad about me. Beth had intricate systems for figuring out if I had been looking at her things—dots of pencil to indicate where she had left a piece of paper, strings tied on the knobs of drawers that would collapse if they were opened. My parents had to lock my Christmas presents in a closet after I peeked so many times that there was no excitement left for the actual opening of the presents on Christmas morning.

I think deep down, I knew I was looking for something to confirm my gut feeling: that I was in danger. I glanced at the list of people Ellie had most recently texted—Debra, Kaivan, her mom, the wedding party group text I was on, a few people whose names I didn't recognize. My finger hovered over the search bar, then I typed "Robin" into it. A bunch of my own texts with Ellie came up, then a text from Isabel asking Ellie for my address to mail me something, then a text from Ellie to Mindy:

Robin is being such a ho about having to get her bridesmaid dress altered. She says it fits fine as is but it definitely doesn't.

Maybe she's concerned about money? You could offer to pay for it.

I don't think it's money. She just thinks weddings are stupid and wants to give me a hard time about everything.

Well, she's not getting married, so I guess I can see how it might feel a little unfair.

What would feel a little unfair?

Doing all this stuff for other people's weddings when she doesn't ever plan on having one.

Omg Mindy, just agree with me and say she's being a ho.

Lol okay, she's being a ho.

I was surprised—shocked, actually—that Mindy had been so sympathetic to my situation. It almost made me want to apologize about the whole vaccination fight, but as I imagined myself doing it, I recoiled. No, I couldn't let Mindy think it was okay not to vaccinate her kids, even if she had been nice to me without my knowing it.

I tapped the Safari icon. The last tab Ellie had open was a message board on the brides.com site. The original poster wrote:

I'm really nervous about my wedding and wondering if y'all have heard of any new wedding charms. We're already planning on doing sage & garlic bouquets, a fifty-ft train, and a mock kidnapping. What else have y'all heard about or done in your own weddings? TIA!

> Have you heard of dressing the groomsmen like the groom and the bridesmaids like the bride? So all the bridesmaids would wear a white dress and a veil, etc. The thinking is they act as decoys to trick the wedding-ruining spirits. One of my girlfriends did this and swears it sealed the deal with her marriage! Good luck!!!

> Okay, the thing I've heard of is kind of unpleasant but someone on a different site said if you sacrifice a female rabbit your marriage will be like, crazy fertile. I know the thought of cutting a cute little bunny's neck is icky but seems like it'd be worth it.

Alarm bells rang through my head.

> Hey OP I've heard of something you can do that will 100 percent *guarantee* your marriage will be happy and will last but I can't post about it here cause it's on the super down-low. Email me at jenthe-winelover@yahoo.com and I'll give you all the deets if you dare.

A call from Aimee came up on the screen and immediately

my stomach dropped. If she was calling Ellie on her wedding day, Aimee must have really had to get in touch with me.

"Aimee?" I said. "Are you okay?"

"Oh, it's you. I've been trying to call." Okay, she was speaking, so she was at least alive. But I couldn't gauge from her voice if something was seriously wrong.

"I don't get any service out here. What's going on?"

"I'm going to preface this by saying I'm okay, but a right-to-life guy with an AR-15 broke into the conference and I got shot in the arm. I'm on my way to the hospital."

"Jesus fucking Christ!" A montage of images flashed by my eyes: the pandemonium of people screaming and running in every direction, Aimee hiding under a chair, or in a closet, or in a bathroom, the unrelenting rhythmic pop of rapid-fire bullets.

"I know. But I'm okay. At least physically."

"You must have been terrified."

"Yeah."

"Did anyone die?"

"I'm not sure officially, but...there were people on the ground who looked dead."

"Jesus fucking Christ."

"Rob?" She raised her voice over sirens in the background. "We're at the hospital now so I have to go."

"Okay, I'm going to the airport right now and getting on the next flight home."

"No, don't miss the wedding. I'm going to be fine."

"Aimee, you were shot by a terrorist. I'm coming home."

"Okay. I love you."

"I love you, too. I'll let you know when I have a flight."

I was hauling myself up off the floor when Ellie stomped out into the hallway, scowling. "What's taking so long?"

"Aimee was shot."

She stopped walking. "What?"

After I told her the details, she closed the space between us and put her hands on my shoulders. "Oh my God, is she okay?"

"She said her wounds aren't life-threatening, but she's about to go to the hospital to find out more. Obviously, I need to fly back to be with her."

"Oh." She bit her lip, and her eyes went distant, like she was seeing the future of her imperfect wedding without her maid of honor. "When?"

"Now, Ellie." I started walking back to my room and she hurried to follow me.

Inside, I tossed my suitcase on the bed and starting filling it with my things.

Ellie grimaced, wringing her hands. "You couldn't wait until tomorrow morning?"

I paused to look at her, and my eyeballs went hot in what felt like preparation to shoot beams of fire at her. "Aimee was shot, and you're worried about your wedding? You really have become the most selfish person ever." I stepped into the walk-in closet to retrieve my hanging clothes, and when I turned around the door swung closed in my face.

"Ellie?" I pressed down on the handle but it didn't move. Did the closet lock from the outside? That would be strange. I jiggled the handle. "Ellie, can you open the door?" I heard something heavy slide across the carpet, then a thump as it was pressed up against the door.

"I'm sorry, Robin, but I can't let you leave right now," Ellie said from outside the closet, her voice muffled.

"Are you kidding?" But I knew she wasn't.

21

Inside the locked closet, my heart started sprinting. I swore I could feel my blood rushing through my veins in hyper lapse. It made me dizzy—I blinked and tried to orient myself, but it was pitch-black, except for the tiniest line of light coming through the crack between the door and the floor. I lowered myself to my knees and took a deep breath.

"I just really need you to stay through the wedding," Ellie said. "Aimee will be okay. You said it yourself."

I pounded on the door. "Ellie, this is crazy. Come on. Ellie? I'll scream, and someone will hear me."

"Scream all you want," she said. "The room is soundproofed."

"Why would the room be soundproofed?" I said, then I

finally started putting the dots together. The missing maid of honor. The worry stone. The lock on the outside of the closet. The mansion was owned by Ellie's family—that had to mean at least one of them was in on it. Could it be Ellie's wedding-obsessed mom? Was she actually the one driving all of this, turning Ellie into a crazy person? Now that she had locked me in a closet, she had officially turned the corner from stressed to psychotic, capable of something extremely unhinged. I shuddered.

"I have to go now," said Ellie. "I'll text Aimee that you decided to stay for the wedding, so she doesn't worry. And I'll come get you before the ceremony. Try not to freak out. Everything will be okay."

"Ellie, please!" I yelled, but the only response I got was the click of the door closing. If the room really was sound-proofed, I might as well test it. I screamed, once, for about three seconds, then waited: nothing. I screamed again, this time upping the volume and the length. Then I felt like I was using up all the air in the closet—could I suffocate in a space this small? I tried to take a deep breath but I couldn't achieve that satisfying sensation of air sufficiently filling the lungs. I tried again and it felt even worse. In a panic, I lowered my head to the carpet and sucked air into my mouth from the crack; the illusion that there was more or better air outside the closet helped me to breathe.

Okay. The last time I had looked at a clock it had been al-most 11. The ceremony would start at 4. I could make it for five hours if I had to, but it would be preferable to get out. How was I going to do that? First, I should probably try kick-ing the door down. I took one more suck of crack air, then stood up and steadied myself. I raised my right leg and measured the distance from my body to the door, ensuring I'd make contact when I kicked. Then I lowered my leg before raising it again and shooting my foot out, heel first. When it hit, it felt like none of my bodily force was transferred to the door, but instead it just boomeranged back into me. Pain vibrated through my shin. I shook my leg and jumped around for a minute, then told myself I should try again, just for good measure. I kicked again, even harder this time, and again it seemed to make no difference to the door. It was heavy and solid and not going anywhere.

Next, I fiddled with the door handle for a while, not entirely sure what I was trying to accomplish but it seemed like something I should cross off the list. Then I tried screaming again while banging my fists against all sides of the closet, in case someone in an adjacent room could hear. I did this for probably five minutes, which isn't a long time to do most things, but it's a long time to scream. Eventually, my arms got tired and my upper lip slicked with sweat and my throat went dry. I wished I had a bottle of water and a toilet—the screaming had dried out my mouth, and my mounting panic had, of course, gone straight to my bowels. The urge to go was getting stronger and stronger. One could hold pee for a while, but holding fear poop was nearly impossible. If worst came to worst, I could squat in the corner and let it out, and it would be messy and it would smell, but it would be out.

I sat down and tried not to imagine giving myself this relief. I thought about Aimee, and whether she would need surgery, and if she did, how I wouldn't be there when she woke up. *If* she woke up. She had never had surgery—what if she had an allergic reaction to the anesthesia? Or what if the anesthesiologist accidentally gave her too much? Or the surgeon slipped and cut some kind of important artery and she bled out? Who would take care of Bean if she died and I was trapped here forever? Who was taking care of Bean right now? I hoped Aimee had thought to call someone, but that was the least of our worries. He could poop on the floor if he had to, like I would probably be doing soon.

To ground myself, I pressed my palms into the carpet and my pinky touched something smooth and cold, and at first I snatched my hand away but then I remembered the worry stone. I picked it up and rubbed my thumb back and forth across the worn groove. *Don't let the brides grind you down. Don't let the brides grind you down.* What if it wasn't just a sentiment but a call to action? *Grind you down. Grind. Down.* I felt along the edge of the carpet in the corner, where I had originally found the stone. It was loose. Underneath, there were floorboards that also felt loose. Normally, I wouldn't have had fingernails, but I had forgotten my clippers, so there was a little bit to work with. I snagged them under the rim of a board and lifted—miraculously, the board came away. Underneath the board was—oh my God—nothing, or so it seemed. I removed more boards until there was an opening about as big as my hand, and I stuck it down as far as it would go, praying I wouldn't feel something furry or squishy or slimy. Still nothing. I removed more boards, until underneath one I felt a rough concrete edge, like it had been scraped with a rock or some kind of tool. *Grind you down.* I laughed, swelling with pride, but then told myself not to count my chickens. I removed all the boards I could, and at that point I surmised, through the touch of my hands (because it was still pitch-black inside), that there was a hole just big enough to fit my body into.

It was exciting but also terrifying. Yes, it could be a tunnel, but maybe an unfinished one, or maybe one that took me somewhere even worse. Even if it got me out, what would I encounter along the way? A dead rat? A live rat? A cold, slithery snake? Stephanie's dead body? I shuddered as I lowered a foot into the hole—I was still only wearing hotel slippers and my getting-ready robe and I wished I had sturdy shoes and actual clothes on. When my leg was almost fully extended, my toe touched what I assumed was the bottom. I swung my other leg into the hole and held on to the opening with my hands until I could lower myself all the way down. A spiderweb stuck to my ankles. I ventured one foot forward and discovered a hole about two feet tall—just high enough to shimmy through on my stomach and elbows.

I stood there for a minute, delaying it, then I took a deep breath and sank down. I reached my arm into the hole and got a few spiderwebs out of the way—all I felt otherwise was cool, semidamp dirt on the bottom and some small pieces of concrete. It smelled overpoweringly of earth. I started crawling, waving a hand in front of me every few paces until it was thoroughly mummified by spiderwebs. My heartbeat reverberated through my stomach, which was pressed into the dirt floor. When I had been crawling for a minute or so, I heard a scurrying noise, followed by a chorus of small chirps. Oh, Jesus. I couldn't tell if it was coming from in front of me or behind me, so I started crawling faster, until I plowed into a soft, warm, undulating mass. I screeched and started to back up, but the rodents were already stampeding over my head, my back, my legs, leathery tails slithering over my calves like the Pied Piper was calling them. I lay still, all my muscles clenched, until the last of them pricked their way down my body. In that moment I wished I would die, or that I would snap my fingers and suddenly emerge outside of the tunnel, but there was nothing to do but keep crawling.

Eventually, the tunnel merged with a wider crawl space that seemed like it was there by design, instead of by the grinding and digging of a trapped maid of honor. The darkness got slightly lighter and when I reached my hand out, I touched stairs. At the top, there was a square line of light around a hatch door and I prayed for it to be unlocked as I pressed my hand against it. I felt it give and started to rejoice, but after maybe an inch it stopped, a metal chain rattling against the pressure. Of course. Why should anything go my way? I sat down on the step and let myself cry for a few minutes, then resolved that I would use all my strength and bust it open. If I believed I could do it, I would do it.

I placed both hands on the door and pushed as hard as I could, until my neck pinched and my jaw clamped and my shoulders seared and my arms shook. Nothing. I stood on my tiptoes and kept pushing until my calves also seared. Nothing. I squatted, then quickly straightened my legs, my hands slamming against the door. Nothing. I grunt-screamed and tried an up-and-down motion, the chain outside jangling wildly against my repeated pushes. Nothing. I screamed so loud and pushed so hard that it felt like my brain might explode from my skull, and then, miraculously, the door swung open.

I thought I saw the silhouette of a person in front of me.

I blinked as my eyes adjusted to the light. A male voice said something in Spanish. I blinked a few more times until I could make out a man wearing a baseball cap with a leaf blower strapped to his back: a gardener. He was putting a key back on a crowded key ring—the key he had used to unlock the hatch door, I realized. He said something else in Spanish and held his hand out to me, pulling me up the steps.

"Thank you," I said, putting a hand over my eyes and scanning the yard for Ellie. "Do you speak English?"

He shook his head, smiling in apology.

"Do you have a cell phone?" I asked. *Teléfono?*

Again, he shook his head. He said something else, and the only word I could make out was *casa.*

Okay, I would have to figure something else out. "Thank you for your help," I said, running toward the parking lot before I remembered I didn't have the car keys—everything was still in my room, including my room key. For a second I thought about just running down the long drive until I hit the main road, sticking out my thumb and hoping someone would stop and take me to the airport, but I wouldn't be able to book a plane ticket without my credit card; wouldn't be able to board a plane without my license.

I would have to ask the front desk for another room key, but based on the soundproofing, I had to wonder if even the staff members were in on whatever was happening. There was no way I'd be able to pick the lock of my door, and all the other bridal party members were in Ellie's suite getting their makeup done, not that I could even be sure if I could trust *them*. I'd have to take my chances and go to the front desk. Before I stepped inside, I took a minute to rub off as much of the dirt as I could from my robe and body, but I still looked like a hot mess. My face was probably even worse, the makeup from the morning smudged and cried off. But strangely, the elaborate swoopy bun still seemed perfectly held in place by the half can of hairspray the stylist had used.

Cranberry juice lady from earlier in the morning was behind the desk. When she looked up and saw me, she literally jumped—I must have looked even worse than I thought. I patted my hair and a dead spider fell to the floor. The woman stared at it.

I stepped up to the desk. "Hi, I'm not sure if you remember me from earlier, but I'm staying in room 113, and I accidentally left my key card in my room." My mouth was so dry it was hard to talk. "Would it be possible to get another one?"

She gave me a tight smile, her foundation creasing into worn lines. "Sure, I'll just need to see your ID."

"Unfortunately, I left that in my room, too. I don't have any of my things." I patted the empty pockets of my robe. "But my name is Robin Hawkins."

She folded her hands on the desk and looked me up and down skeptically. "*Unfortunately*, without ID there's no way for us to verify that you are who you say you are. I'm sure you understand."

"You don't remember me from this morning? I'm the maid of honor in the wedding this weekend—"

"Oh, why didn't you say so? I'll just call the bride." She picked up the phone and dialed.

"No, no, no, please don't do that—" I lunged over the desk, then stopped myself from grabbing the phone out of her hand.

She held her pointer finger in front of my face. "Hi, Ms. Kowalewski? I'm sorry to disturb you, but we have a woman here who says she's your maid of honor and she's locked out of her room, but she has no ID."

My stomach squelched. Should I just make a run for it? But I had been over this; there was no way to get back home without my things.

"All right, thank you, Ms. Kowalewski." She hung up the phone and gave me another tight smile. "She's going to come down."

My intestines started boiling and my mind went frantically blank. I couldn't think of a single good option for what to do. My toes twitched inside my slippers but my feet stayed stuck to the floor. I was like a deer, frozen by oncoming headlights. Should I tell the concierge to call 911? Was locking a person in a closet actually a crime? Even if the concierge believed me, it would turn into a whole thing. The police would show up, I'd have to give a statement, and I'd probably be detained for hours. The best option was to just get my stuff and get out as quickly as possible.

"My goodness, what happened to you?" I heard Ellie say. She was wearing her getting-ready robe and her makeup was halfway done, dark contouring lines tracing her cheekbones and just one eye encased in black. "Don't worry about giving her another key. I have one," she said to the concierge. She hooked her arm through mine and pulled me down the hallway, then through the door of my room. My eyes immediately went to the chair next to the bed, where I had remembered leaving my New Yorker tote bag. It wasn't there. When Ellie saw that the dresser was still in front of the closed closet door, she frowned. "How did you get out?" She heaved the dresser out of the way and opened the closet door, peering inside. "Holy shit, is that a tunnel? Well, that would explain why you look the way you do."

"Where's my stuff?" I said, flinging blankets off the bed and opening all the drawers of the dresser and crouching to peer under all the furniture.

When I admitted temporary defeat and raised my head from looking under the bed, Ellie was standing there holding a glass of water. "You must be dying of thirst. I'm sorry I forgot to leave any beverages in the closet."

I grabbed the glass from her and brought it to my lips as fast as possible, greedily guzzling as water spilled out the sides and dripped down my chin. The glass was empty almost immediately.

Ellie clapped her hands and laughed. "That was too easy."

A weird sinking feeling pulled at my body, like the earth's gravity had gotten stronger. I put a hand on the bed to steady myself. "What was too easy?"

"You've got to hydrate," she said, imitating me with a hand on her hip and a pointer finger in my face.

I swallowed a mouthful of spit, then touched my throat. "What was in the water, Ellie?"

She batted her long, false eyelashes at me. "Just a little bit of poison."

It felt like I was zooming through the floor and the soil and the layers of rock beneath that and the core of the earth until I busted through the other side, upside down. Fuck, fuck, fuck. I had never made myself puke before, but if there was any time for it, it was probably now. I stuck my pointer and middle fingers down my throat but couldn't get myself to gag.

"Don't bother with that," Ellie said, leaning down and rub-bing my back. "It's already in your system. But don't worry, it's slow-acting. You won't feel any symptoms for twelve hours, probably. And by that time I'll have given you the antidote."

I took a breath. "There's an antidote?"

"Of course, silly." She booped my nose with her pointer finger. "I wouldn't just flat-out poison you."

"Right," I said. "That would be crazy."

"If you hadn't tried to escape I wouldn't have had to do this," Ellie said admonishingly. "Just stay until the end of the reception, then I'll give you the antidote—as long as you don't try anything else. No more escape attempts. No tell-ing anyone—that includes the police. They wouldn't know what kind of antidote to give you anyway, since I wouldn't tell them what poison I used."

The falling sensation had lessened to the point that I was finally able to stand up. My brain suddenly kicked into gear like the power turning back on after a temporary outage. "I'm not sure I believe you."

"Rob, I'll give you the antidote, I promise." She held her pinky out to me.

I waved her off. "No, I'm not sure if I believe there was poison in that water at all."

She smiled and looked me dead in the eyes. "If you think I'm lying, you're free to leave." She made a Vanna White ges-ture with her arm in the direction of the door.

I stepped past her and gripped the cool metal doorknob, then turned back to look at her, searching her face for some kind of tell.

She held her features completely still, statuesque.

We stayed like that, each waiting for the other to call our bluff, for a full minute. Half of me thought Ellie would never poison me, and the other half thought she definitely would. This was the person who'd been my friend longer than anyone else; the person who had made me feel so safe when I was at my most vulnerable; the person who was second on my iPhone Favorites, right under Aimee. On the other hand, this was the person who had been shoved toward marriage her whole life; the person who seemed like she was coming unhinged bit by bit over the course of the weekend; the person who had *slit a rabbit's throat* the night before. I could hold out until late tonight. Aimee would understand when I told her the story. If I was alive to tell her. If she was alive to hear it. I begrudgingly let go of the doorknob.

22

"We've got to get you cleaned up," Ellie said, steering me into the bathroom and turning on the shower. She tested the temperature with her fingers, like even though she had maybe poisoned me and was definitely keeping me here against my will, she was concerned about the water being too hot or too cold. When she deemed the temperature just right, I stepped in and tried to divert my mounting panic attack by focusing on the sensation of scalding-hot water pounding my scalp. Ever since Ellie claimed she had poisoned me, I had been monitoring every feeling in my body—the shortness of breath, increased heart rate, sweaty palms, dry mouth, dizziness, twisting stomach, trouble concentrating—and questioning if it was the poison or just the anxiety of the imagined poison. I forced myself to take long breaths in and out until my heart felt like I was going for a light jog, not sprinting up a hill. Then I spent the whole shower going back and forth between belief and disbelief about the poison, between accepting that I had to stay and making plans to escape. But every escape plan ended with Ellie not giving me the antidote, and I couldn't risk that. I'd just have to get through the wedding without pissing her off any further. Even though it was repugnant to me, the *safest* route of action would be to placate her and pretend I was somehow happy to be there. Maybe if I faked it hard enough, she would at least give me my phone back so I could talk to Aimee—Ellie had told me my stuff was locked in the safe in her room, and she'd return it when she gave me the antidote. I turned off the shower, then pushed my mouth into a serene smile before pulling back the curtain.

"Feeling better?" Ellie said.

"Much," I said, turbaning a towel around my head. "I was thinking…if I fly back tomorrow as planned, it's less than a twenty-four-hour difference. If Aimee needed surgery I would've missed it, anyway, and she said her wounds weren't serious. She even told me not to leave. So even though you forced me into it, I think staying was the right choice."

Ellie narrowed her eyes at me. *"Really."*

I nodded decisively. "I would have regretted it if I had left. You're my best friend, you're getting married, and I want to be here."

She blinked rapid-fire as her eyes went watery. "I wish you weren't saying that just because you want the antidote."

"I'm not. Really." I reached out and squeezed her shoulders, even though the last thing I wanted to do was touch her.

She held my gaze with her narrowed eyes for a few seconds, then sighed. "Whatever. Let's go get your makeup done." She held her hand out to me.

I took it and let her lead me out of the room.

When I came back to Ellie's suite, everyone crowded around me with hugs and I'm sorrys—Ellie had told them about what happened to Aimee, and to explain my absence, she had said I needed some alone time to process everything. I guess being locked in a closet could technically be categorized as alone time. Once everyone stopped fussing over me, my eyes went straight to the closet, where the safe containing my things was waiting. I itched with the desire to try to break into it but of course, that road led to no antidote so I forced my mind to put up a barricade. There wasn't enough time for Mia to redo my makeup since she had to finish doing Ellie's, so Blair volunteered to do mine. "I watch so many YouTube tutorials I'm basically a makeup artist, anyway," she said.

I sat down and reminded myself to act like a person who wasn't being held against her will. I was happy to be here. I was breathing normally. My heart was beating leisurely.

As Blair was patting foundation across my cheeks, her phone dinged with a text message. She glanced down at it, then said, "I knew it!"

"Knew what?" I asked.

Her face perked up the way it always did when she talked about men. "So like five minutes ago I posted a picture on Instagram of me and the really hot groomsman, and now the guy I've been seeing back home finally texted me asking how the wedding is going, just like I knew he would when I posted the picture. He keeps saying he doesn't want to be exclusive, but then he gets jealous whenever I'm with another guy."

I widened my eyes. "Wow, you treat dating like tradecraft."

She paused, the foundation sponge in midair. "What's that?"

"What spies do."

She sighed, irritated. "What does that mean, *what spies do*?"

I thought about how to explain it. "Did you ever watch *Zero Dark Thirty*? All the shit they did to find Osama—tapping his top guy's cell phone, organizing a fake vaccination drive where he lived so they could get DNA from his kids—all that was tradecraft. So you basically treat finding the leader of al-Qaeda the same as finding love."

Blair laughed bitterly. "Yeah, you work your ass off to land some crazy dude with a violent streak who's fucking five other women. Sounds about right. I swear, sometimes I wish I was a lesbian." She gave me a conspiratorial smile.

The rage lighter inside me flicked, then whooshed into flame. Straight women saying they wished they were a lesbian was one of my number-one triggers—it made being gay seem like a fallback choice instead of an inherent part of someone's identity, it stereotyped lesbian relationships as uncomplicated, and the women who said it to me were never actually open to the idea of sleeping with another woman. As I opened my mouth to say all of the above, the post-yoga conversation with Isabel nudged into my mind. I briefly considered keeping my mouth shut and letting it go for the sake of my health, but holding it in made me feel like I might internally combust, and that couldn't be healthy, either. I decided to compromise—something between a heated rant and staying completely quiet. "So why not give it a try?" I said, laboring to keep my voice light.

"Cunnilingus," Blair said, pulling her mouth down and sticking out her tongue like she had just eaten something gross. "I just couldn't."

"Well, that's a pretty big part of being a lesbian. So it sounds like you *don't* wish you were one."

She shrugged. "I guess you're right."

It hadn't been quite as satisfying as the full rant would have been, but it would suffice. The flame died down to a simmer.

The hours until I could leave dragged on. Underneath my happy-to-be-here act, I just kept thinking *Aimee, Aimee, Aimee, Aimee, Aimee.* Had she had surgery? If so, was she awake? Had she read the text Ellie had sent about staying for the wedding? Did she have a sense that something about it was fishy? Or did she take it at face value, disappointed that I had stayed even though she had told me to? Because of course she had wanted me to come back. When you've been through something traumatic, you want your partner there. It was killing me that she might think I would choose not to go to her. But every time I started thinking about leaving again, I'd look up to find Ellie's eyes locked on me.

When my makeup was finished, Ellie's and Kaivan's moms arrived, fresh from a local salon where they had their hair and makeup done. Kaivan's mom looked like she was headed to the Oscars, in a long, navy blue, lacy gown with side-swept hair and makeup that managed to look understated even though up close you could tell she was wearing quite a lot. Ellie's mom looked like one of the mothers closeted celebrities bring to the Oscars, stuffed into a shiny dress she'd never otherwise wear, her grayish-blond hair teased and bouffanted, her grayish-blue eyes almost completely lost behind thick liner and shadow. After the rabbit killing, the closet debacle, and the possible poisoning, I eyed her with suspicion and tried to avoid getting trapped in a conversation with her, but she caught me coming out of the bathroom.

"Aren't you so excited for our Ellie?" she said as she barreled me into a hug. She still smelled like their house in high school: dryer sheets and a touch of cinnamon with a strange plastic-y after scent.

"Mm, so excited," I said, trying to pull out of the hug, but she held me so tight I almost couldn't breathe. My heart knocked against her formidable breasts.

She sighed as she finally released me. "You know, ever since I found out I was having a baby girl, I've pictured this day."

"Really? What if Ellie hadn't wanted to get married?"

She waved her hand in the air like I was talking nonsense. "Oh, she's always wanted to get married. She's just had such bad luck, you know? It's hard to meet a decent man these days, much harder than when I was young. Every time she talked about someone new I'd get my hopes up and think he was finally the one, and then he'd let us down. So many letdowns." She clucked her tongue. "Every time I would catch up with one of my friends, they'd tell me one of their kids just got married. And then they'd ask about Ellie and I'd have nothing to say, you know? I prayed and prayed and then finally, God sent us Kaivan." She reached up to touch the cross necklace she still wore after all these years and patted it like she was patting God on the back for a job well-done. I had almost forgotten how religious she was; how uncomfortable it made me. When I put it together with the rabbit, the closet, and the poison, it made the back of my neck prickle. If I could have gotten a word in, I might have asked her a leading question, something that would have shown me if she was the evil puppet master or just yet another wedding-obsessed, grandkid-obsessed mother, but there was no way to get a word in with Ellie's mom. "Now they can go forth and multiply," she went on. "I told her I want at least three grandbabies to keep me busy." She took a breath and I thought maybe she was finally about to ask me a question about myself. "Have you seen the dress?"

"What dress?"

She barked a laugh. "The wedding dress!" She didn't even wait for me to answer before plowing on. "Oh, it's gorrr-geous." She grasped my arm and leaned in like she was telling me a secret. "You can thank me when you see it, because I chose it. I chose most of the things for this wedding. Ellie probably complained about me being one of those momzillas, and now that we're through it I can admit I probably was." She ran a manicured pinky nail underneath her eye. "You know, I think because her dad and I got divorced, I looked at this as my second wedding, my chance to get it right. And if everything is perfect maybe they'll stay together forever, you know?" At this the back of my neck prickled again. *How far would you go to make it perfect?* I asked her in my head as she went on and on. "I always worry that our divorce really *affected* her, that it was the reason she wasn't meeting the right man, but thank God I don't have to worry about that anymore!"

I butted in. "So you think Kaivan is the right man?"

"You know, when you're thirty-four, any man willing to marry you is right!" She laughed and slapped my arm so hard it stung. "No, I kid, I kid. I think he's a great guy. And look how well he's doing with his apps and all that. I don't understand any of it, but I understand money, and let me tell you, Ellie will be well taken care of." She winked at me, then before she could keep going, thank God, Ellie emerged from the bedroom in her getup.

It was the first time she had let anyone other than her mom see the dress. Everyone gasped and brought their hands to their hearts, while I brought my hand to my mouth to cover what I was sure was not the appropriate facial expression. Ellie was wearing a long ball gown with cascading layers of lace that pooled around her feet, and the top of the dress was mostly that sheer material that was meant to fool people into thinking it's your skin, with a few strategic lace flowers to cover the most scandalous parts of her breasts, but you could still see a lot of them. It wasn't the kind of dress I had imagined Ellie in at all, more like something a New Jersey ex-stripper would find in a David's Bridal, even though I was sure it was very expensive. Knowing Ellie's mom had chosen the dress made it seem even more ludicrous. Ellie's drag queen makeup added to the effect, with overly defined brows and fake lashes so long and voluminous they probably created a breeze when she blinked, and foundation like the top layer of pudding left in the fridge overnight. Her hair was in one of those complicated swoopy updos that probably required hundreds of bobby pins and a whole canister of hair spray.

Everyone gathered around Ellie in an imitation of a hug, careful not to muss her dress or her makeup, and told her she looked beautiful and gorgeous and stunning and sexy. *Uncomfortable* was the word I would have used.

"You…" I searched for something to say that would sound sincere but wouldn't be a lie. "Are a sight to behold," I said, squeezing Ellie's hand.

"Can you help me go to the bathroom before we take pictures?" Ellie asked me. "I don't want my dress to fall into the toilet."

I nodded and followed her to the bathroom. *Happy to be here, happy to be here*, I repeated in a parrot-like voice in my head. Ellie said she had read online about the best way to pee, which was to sit backward on the toilet so the front of the gown could rest on top of the tank, and someone would stand a few feet away holding the bottom of the gown.

"I really am glad I stayed," I said as I piled lace into my arms and Ellie precariously lowered herself onto the toilet seat. I could see her face reflected in the mirror as she scowled.

Urine tinkled into the toilet. "Yeah, right," she said. "You probably think I've fully lost it."

"I don't know," I said. "After talking to your mom today I think I'm starting to understand it. She seems even more wedding crazy than you. Add that pressure to the societal pressure and eventually, you're going to blow." I had said it to humor her, but as the words left my mouth I felt their impact—if I had had a mom like her, I might have lost it, too.

"That's very understanding of you," Ellie said. The urine

trickled to a stop. "Do you still think Kaivan isn't the right person for me?"

Some of the lace escaped my hands and I rushed to gather it back up. I thought about what this version of Robin would say, this non-feather-ruffling Robin. "It doesn't really matter what I think," I said. "Only you can know that, and if you think he *is* the right person, then I'm truly so happy for you."

In the mirror Ellie smiled sadly. "Do you know how nice it is to hear you say that, even if it's a lie? Imagine if you had just been able to say that to me a year ago, when I told you we were engaged." She shook her head.

"I wish I had," I said. "I'm learning that I don't always have to say exactly what I'm feeling."

An airy fart echoed in the toilet bowl. "Oh my God." Ellie covered her face with her hands and laughed. "I can't believe this, but I think I have to shit."

"Okay," I said. "Do you want me to keep holding your gown? I think if I leave you might get poop on it."

"Can you?" Ellie grimaced in an amused way. "God, how terrible for you."

I waved her off. "Hey, it's not as bad as being locked in a closet and having to crawl through a rat-infested tunnel to get out."

There was a staccato plop in the toilet as Ellie made a horrified face. "Seriously? It was rat infested?"

"They crawled over every inch of my body. Probably like fifty of them." I shuddered, remembering it, but it seemed kind of funny now, and I found myself laughing.

"Jesus!" She rolled some toilet paper, gagging and laughing at the same time.

"Are you gagging about the rats or your poop? It smells like a skunk sprayed onto a hard-boiled egg." We were both shaking with laughter at this point.

Ellie compulsively wiped a pointer finger below her eyes, worried about her makeup. "Hey! It's a stress poop. They always smell worse."

"Oh God." I choked. "It's hard to breathe out of your mouth when you're laughing. At least I can't see anything underneath your gown. It's like a privacy shield."

"You know, I can't believe more brides don't talk about this. Or is 'wedding jitters' just a euphemism for diarrhea? It's like a cruel joke that you can't go to the bathroom by yourself because you're wearing a gigantic white dress. I've heard everyone shits when they give birth, too. All these momentous occasions, marked by shit." As if to add a period to her sentence, there was a fart that sounded like a motorcycle starting up followed by another few plops in the toilet.

"I have some Imodium in my bag. You should probably take one. Or like, five."

"Of course you have Imodium. Is it in your little plastic baggie pharmacy?"

"Yup, along with my Pepto chewables, earplugs, dental floss, panty liners, Tide pen, Band-Aids, and hand sanitizer."

"Okay, I have to wipe," Ellie said through little gasps of laughter. "Can you lift my gown up a little higher?"

I raised my arms and turned my head.

"Man, this reminds me of high school. Remember when we would stay in the room while the other one pooped? Why did we do that?"

"I think we just wanted to feel close to each other, you know? As close as possible."

Ellie smiled, her eyes faraway like she was back in the past. "Yeah. Sometimes I think that was the closest I've ever been to another person. It feels like you're not allowed to have friendships like that anymore, once you get older and romantic relationships get more serious. And I know a lot of people call their spouses their best friend, but it's just not the same."

"I think this is the first time I've really felt close to you all weekend. I guess it took getting back to our roots." I wasn't sure if I was still lying or if I meant it. Jesus, I might have meant it. Was I developing Stockholm syndrome?

Ellie flushed the toilet, then found my eyes in the mirror. "I love you, Rob. I know everything I've done this weekend might make it hard to believe, but I do."

"I love you, too, Ell." I cleared my throat. "Is there any chance I could have my phone back, just for a minute, so I can talk to Aimee and find out if she's okay?"

She looked away, then yanked her dress out of my hands. "No. I'm sorry."

23

It turned out that the photographer was able to borrow some equipment from a friend, so after Ellie and Kaivan took 437890547892 pictures (holding hands on the beach; kissing in front of a palm tree; fake laughing on a cliff; Kaivan carrying Ellie through the doorway of the mansion; Ellie whispering a secret in Kaivan's ear; Kaivan kissing Ellie on the forehead; Ellie's veil blowing in the wind; Kaivan facing the camera and Ellie facing away, smiling over her shoulder to showcase the sheer back of her gown; Kaivan twirling Ellie in a circle; etc., etc., etc.), it was finally time for the ceremony. We all stood bunched behind the door that opened to the aisle, clasping hands like we were one big happy wedding party as Mindy said a prayer, asking God for His blessing for the bride and groom. I wondered if God had given Ellie His blessing to lock me in a closet and poison me, or to make me believe she had.

"How do I look?" Ellie asked me after the prayer was over and everyone had joyously yelled amen, even me.

Ellie looked like an iteration of every blonde, white bride who had come before her, and I thought about how many women were also getting married right now across the country—probably at least five thousand, maybe even ten—and how all the ceremonies and receptions would be nearly identical, and I saw all of them unfolding simultaneously in a Russian doll-esque fashion, each one containing the other, but I managed to tell Ellie she looked beautiful as I helped her lower her veil and arrange her train.

Then we all lined up in the order we would walk out, the bridesmaids and groomsmen linking arms jovially. The groomsman standing next to Shaun gave him an uncomfortable smile, like he thought linking arms with Shaun would make him gay. Outside, the processional music started playing, a harp strumming "Prelude in C Major" by Bach. I tried to focus on the music to distract myself from my anxiety. Even if it had become a wedding cliché, it really was a perfect song. The repeated broken chords made every note feel logical and inevitable, and from beginning to end, the composition took you on a journey through the full range of human emotion: from certainty to uncertainty, from lightness to darkness, from hope to despair, then back to certainty, lightness, and hope. It made sense that people chose it for their wedding song, since it could seem to represent an entire marriage.

"Psst!" The flower girl, Ellie's cousin, pushed a finger into my back. "It's your turn!"

I took an abrupt step onto the aisle that was a plastic white material like a slip 'n' slide as my feet wobbled in my heels and my hands shook slightly around the garlic-and-sage bouquet. The sun came out from behind a cloud and saturated everything with vibrant color the way an Instagram filter would—the bright green lawn and the sparkly turquoise ocean looked almost neon. The palm trees swayed in the breeze like they were dancing to the same midtempo song. The clouds were perfectly shaped cumulus ones, cartoon-esque, and I pictured a squat little Mario jumping under one of those question-mark boxes and bopping it with his head, releasing a mushroom that turned him into a normal-size man.

Mario made me think about Beth, the two of us playing Nintendo in our musty basement surrounded by a rainbow of pickled vegetables in dusty jars. Beth always won, whereas I was more interested in exploring, climbing up the vines where you could run across the clouds and collect dozens of coins or shooting down those pipes that would take you underground. Looking for ways out of the regular world while everyone else was just trying to get to the next level. I felt completely separate and alone from the wedding guests who surrounded me, turned around in their white folding chairs staring at me. I felt like I had been gone for a year. I missed Aimee and Bean and my friends and my bubble. I just wanted to go home and to not be poisoned and Aimee to be okay. Instead, I took my place under the altar wrapped with wildflowers and draped with gauzy white fabric cinched in the middle like curtains around a window.

When Ellie walked out with her mom, she seemed perfectly comfortable being stared at. She held her head high and tilted her chin upward, smiling serenely for the photographer, her fifty-foot train swooping behind her. Ellie's mom was beaming—literally, her face was shining like a second sun as she lived the moment she had dreamed of ever since the ultrasound technician told her she was having a girl. She reluctantly let go of Ellie and took her seat at the front as Ellie took her place under the altar, handing me her sage-and-garlic bouquet and taking Kaivan's hands. He lifted her veil and whispered that she looked beautiful.

The minister cleared his throat and started talking about God. After Ellie's dad died, she had found religion again and now went to church every Sunday. It reminded me of the first time I went to Ellie's house and, naturally, we had our first disagreement. Ellie told me she had felt God's love when she met me; that she thought He had sent me to her. Looking back, it was probably one of the most loving things anyone had ever said to me—to equate my friendship to the love of God. And instead of hearing what Ellie was saying, about how important I was to her, I just thought Ellie was naive and simple and fought with her about God's existence, wanting her to agree with me.

Ellie pulled a piece of paper from the chest of her gown and unfolded it, reading her personalized vows to Kaivan. "Growing up in a military family, I moved every few years and constantly had to make new friends. I learned pretty quickly that the easiest way to get people to like you is to match yourself to them. So for most of my life, I honed this skill and lost myself in the process. But then I met you, and you saw through it. You were the first person who pushed me to really be myself, who assured me you wanted *me* and not a reflection of yourself. So when I met you, I met myself. When I loved you, I loved myself."

Ellie got choked up then. She blinked and tears rolled down her cheeks. Everyone in the audience was sniffing and pressing tissues to their eyes. I felt more dumbfounded than weepy. There was no way I could doubt it now—Ellie loved Kaivan, and for good reason. A guy I thought was the scum of the earth had apparently done what I had failed to do: accept Ellie for who she was. Was it why she had poisoned me, or claimed to? Was I such a bad friend that I made her want to kill me?

I thought back to that first time meeting Kaivan when we were all discussing *Jane Bond*, and how I assumed he kept asking what Ellie thought because he wanted her to agree with him—but he actually just wanted to know what Ellie truly thought, without being influenced by anyone. Could I say the same, that I had ever encouraged Ellie to explore an opinion that might be different from my own? Deep down, didn't everyone want reflections of themselves? We just wanted to think it was an organic connection—that two almost completely similar people in this great big world *happened* to find each other. And we would feel betrayed if we discovered that the other person had merely been faking the similarity all those years, even though we would probably stop liking them the instant the fake-similarity ceased. We would tell ourselves it was about the lying but really it was about wanting the reflection.

This rumination made me miss Kaivan's vows. The minister said some more stuff about God and then they were pronounced husband and wife, Mr. and Mrs. Ellison. After some prewedding indecision that I sensed was mainly for my benefit, Ellie had decided to take Kaivan's last name. Ellie Ellison—that was how important it was to her for people to know she was married. Her maiden name was Kowalewski, which harkened back to her Polish ancestors whom Ellie's mom had told me were blacksmiths. All that identity, erased. Although Ellie's maiden name was just the name her mother had taken from her father, and her mother's maiden name was just the name Ellie's grandmother had taken from her grandfather, and so on and so forth. If you traced history all the way back to the beginning of surnames, I doubted there was a woman who had her own. So the idea of a woman's identity being tied to a surname was yet another instance of not being able to untangle ourselves from the patriarchy. When I was in college and first becoming aware of all these things, I was so dispirited at the impossibility of a woman ever finding her true surname that I had considered changing mine to something made up that had no history at all. Sometimes I still thought about it.

At the reception in the dining room, white fabric was draped from the ceiling in the shape of a blooming flower with a massive chandelier as the pistil, and white globe lights accentuating the edges like drops of dew. On each table there was a triangular gold-and-glass terrarium centerpiece filled with sand and a succulent—a last-minute replacement to flowers floating in water after the blight at the farm. Ellie and Kaivan did their first dance to "At Last," and with the second-

choice singer whose voice was a little more high–pitched and
thin, it sounded off. Maybe the wedding singer *had* mattered.

After absently smiling and nodding through every conversation, deep breathing through the nosedives my stomach
kept making, and watching my salad go limp on my plate,
it was finally time for my speech. I stood up and blinked a
few times, waiting for the black spots to disappear from the
edges of my vision, then unfolded the piece of paper dusted
with orange from all the Doritos I ate on the plane. At that
moment I would have done anything to get out of making
that speech—let a Men's Rights Activist win an argument,
watched all three Fifty Shades movies, gotten a Monistat-
resistant yeast infection. But since none of those options presented themselves, I took a deep breath and started reading.

"Hi, everyone, for those of you who don't know me, I'm
Robin, Ellie's best friend from high school and her maid of
honor. I'm so happy to be here tonight to celebrate Ellie and
Kaivan." God, I felt like a plastic pull-string doll. I couldn't
bring myself to look at Ellie. "The first time I met Ellie, she
showed up to a debate club meeting where we were discussing whether profanity in movies was bad for society and I
was on the pro-profanity team. I must have impressed Ellie
with all my swearing, because after that we became friends."
Light chuckle from the audience. "For the rest of our time in
high school, we were literally inseparable." I skipped over a
few crossed-out lines about coming out to Ellie and popping
each other's zits and trying to make ourselves have the same
dreams, since it had all felt too intimate for a wedding speech.
"The thought of splitting up to go to college was unbearable,
so we applied to the same schools and both ended up getting

into our first choice." Here I of course left out the big fight over the paper, the time apart, and the reconciliation after Ellie's dad died, instead opting for the breeze-over: "Over the years, Ellie and I have laughed together, cried together, and laughed until we cried." People were starting to shift in their seats and tip back their empty glasses for the last drops of alcohol. "Ellie is one of the most loving, accepting, and open people I've ever known. She's always trying new things, so it makes sense that she met Kaivan at a pottery class." This was the lie they told everyone about how they had met, instead of the embarrassing truth of Spouse Spotter. "That night Ellie made a truly terrible bowl but met a terrific husband." Light "awwws" from the crowd. "This wedding and this marriage is what Ellie has always wanted, more than anything else, for her entire life. I hope it makes you happy, Ellie." I hadn't meant for it to sound sarcastic, but it came out sounding that way, and everyone in the crowd clapped half-heartedly as I finally forced myself to glance at Ellie.

She was looking at me like I had just given the worst maid of honor speech in the whole world. As I was about to look away, I saw something else written on her face—a mix of regret and desperation and hopefulness that sent a shock through my stomach. It reminded me of the way she had looked at the rabbit before slitting its throat. My gut told me that maybe Ellie really *had* poisoned me. And maybe she wasn't planning on giving me the antidote at all.

24

For a while I argued back and forth with my intestines, even though Isabel had said our gut was smarter than our brain. The more I thought about it, the more it dawned on me that Ellie had probably been trying to kill me all weekend: I hadn't imagined the hand pushing my head down during the surfing lesson; my allergic reaction to the chickpea tagine wasn't due to a chef's negligence; the rabbit sacrifice was just a precursor to a larger sacrifice; Ellie—sleeping or awake—had meant to suffocate me in the middle of the night; and she had forced me to stay here, via the locked closet and the poison, because she hadn't been able to kill me yet, but she knew she needed to.

If I could get Ellie to admit that her plan was to off me, I was convinced that I could talk her out of it. She would listen to me the way she had always listened to me. For the rest of the reception, I watched her closely. When she wasn't being barraged by hugs and well-wishes from distant relatives, she was surrounded by a circle of gyrating women on the dance floor. When the night was almost over and she finally had a moment to herself, she slipped out the back door. I tailed her as she went up the stairs, down the hall, and into her suite. I stood outside the door for a few minutes, listening. The TV turned on. The water in the bathroom ran. When it stopped, I knocked.

Ellie swung the door open. "Oh, it's you." Up close, her makeup looked faded, and one of her fake eyelashes tilted to the side, about to fall off.

"I have to talk to you," I said.

She opened the door wider and stepped to the side. The room smelled strongly of mint. *Sex and the City* was on TV, the show Ellie watched whenever something was bothering her and she needed to be comforted, and Charlotte was saying, "Maybe we can be each other's soul mates. And then we can let men be just these great, nice guys to have fun with." I rolled my eyes and sat on the edge of the bed, then saw the source of the smell on the bedside table: a Bath & Body Works stress-relief candle scented with eucalyptus and spearmint.

"Are you feeling stressed?" I said, gesturing to the candle. "Why are you up here instead of enjoying the reception?"

"Oh, no reason." She stood next to the bed, her eyes darting around the room.

"Is it because you're not going to give me the antidote?"

"I guess I can tell you now," she said, her eyes finally resting on me. "I never actually poisoned you. At that point I was still in denial about what I'd have to do."

My stomach audibly squelched. "But now…"

She sighed and pressed two fingers into her temple. "You know what I'm going to say, Rob."

"I want to hear you say it."

"I…" She swallowed and then calmly said, "I have to sacrifice you."

It was a strange relief to finally hear her admit it. "Thanks for telling me the truth."

She huffed a laugh. "You're welcome."

I laughed, too, then mocked myself in a dumb voice. "Thanks for telling me you're going to kill me! Thanks so much!"

We both laughed hysterically for about ten seconds. When we trailed off, I said, "Is your mom making you?"

"No, but she's the one who brought up the idea. There's this Polish folklore about a wila—that's the evil spirit of a dead maiden—who takes over the body of a bride and tells her to kill her best friend, or else her marriage will be cursed. Then I started seeing all this stuff on the dark web about how murdering your maid of honor was the most effective wedding charm out there."

"How is it supposed to work? Like, what's the reasoning behind it?"

She shook her head, grinning. "Ah, so this is when you try to logically argue your way out of being murdered. That's so classic Robin."

"Come on, just explain it to me." I patted the bed next to me.

She sat down and sighed. "You're going to say it's stupid."

"Try me."

"So they say the reason so many marriages are failing—"

"Sorry, who's they?"

She sighed again. "I don't know. All this information is passed through an anonymous whisper network, so it would be impossible to trace it back."

"Okay, go on."

"Okay. So they say the reason so many marriages are failing is because the relationship between the spouses has lost its purity. A husband is supposed to be everything to you, but there are other people in the bride's life fulfilling roles that the husband should fill. That will weaken your marriage." She was talking like a kid delivering an oral book report on a subject they didn't fully understand. "To fully commit to your husband, you have to end the relationship that was previously your closest. Which is usually your maid of honor."

"Does Kaivan have to kill his best man, too?"

"No," she said like it was obvious.

"Why not?"

"They say women have closer relationships with their friends, so it's the bride's problem to solve."

I snorted. "Well, that seems totally sexist."

She threw her hands up and let them fall into her lap. "See, I knew I shouldn't have told you."

"So the idea is I'll ruin your marriage because you and I will be too close?"

She shrugged. "Something like that."

"Couldn't we just like…stop speaking?"

On the TV, *Sex and the City* started skipping, Carrie stuck in a robotic loop of bringing a spoonful of ice cream to her mouth. Ellie must have been watching a DVD. "Some women tried that and they still ended up getting divorced."

"And the women who killed their maids of honor have all lived happily ever after?"

"I don't know. This charm hasn't really been around long enough to prove if it works till death do us part." Ellie hit the eject button on the DVD player, then vigorously rubbed the disc against her dress. It fell out of her hand and when she leaned over to pick it up, she accidentally stepped on it. A crack echoed around the room as the disc separated into jagged pieces.

"And yet, you're willing to try it?"

"I don't know, Robin! Maybe, for once in your life, you need to accept that you can't change somebody's mind. I'm my own person, and this is my decision." Ellie picked up a triangular piece of DVD with a sharp tip. She turned it over in her hands, then her eyes zeroed in on the side of my neck. She stood up and took a step toward me.

Instinctively, I put a hand to the spot on my neck Ellie was staring at. My jugular vein jumped beneath my fingertips. "Ellie, you don't have to do this."

In the darkness of the room, her pupils seemed to have taken over almost her whole iris. She took another step toward me. She raised her arm, the knifelike piece of DVD aimed perfectly, and I realized we were past the point of talking. She was truly going to try to kill me and there was nothing I could say to stop her. I had never actually feared for my life before—all the times Ellie had tried to off me earlier in the weekend, I was too dumb to realize what was happening. Now I finally understood. The way it felt, the terror of impending doom, was how it felt every time I got into an argument—like I was fighting for my life. Like if someone disagreed with me, it would mean my demise. Just like Alonzo had said, only I had thought I was above it. And just like Isabel had said, I was hurting myself—at this point, I was essentially *killing* myself. But I wasn't dead yet.

I fell back on the bed and rolled to the side. Ellie lunged at me and I rolled to the other side, but before I could contemplate my next move she jumped on top of me, straddling me and pinning me down with her prewedding workout Soul-Cycle thighs. I had about one second before she tried to stab me again. What could I do? *What could I do?*

Her dress! She would hate that. I brought my hands to the neck of her gown that was made out of that sheer faux-flesh material, and with each hand, I pulled as hard as I could in opposing directions until I heard the satisfying rip of the fabric. The tear went all the way down to just below her breasts before it hit a lace applique flower. Ellie looked down at her chest and screeched like the rabbit had right before she killed it.

"Eight thousand dollars!" she screamed, which I guessed was the cost of the gown, before she raised her arm above her head again. I braced my hands against her forearm, but she had gravity on her side, and each second the point of the DVD shard descended closer and closer to my neck. We both strained with effort—a vein underneath Ellie's eye bulged like a worm was just underneath the surface of her skin. Eventually, the muscles in my arms turned to jelly and I had no leverage left. The sharp tip of the DVD pierced the skin of my neck.

This is it, I thought. Death by *Sex and the City* DVD. I

would never see Aimee—*if* she was alive after possibly having surgery—or Bean or my parents again. Beth and I would never have another chance to reconcile. A *missing* flyer with my face on it would go around for a while, then they'd all get thrown away or stapled over or rained on until you couldn't read them anymore. I would never be found and eventually, they'd have a funeral. If Aimee was alive, maybe she'd become obsessed with researching my case. Maybe she'd figure it out but no one would believe her. Then I heard a brittle snap— the shard of DVD had broken in Ellie's hand. I brought my fingers to my neck, expecting to feel a warm gush of blood, but my skin was dry. The DVD had only scratched me!

Ellie and I both took a second to recalibrate. She blinked repeatedly and the fake eyelash that was in the process of coming unglued looked like it was hanging on for dear life. I took a deep breath and blew the strongest gust of air I could at her eye. The lash fell sideways in front of her iris and teetered there, obscuring her vision. She brought a hand to her eye and in that moment I was able to sit up, but she still had my legs pinned. What now? What could I use as a weapon? The necklace Ellie had given me as a maid of honor gift—it had a long gold chain and a little chunk of amethyst, my birthstone, as the pendant. I pulled it over my head and in the same motion lowered it over Ellie's; then I crossed the chain around her neck and pulled as hard as I could in either direction.

Ellie dropped the DVD and brought her hands to her neck, trying to get her fingers underneath the gold chain. When that failed, she just started thrashing around. I struggled to keep the chain tight around her neck. Her eyes watered and I wondered if she was crying or if it was just an effect of the strangulation. *It's not Ellie; it's a crazy person who's trying to kill you,* I told myself as I kept pulling the chain and her face got redder and redder. Eventually, she stopped thrashing. Just when I was worried I might actually kill her, the chain broke and my hands flew apart. She had spent eight thousand dollars on her dress and the necklace was probably under fifty. "Cheap piece of shit!" I yelled.

Ellie gasped and coughed as she crawled off the side of the bed. My eyes landed on the Bath & Body Works candle burning on the bedside table. I jumped on top of Ellie, then grabbed the candle and tilted it so the flame licked the hem of her gown, but the fabric just turned brown and melted instead of catching fire. Ellie kneed me in the groin and I rolled off her, dropping the candle. It fell at the edge of the bed and the corner of the duvet started to smoke, then a few tendrils of flame jumped to life. They crawled up the bed, then swept across it, growing in size until the whole bed was flickering orange and yellow. Minty smoke filled the air but no fire detectors went off.

I decided to make a run for it—out the door, down the hallway, down the stairs, out the back door, past the lawn with the rows of white chairs and the altar, to the rocky cliff with the churning ocean at the bottom. It seemed incredibly irresponsible that a wedding venue wouldn't put a fence at the perimeter of the cliff, to stop people from going too far. I peeked over the collapsing edge and my stomach lurched with a vision of my body lying at the bottom, crumpled against the sharp rocks, then eventually carried out to sea by the tide. I licked my lips and tasted salt. It would be easy for Ellie to say it had been an accident.

25

I stood on the cliff, cursing my panicked decision making. Why had I run out the back and not the front, where my rental car was parked? Why hadn't I gone back to the reception where there were hundreds of witnesses? How had I ended up in the worst possible place, a narrow, rocky headland that extended past the rest of the coastline? To change course now, I'd have to run back down the headland, where I would collide with Ellie. She was coming toward me fast. I was trapped.

I had thought maybe the fire would end things, or at least deter her, but she still looked focused as ever. With each step she took, my brain became swimmier and swimmier, drowning in the surreality of the situation. The moon was a perfect circle the color of peach ice cream. It threw an iridescent rose-gold path onto the ocean that continued exactly where the wedding aisle left off, like you could just keep walking off the cliff directly onto the ocean. I wished I could walk on water as I helplessly scanned the property, praying an employee was outside cleaning up or someone was having a cigarette or a couple had sneaked off to make out, but it was just me and Ellie. The bass from "Uptown Funk" reverberated from the dining room on the other side of the building, so no one would even hear me if I screamed.

When Ellie was a few feet away, she stopped, panting. Her gown gaped open at the front where I had ripped it, and her neck was still indented with the angry red line from the chain of my necklace. She looked at me unwaveringly and it struck me that this wasn't hard for her. She wasn't torn up about it. And why should she be? I thought back to her wedding vows—I had never accepted her for who she was, and this was her finally not accepting me. It was my greatest fear made literal: rejection as death.

Even if we were in some alternate universe and Ellie *wasn't* about to murder me, this wedding would still signal the death of our friendship—she was on the first rung of the ladder, and I was left standing at the bottom. As she climbed, it would get harder and harder to see or hear each other: I'd crane my neck and she'd yell down at me but I wouldn't be able to make out the words. It would be so much easier if she just stayed friends with the people who were up there with her; if I just stayed friends with the people on the ground with me.

She took a step toward me. I glanced over my shoulder:

there was room for me to take two, maybe three steps back before I would slip against the crumbling earth and plummet to the bottom. Good thing I had a fear of heights. I held my hands in front of my body, palms facing her. My throat was tight; my eyes hot.

"Ellie, am I really that terrible? That you could kill me with no regrets?"

"Of course I'll have regrets. But marriage is about sacrifice." She took another step toward me.

I took a small, tentative step back. My eyes were so full of tears I could barely see. I blinked, letting them slip out. "You could live without me, just like Beth?" Saying it out loud, a dark blue wave of sadness swept through my body, dizzying me. I lowered myself to my knees. The day Beth rejected me was like my personal big bang: the explosive origin of my rage, and after that it just kept expanding. I had thought at some point I would find a measure of closure about our estrangement. But no matter how many years passed, no matter how much therapy I had, I knew I would never be over it. The day I died—which hopefully wouldn't be this day—I'd still be waiting for an apology from Beth. For the acceptance I deserved. And until that day, every cell in my body would be packed to the brim with anger. Unless I found some way to change. It was now or never, literally. "What if I promised to be better? Less judgmental, less argumentative, more accepting?"

Ellie laughed morosely and came closer. "It's a little late for that."

I scooted backward, small rocks in the dirt grinding into ⁓s. The rhythmic crash of waves that was normally so soothing now sounded horribly ominous. They counted down the seconds to my impending doom. My foot dipped over the edge of the cliff, a cold breeze whooshing around it. That was it—as far as I could go. My body lilted back and forth dangerously. The waves smacked against the cliff and I swore I felt the ground underneath me shake. "I mean it, Ellie. From the bottom of my shitty heart, I'm sorry. I promise I'll try to be better." I held my arm out, pinky up, waiting.

Ellie's face softened into a peaceful expression. "I'm sorry, too." She extended a hand toward me, I assumed to link her pinky with mine, and relief flooded through me like a sweet drug. I'd get a chance to change. I'd get to see Aimee and Bean again. I'd get to go back to my life. But her hand sailed past my waiting one and landed on my shoulder, where she applied a moderate amount of pressure—something between a shove and a nudge—and that was all it took to send me plummeting backward through the dark abyss toward the jagged cliffs below. The feeling of falling reminded me of the trust fall, how scared I had been and how reassuring it was when my back smacked into the solid arms of the bridal party members. I waited to feel what my back would smack into this time.

26

I tried to open my eyes, but they felt weighed down by something small yet extremely heavy, like a fishing weight or a bullet. Close by, there was a steady beeping sound, and farther away, other steady beeping sounds bumped up against each other and someone fuzzily talked over an intercom. The air was cold and smelled like antibacterial soap. I tried to turn my head, but something held it firmly in place. I lifted a hand to touch whatever was there, but my hand was immobilized, too. Was I dead? I focused all my energy on lifting my eyelids. It felt like I was bench-pressing a hundred pounds, but eventually, they rose to reveal a bright fluorescent-lit hospital ⌐ and Aimee sitting next to me, her hair greasy and her ⌐er eyes naked of eyeliner. Her arm was in a sling.

"Thank God you're awake," she said, leaning in to kiss my extremely chapped lips and stroke my face.

"Aimee, what are you doing here?" It was almost impossible to talk because my tongue was so parched it felt freeze-dried. I motioned to the cup of water sitting on the bedside table. Aimee held the cup to my mouth and I gulped it down until it was gone.

"I flew here after Kaivan called and told me you were in an ambulance," said Aimee. "Do you remember what happened?"

I surveyed my body. Almost the entire left side was encased in a white cast. I blinked and my head spun as I relived the feeling of falling, and how I made a last-minute decision to turn onto my side and tuck in my head, but I couldn't recall the moment of impact or anything after. What I remembered best was Ellie's calm face right before she pushed me. The EKG next to me beeped faster. "Ellie pushed me off a cliff." It felt utterly ridiculous to say it out loud.

"Apparently, you fell almost fifty feet, but thank God you landed on sand so it really broke your fall. You only have a sprained neck, a broken elbow, and a dislocated kneecap."

"Oh, is that all?"

"It could have been way worse, sweets. You could have died."

"How are *you*?" I asked. "Did you end up needing surgery?"

"Nope, they just removed the bullet, stitched me up, and sent me home. Isn't it funny that I came out of a terrorist attack in better shape than you came out of a wedding?"

"It's hilarious," I said.

Aimee clasped the fingers of my uncasted hand. "It's fucked

up, is what it is. Ellie tried to *kill* you. That's one of the wildest things I've ever heard. Thank God Mindy saw it happen, or else they'd probably say you were making it all up."

"Wait, what? Mindy saw it happen?"

"Yeah, she had gone outside to call her husband and then saw what was happening. She actually had to hold Ellie at gunpoint to stop her from fleeing the scene. She already gave her statement to the police. Speaking of, there are two officers here who've been waiting for you to wake up. Can I go get them?"

I started to nod, then stopped when a white-hot laser of pain shot through my neck.

Aimee stuck her head out of the room and waved in a man with sprawling eyebrows and a woman with a slicked-back ponytail, both holding disposable cups of coffee. "Hi, Robin," said the woman. "I'm Officer Simon and this is Officer Ramirez. We've been waiting for you to wake up so we can get your account about what happened. Does that sound okay?"

I was about to nod before I remembered not to. "Yes," I said instead.

The officers pulled up chairs next to the bed and sat down. Officer Ramirez took out a notebook as Officer Simon kept talking. "We'll try not to take too much of your time, so you can get back to resting. How are you feeling?"

"Do you mean physically, or emotionally?" I asked.

Officer Simon smiled sympathetically. "Let's start with physically."

"Pretty out of it," I said. "And in a good amount of pain." My whole left side was throbbing so hard it felt like bass vibrating through a speaker. I tried to think of how I would answer the question of how I was feeling emotionally. I couldn't really make sense of it. What are you supposed to feel after your best friend tries to murder you? Shock? Sadness? Rage? Confusion? Betrayal? I didn't feel any of those things, really—just numb.

"I'm so sorry this happened to you," said Officer Simon. "I'd like to hear the whole story, everything you can remember, even if you don't think it's important."

I blew air out from between my lips. "God, where do I even start?"

"Maybe we can start at the beginning of the wedding weekend, then go back and fill in any gaps if we need to. Does that sound good?"

I took a deep breath and told them everything: Stephanie Bennett, the missing bridesmaid from the weekend before, the surfing lesson, the chickpea tagine, the slitting of the rabbit's throat, the sleepwalking, the closet, the tunnel, the poison, the showdown after the wedding, the push off the cliff. A part of me felt guilty, like I should have been trying to protect Ellie by withholding certain details or minimizing things. "What'll happen to Ellie?" I asked.

"It depends," said Officer Simon. "She already confessed to the crime, which is good."

"And the crime is…"

The officer looked at me like I was simple. "Attempted murder."

"God." Dizziness surged through my head. "How many years do you get for that?"

"That'll depend on whether it's first- or second-degree.

Mrs. Ellison's lawyer is arguing for second-degree, based on temporary insanity."

I laughed, then stopped. "I could actually buy that. She really did seem insane. How many years do you get for second-degree?"

"Anywhere from five to nine years."

I tried to decide if this sounded too long or too short. Again, I felt weirdly guilty. "She might not be able to have kids," I said suddenly.

"Sorry?"

"All she ever wanted was to get married and have kids. She'll probably be in prison until it's too late, fertility-wise."

Officer Simon looked at me like I was the insane one. "Well, maybe she should have thought of that before she tried to kill you."

Ellie ended up getting five years in state prison. In connection to investigating her case, the police figured out that twelve other missing women, including Stephanie Bennett, had been murdered by brides. "The Bridezilla Killas," the newspapers called them. For a while after the news got out, women were too afraid to say yes to being bridesmaids or maids of honor, so wedding parties essentially stopped being a tradition. It was like a domino effect after that—*if we're not having a wedding party, then do we really need a bachelor and bachelorette party? Do brides really need to wear a virginal white dress and a veil? Do we really need to register for an upgrade of all our kitchen items?* The industry took a huge hit. If people did get married, they tended to have a small ceremony or go to city hall.

And the world didn't end. The economy actually improved,

with people spending more on entertainment, dining, and travel—experiences that helped you enjoy your time with your partner, instead of saving for one big day. But after a span of months everyone either forgot about the Bridezilla Killas or simply stopped caring, and the wedding industry rebounded—not to where it was when Ellie got married, but to where it was before that, when things were "normal."

Ellie tried calling me almost every day for the first couple weeks after she went to prison, but whenever I heard the automated voice saying it was an inmate, I hung up. Mostly because I didn't know what to say, because I still didn't know what I felt. A part of me felt bad for Ellie, like it wasn't her fault that her mom and society had brainwashed her into becoming so obsessed with marriage. Too bad you couldn't put *society* in prison. Or at least the National Organization for Marriage lobbyists, or the media conglomerates who carried out their orders, or the businesses that benefited from the wedding-industrial complex. Another part of me was furious, and another part of me was intensely sad, and another part of me was weirdly grateful, because it had finally forced me to reckon with the worst parts of myself.

27

About six months after Ellie went to prison, a thick envelope came for me in the mail. My heart snagged when I opened it and saw Ellie's bubbly script, written in pencil on lined notebook paper like we had used in school.

Dear Robin,
I'm writing this letter to try to explain why I did what I did. I'm not hoping that it'll make you forgive me—I've given up on that—but I'm hoping at least it'll help you understand. You can use it for your dissertation—I can be your psycho case study. I've had a lot of time to think in here, and I hadn't realized just how brainwashed my mom and

society had made me about marriage. So I went back, basically from birth, and tried to figure out how I got here.

My parents told me that my third word, after "mama" and "dada," was "wedding." Probably because there was nothing I liked better (and nothing my mom liked better) than to flip through the faux-leather photo album with this label, oohing at my mom's long white dress, the wildflowers in her hair, the sparkly ring on her finger, and the colossal tiered cake. My mom would sigh wistfully and say things like, "Look how thin I was," or "Happiest day of my life," or "I wish I could do it all over again."

My favorite before-bed story was how my parents met: my mom had set her girlfriend up on a blind date with my dad, who was just an acquaintance at the time. When the friend told my mom she was going to back out, my mom decided to go in the friend's place. When she showed up at the diner, my dad said, "I'm glad it's you."

"And the rest is history," my mom would always say, planting a kiss on my cheek and turning out the light. One summer my mom bought me a lacy white dress and I refused to take it off for weeks, calling it my wedding gown. When I spilled Hi-C on it and my mom couldn't get the stain out, I cried so hard that I puked.

From a really young age, my mom was hyper-focused on my love life. Even before I started going to school, whenever I had a male friend, my mom would always ask me if he was my boyfriend, and she'd make us pose for pictures with him kissing my cheek, and she'd make comments to his parents like, "Can't you picture them married someday?" Then once I started school it got even worse. Other *parents would ask their kids about their teachers or what they learned that day, and my mom just wanted to know if there were any cute boys in my classes or if a boy had asked me to be his girlfriend yet or if there were any other girls who had boyfriends.*

My favorite movie growing up was The Little Mermaid, *and I would make all my male friends play a game where I flopped around on the ground, my feet stuck together like they were a flipper and my hands clasping my voiceless throat, until the boy kissed me and transformed me into a speaking human. I couldn't get enough of each Disney movie that followed:* Beauty and the Beast, Aladdin— *all of them ended with those cartoon mouths mashed together in a lipless kiss, followed by an extravagant wedding.*

After that came my favorite rom-coms: She's All That, *in which Freddie Prinze Jr. makes a bet that he can transform an unpopular nerd, the notoriously heinous Rachael Leigh Cook, into the prom queen. The whole movie basically exists for the post-makeover scene where Rachael Leigh Cook walks down the stairs in that strappy red dress while the camera pans up her body and "Kiss Me" by Sixpence None the Richer plays. She trips on the last step because she's still a nerd at heart! A hot nerd who forgives Freddie Prinze Jr. for his lies and agrees to be with him. In* There's Something About Mary, *Cameron Diaz—a woman so hot she drives every man she meets to insanity—ends up falling in love with her stalker.* 10 Things I Hate About You *features Julia Stiles as a mean, tough girl who just needed to fall in love with a guy paid to date her in order to realize she's soft and sweet. Every movie culmi-*

nates in a kiss and a woman deciding it didn't matter that the man lied to her. Why didn't I see how messed up that was at the time? I remember you never liked those movies, so I'd watch them alone in my room before bed every night, falling asleep to dreams about when it would be my turn.

By the time I was sixteen, I had my wedding all planned out—you probably remember the sketchbook I had with all the lists and drawings of everything. It would be nautical themed, on a boat just like Ariel and Eric's, with little anchors sewn around the train of my gown, and my bridesmaids would wear ruffly blue dresses that looked like waves of the ocean, and the cake would be in the shape of a seashell, and the flower arrangements would be beach roses and seagrass, and the table toppers would be sand, sand dollars, and tea lights in wide glass bowls. The man by my side would be Brad or Patrick or Ryan or Chris or Matt—I crossed out names and replaced them each time my crush changed.

My mom was thrilled when I got my first serious boyfriend, Brian, in high school—more thrilled than when I'd gotten As on my report card or when I won first-place medals on the track team. She constantly asked me invasive questions about our relationship, like if we had said I love you yet, what we had done sexually, if we had had a fight. If she wasn't asking questions, she was giving me unsolicited advice about how to make sure he didn't break up with me: keep him wanting more, always look your best, be interested in what he's interested in, etc. Whenever he'd come over she'd always ask him if I was keeping him happy. When we broke up six months later, the first thing she said to me was, "What did you do?" Like it was my fault some-how. Then she literally cried, saying she had been sure he was the one. Every time I had a boyfriend this cycle would repeat: the invasive questions, the advice, the crying over the breakup.

Then you know what happened right after I left for col-lege. I knew something was wrong when my parents came into my room and the first thing my mom said was, "You know how much we love you, don't you, honey?" in this shaky voice. My dad had been diagnosed with ALS the year before and his symptoms had been getting worse, so I thought they were going to tell me he was dying—that he had however many days or months left. Instead, they told me they were getting a divorce because they had fallen out of love. To me, that almost seemed worse than if my dad was dying. I was so fucking mad, mostly at my mom for abandoning my dad, even though they said it was a mutual decision. I called her a heartless bitch and I still remember the way her face collapsed after I said it.

I know some kids with divorced parents get disillusioned about marriage, seeing it as a sham and deciding not to do it themselves. Or at least becoming slightly more wary of the institution. But I just got even more hyper-focused on mar-riage after my parents got divorced, like it was my wrong to right. Like a successful marriage for me would somehow offset my parents' failure. In college I scared off a lot of guys by asking a million questions about the future on the first or second date: what age do you think you'll be ready to get married, do you think divorce is okay, how many kids do you want, etc. So I started dating older guys, most notably *my twenty-eight-year-old psych professor, who wore Italian leather loafers and had this gorgeous apartment in the Back Bay and would read Nietzsche out loud to me in bed, which I now realize was just dumb fucking posturing. But at the time it convinced me he was an Adult, a man ready to Settle Down, so I gave him my virginity, a thing I did not take lightly. I remember being really sad that I couldn't tell you—this was when we weren't talking. Shortly after that I found out he had been sleeping with at least three other female students. I got him fired and then didn't get out of bed for a month.*

After that I created this "marriage material" checklist for all potential boyfriends, including things like "knows how to manage his finances," "is romantic," and "has a five-year plan." After every breakup the list would get longer and more specific: "has a good relationship with his mother," "is spontaneous but not too spontaneous," "doesn't play video games for hours every day," "will take care of me when I'm sick," etc. Sometimes I would even pretend to get sick early on in a relationship, and if the guy didn't show up at my door with chicken soup by the end of the day, I'd dump him. Most men didn't last more than a few months. One or two lasted around a year, at which point the relationship inevitably crumbled under engagement pressure from yours truly.

By the time I was in my late twenties, I didn't feel any closer to marriage and I started to panic. My mom was always telling me time was running out, that all the good men were going to be taken soon, that I was only getting less desirable and less fertile as the years went on, that she wanted grandchildren soon, that there must be something wrong with me, etc. "My friends all tell me their daughters are getting married and having babies, and they ask about you and I have nothing to say!" I asked myself what was more important: finding the perfect man, or getting married? It was clear to me I wouldn't be able to accomplish both. So I got rid of the checklist and instead I looked for guys who just seemed ready to marry, despite their other flaws. You remember Patrick? The guy who put me down whenever he could, criticizing my roast chicken or my taste in movies or my spelling but promised we'd get engaged after a year of dating? God. And I put up with all of it until his proposal, which included all the things I'd need to change about myself before we got married, at which point I called it off and then didn't get out of bed for so long that I lost track of the days.

I started seeing that therapist, Dr. Frank, who told me I was hyper-focused on marriage because it allowed me not to focus on myself as a person, and what would make me happy besides marriage. At first I vowed to never go back, ranting to everyone that Dr. Frank only claimed happiness could be found outside marriage because she was married herself. But the thought still got into my head, and while I rode the subway or lay in bed at night or sat through work meetings I found myself asking: what would make me happy, if in some alternate universe marriage was off the table? I hate to admit that even now, it's a difficult question. You know I had never really felt a calling toward anything, which was probably why I ended up working in HR. I didn't love the job, but I didn't know what else I would do, especially in my thirties, when starting over would require starting at the bottom of the pay scale. I took a career quiz and it told me I should work in human resources. LOL/ loudly crying emoji. Everyone around me seemed to have figured it out: at the ad agency where I worked, the copywriters were all writing novels, the designers were making their own art, you were teaching young people about feminism, Lanie was a social worker at a psych hospital, Cassandra was an editor at a fashion magazine, Jill was even a goddamn architect.

I knew I wasn't a creative person; I didn't feel compelled to make art *of any kind. Every time I even write the word* art, *in my head I say it in this sarcastic, stuffy voice with my pinky up. And my hobbies at that time—yoga, making time-intensive foods like yogurt or bitters or bread, making beaded jewelry, DIY home projects, watching every reality TV show on Bravo—felt like pastimes, nothing further. You know how my hobbies changed all the time—I was constantly trying new things to try to find my passion like knitting or Zumba or bonsai or coding or hiking or painting or trivia or pottery or acting or ice-skating or meditation or even Renaissance fairs. But nothing ever stuck. I would try something out for a few weeks or months, then lose interest and move on.*

After my thirtieth birthday, like the literal day after, I started being served these articles in my Facebook feed with headlines like "Single Woman Chokes and Dies While Eating Dinner Alone" or "Female Fertility Decline Begins in Late 20s." Spouse Spotter even put these targeted ads on Facebook that used your birthday to figure out your age.

The ad was a huge red countdown clock that would tally the days, hours, and minutes until you became rotten, and every day I'd watch, transfixed, as the numbers dwindled. I contacted Facebook and tried to get them to stop serving me the ad, but they said there was nothing they could do about it. Every person Instagram suggested I follow was an engaged woman planning her wedding or a woman who had just gotten married, and by contrast, the ads in my feed were for cookbooks called "Cooking for One" or T-shirts that said something like "Cat Lady." When I'd turn on the TV, every show was a sitcom about a married couple or a reality dating show or a renovation show about a husband-and-wife duo or crime procedurals about single women getting brutally murdered. Wedding planning companies would send me direct mail that was designed like fake wedding invitations with a blank space where the groom's name was supposed to go. I know this shit sounds way too obvious but… it was effective.

So one day I gave up and clicked the Spouse Spotter countdown ad I had been served 43789234 times. Within the first month, I met Kaivan on there. He had an MR of eighty-nine, one of the best I had seen, and in his profile he said he didn't believe in divorce. He didn't meet all the criteria on my personal marriage material checklist—he had never (like, ever) cleaned the kitchen stove and he was super impulsive with his finances, new Amazon packages arriving on his doorstep nearly every day—but he did bring me soup when I was sick, and he listened to me in this really attentive way, and he seemed readier to commit than most other men. I decided to just accept it: my passion was marriage and creating a family. And I would pursue it just like any other passion: doggedly, as if it was the one thing that would make me happy.

After a few months of dating, after we had said we loved each other, I started dropping hints like showing him rings from the engaged women I had started following on Instagram, saying something casual like, "That's a gorgeous ring, isn't it?" I would tell him about coworkers who had gotten engaged and emphasize how they seemed sooo happy. Sometimes I even made the coworkers up to make it seem like everyone was getting married. When he got bedbugs, I convinced him to move in with me and after that I would say things like, "It's so nice waking up next to you every single morning. Wouldn't you like to do this for the rest of our lives?" I mean, I knew how I sounded; I just couldn't stop. Every time we went out to an especially nice dinner or took a weekend trip, I'd get my hopes up that he was going to propose, and when he didn't, I'd go on a rampage but not tell him why. I've never told anyone this, not even you, but after about six months I told Kaivan I had a NuvaRing even though I didn't, hoping we'd get accidentally pregnant and it would force the issue. But when it didn't happen after a few weeks, I was feeling guilty enough that I went back on the ring. I really did think he was the one, and I didn't want our life together to start out with some massive lie.

He proposed after ten months. When I told my mom, I swear to God it was the happiest I had ever seen her. "Finally, the curse is lifted!" she said. At first, I felt this massive gush of relief—I swear, muscles I had been tensing since puberty finally released and this big chunk of my brain that had been flashing code red at me just turned off. I slept like I had never slept. My stomachaches went away. I took walks and felt like I was seeing the true blue of the sky for the very first time. Then one of my coworkers, a real one, came in crying and told me her fiancé had called off their wedding. He hadn't been ready, he said. He had felt pressured. It sent me into a total tailspin. What if Kaivan did that?

So I became fixated on planning the perfect wedding, since it was something I could control. I felt powerful when I chose the font for the invitations, or when I chose a cake flavor. Like they were nails I was hammering into the eternal bond between Kaivan and me. When I started hearing about wedding charms from my mom or on the wedding boards I'd read, I was tempted, because they promised even more control, but I was afraid of being judged by people like you. So I didn't initially incorporate any of them into my wedding planning, but I read about them and made little mental notes about things I could do at the last minute if I felt like I needed to.

New charms were popping up all the time, and with the more extreme or weird ones—the ones that would never be written about in a publication or talked about on the news—there tended to be a heavy cloak of secrecy around them. To learn about them, you had to email someone and literally sign an NDA before they'd tell you what they were. I told myself it was just curiosity, but I emailed about all of them. When I read the one about sacrificing your maid of honor, the hair on the back of my neck stood up.

If I'm being 100 percent honest, I did think about you and your shitty reaction when I told you Kaivan and I *had gotten engaged, but in a completely hypothetical way. Like, oh, if I was a different person, a completely psycho bridezilla, I could justify killing Robin because of what she said that night. I'd probably do it in a way that made it look like an accident, like pushing her off a cliff. But then I'd have to retrieve her body and lug it back up the cliff to offer her organs to the wedding gods. That would be inconvenient. Eh, no matter, it's not like I'm going to actually do it. But sometimes I would find myself thinking about it, devising methods even though I had no intention of coming even close. Putting nuts in your food. "Accidentally" tripping you. Drowning you in the ocean. I started dreaming about it a little too frequently, and I'd wake up covered in sweat, my hands clenching.*

I didn't start thinking about it for semireal until the beginning of the wedding weekend, when everything started going wrong with the flowers and the wedding singer and the photographer—it just seemed like a sign that the wedding was cursed and I started to feel really out of control. Plus, you were getting into fights with everyone and not being sympathetic about all the wedding-related catastrophes and in general being up on your queer high horse, judging everything. When we were out in the ocean surfing it started as a joke, because I could tell you were so scared, and I was still a little mad at you for being insensitive about the wedding singer—I was going to hold your head under for a few seconds and then let go and laugh when you came up sputtering. But every second that I planned to let go I just didn't. It was like some invisible force was keeping my hand there. Then a wave came and knocked us over and knocked me out of the trance and I was like, thank God! Thank you, wave! Then during the rehearsal dinner, after you had made Kaivan talk about his face filter—which of course I knew was racist, but Kaivan and I had already had a long discussion about it and I didn't want to get into it again—I was walking through the kitchen and the cook asked me to taste your tagine. I told him it seemed like it was missing something, some creaminess, and he suggested almond butter. I debated it for a few seconds, then told him that was a great idea. It wasn't that much almond but-ter, anyway; I thought it would probably just make you a little sick and that way you'd be tuckered out and would stop picking fights with everyone. When I came into your room in the middle of the night I pinky swear I really was sleepwalking, but I think even my subconscious knew what I was planning to do. It was like I was trying to warn you. When I locked you in the closet it was partially because I really did want my best friend there on the biggest day of my life, and partially because I didn't want the picture-perfect ceremony and reception to be marred by your ab-sence, and partially because if you left then I'd really never be able to sacrifice you, and what if I needed to? I already told you I didn't actually poison you; I just had to think of some way to make sure you'd stay after you escaped from the closet and thankfully, you believed I would do some-thing that unhinged. The only time I really meant to kill you was the last time, when you came to my room to try to talk me out of it, like I would just do whatever you wanted for the millionth time because I wasn't my own person. Our whole friendship had always felt like it hinged on me mir-

roring you, and I was so tired of it. I guess you could call me pushing you off that cliff a claim of selfhood.

I'm so relieved you didn't actually die. When I look back at the wedding weekend now, I feel like I truly was temporarily insane. I know people think it was a bullshit defense but I wouldn't have lied about that. I think most women would say they feel at least a little insane on their wedding day—it's just that no one talks about it. Society tells you over and over and over how important it is for you to get married and then expects you not to go crazy? To not do anything possible to make the marriage last?

I don't really know what else to say. I guess I could say I'm sorry for the millionth time, and I'd still mean it. But like I said, I don't expect this letter to make you forgive me. I mainly wanted to give you the whole story, so you could include it in your dissertation like you wanted. A small thing I can give you.

I love you,
Ellie

28

Two or so years after I get Ellie's letter, I fly to Los Angeles for an academic conference, and when it's over, I have a free day before flying back to New York. California brings back a lot of memories from the wedding, and I can't stop thinking about Ellie. We still haven't spoken. The return address on her letter was a women's prison in Corona, only about two hours from LA, and when I call about visitors, the automated voice says they're allowed that day. So I get in my rental car and go see my best friend who tried to kill me.

The visitation room reminds me of an elementary school cafeteria, with checkered linoleum flooring and long wooden tables lined with uncomfortable plastic chairs. There are two vending machines in the corner, and on the off-white walls there's an American flag and, bizarrely, a large painting of a blooming cherry tree next to a lake dotted with swans. It somehow makes the room feel even sadder.

As I sit at a table waiting for Ellie, I watch the people around me: an inmate with pencil-thin eyebrows and blotchy skin plays checkers with a young boy, presumably her son, while the man next to the boy stares at his phone. An old woman with a sweatshirt that reads "The galaxy's greatest grandma" shares a bag of pretzels with an inmate who has a little constellation of stars tattooed on her cheek.

When Ellie comes out and sees me, she drops to the floor and covers her face with her hands. Then she gets up and runs, wrapping me in a tight hug until a guard separates us.

We sit down at the table. "What are you doing here?" Ellie says, her eyes wide with shock. She looks better than I would have imagined—her blond hair seems freshly highlighted and washed, her skin is clear but a little pale, and her body seems the same as it always was, although it's hard to tell underneath the loose orange jumpsuit she's wearing.

"I don't really know, honestly. I came for a conference, and then I kept thinking about you." I push a bag of Cheetos from the vending machine across the table. "I got these for you."

Ellie smiles tentatively and pops open the bag. "God, it's so good to see you. Did you get my letter?"

I nod.

Ellie places a single Cheeto on her tongue and rolls her eyes up in ecstasy. "Did you use it for your dissertation?"

"Yeah, Professor Gaffney finally told me it was very sexy, which I guess was true because I ended up getting an agent, and after making a bunch of changes, we actually sold it a few months ago. To one of the big publishing houses and everything."

Ellie smacks my arm. "Holy shit, Robin! That's huge." She seems genuinely excited for me despite her current circumstances.

"Sorry, I don't know if that's weird. A book that's partially about you and...what you did."

Ellie is now eating the Cheetos rapid-fire. "Hey, I told you you could use it. And I kind of owe you."

"I don't know. I feel like I kind of owe you, too."

"What do you mean?"

Someone yells across the room, and a guard walks over to quiet them down. I wait for it to pass. "Your vows at the wedding, about Kaivan being the first person to want you and not a reflection... It made me feel like I had failed you as a friend. Because I think I did want the reflection."

Ellie nods. "Well, you wanted an almost-reflection. Not a hundred percent, like when we both turned in the same paper, but close enough. Saying the same thing but in a different way. Tomato, tom-ah-to, you know?"

"I wish you had told me."

She lets out a short laugh as she licks the Cheeto buildup from her fingers that look like bright orange sewing thimbles. "What? That our friendship depended on me matching you?"

"Yeah. If I had known, I would have told you to stop pretending and just be yourself."

"I don't think I knew who that was, at the time. It was only when I met Kaivan and he told me to stop agreeing with him all the time that I looked back and realized what I had been doing."

"I feel like I must have known what you were doing subconsciously, too. And I let you, because my need to be agreed with was that strong. That night after the wedding was the first time I've ever really thought my life was in danger, and the way it felt in my body was the same as every time I get into a fight. That's fucked up, right?"

"Yeah, but it makes sense." Ellie roots around in the bag for more Cheetos, but they're gone. "Everyone has their ways of keeping control. For you, it's your opinions. For me, it was climbing the ladder, as you call it. Marriage, house, kids. But being in here has thrown off the grand plan. It's forced me to let go. I can't live in that nice house we bought. I may not be able to have a biological kid. Kaivan might meet someone else, even though he keeps swearing he won't. I have to make peace with these things, let my life take a different course than I was planning, or else I'll lose it."

"Wow, sounds like prison has been kind of good for you. Zen'd you out."

Ellie laughs. "I wouldn't go that far."

"I'm trying to be a little more Zen these days, too," I say.

Ellie squawks. "You, Zen? I can't really picture that."

Next to us, a middle-aged woman wearing a string of pearls and khaki pants looks at her watch and sighs, then stands up and gathers her things to leave. She had been there when I sat down.

I tut my tongue. "I said I was *trying*."

"And what does that involve?"

"I joined a rage-a-holics anonymous group. We end every

meeting by saying the serenity prayer, but we replace God with ourselves: Self, grant me the serenity to accept the things I cannot change, the courage to change the things I can, and the wisdom to know the difference."

"And do you? Have the wisdom to know the difference?"

I sigh. "Some days yes, some days no. I went on a silent meditation retreat, too."

She smacks the table. "No *way*! What the hell was that like?"

"Miserable, but enlightening. When you meditate, you're supposed to notice sensations in your body but not react to them, so it teaches you not to react to things in daily life. Like other people's opinions, for example." I smile. "Like I said before, it works some of the time."

She shakes her head. "I can't believe you're undergoing this complete transformation and I'm not around to see it." She looks down at the table, and when she looks up again her eyes are glassy, her bottom lip wobbling. "I really miss you, Rob."

"I think I miss you, too, which is really weird to say to someone who tried to kill me."

Ellie laughs as she fiddles with the empty Cheetos bag. "Can I call you sometime?"

"Sure," I say. "I'd like that."

"You promise you'll pick up?"

"I promise," I say, and extend my arm across the table, pinky out. Ellie hooks her pinky around mine and we both lean in to kiss our hands, eyes locked on each other, the way we had done when we were young and inseparable.

★ ★ ★ ★ ★

ACKNOWLEDGMENTS

As always, thank you firstly to Ashley, who hates weddings as much as I do. I loved our city hall ceremony (no vows on Fridays) and potluck celebration and I love being with you every day, ranting about all the other things we hate. Thank you to Alexa Stark, my agent, for helping me keep my head on straight and always finding a way to sell my wacky work. Thank you to John Glynn, my editor, for helping me turn this into the wild thriller it is today and for being almost ridiculously easy to work with—I truly didn't know it was possible to feel this respected and cared for as an author! Thank you to my publicist, Leah Morse, and my marketing manager, Pamela Osti, for getting the word out and getting the book into readers' hands. Thank you to Charlotte Phillips and Sean Kapitain for designing a cover that's literally blazing with sinister sarcasm, reflecting the tone of the book so perfectly. Thank you to Cicely Aspinall, my UK editor, for your brilliant ideas—one of which was the title of this book! Thank you to the whole HQ team for bringing this book across the pond. Thank you to Seema Mahanian for the early encouragement and helpful feedback. Thank you to initial readers Marisa Clark, Jason Thayer, and Abigail Lloyd. Thank you to my generous blurbers Amy Jo Burns, Chelsea Bieker, John Fram, Micah Nemerever, and Peter Kispert. Thank you to all of the booksellers and bookstagrammers who help spread the good word—us authors owe you so much! Thank you to my real-life high school BFFs Abigail Lloyd & Rebecca Purser for inspiring so many of the friendship flashbacks. Thank you to everyone who shared their bridesmaid horror stories. Thank you to my dog Whiskey for always being by my side as I write and for forcing me to take breaks for walks. And thank you to my parents for never pressuring me to get married, have a wedding, have grandkids, or do anything else related to societal expectations—it's probably a big reason why this book exists.

ONE PLACE. MANY STORIES

Bold, innovative and
empowering publishing.

FOLLOW US ON:

@HQStories